Castle Walls

Castle Walls

D. Jordan Redhawk

P.D. Publishing, Inc.
Clayton, North Carolina

Copyright © 2006 by D. Jordan Redhawk
SECOND EDITION

All rights reserved. No part of this publication may be reproduced, transmitted in any form or by any means, electronic or mechanical, including photocopy, recording, or any information storage and retrieval system, without permission in writing from the publisher. The characters herein are fictional and any resemblance to a real person, living or dead, is purely coincidental.

ISBN-13: 978-1-933720-01-2
ISBN-10: 1-933720-01-8

First Printing 2003 (ISBN: 0-9741378-1-2)

9 8 7 6 5 4 3 2

Cover art and design by Stephanie Solomon-Lopez
Edited by Day Petersen/Linda Daniel

Published by:

P.D. Publishing, Inc.
P.O. Box 70
Clayton, NC 27528

http://www.pdpublishing.com

Acknowledgements:

Many thanks go to the following people:

To my editors — K. Simpson, Day Petersen, and Linda Daniel. Special thanks to Cindy Cresap for the extensive editing she did for the first edition. I couldn't have done it without her.

To Nancy Ashmore, a.k.a. Medora MacD. She's a technical editing goddess and deserves much praise.

To Stephanie Solomon-Lopez for a number of things. Her last minute assistance and Mac programming genius helped me through a computer swap during the first round of edits. To top it off, her cover design is absolutely spectacular!

To Janet Redhawk for a full on brainstorming session to help me flesh out the original story. Many of the fourteen additional scenes added for publication were her suggestions. You rock!

Additional thanks to April Eymann, Amanda Baughman, Ellen Wright, Gerri Baker and Amanda Lam from the Forward Motion Writing Community for a stimulating discussion of medieval politics.

DEDICATION

To my wife, Anna Trinity Redhawk — it's still good.

To the troupe of Cirque du Soleil's Saltimbanco — they fanned the flames that had already begun.

Prologue

Moist fog, muffled sound, a minstrel's voice calling.

Blindly, she focused on the song and its sedate beat, moving with care over the uneven terrain. As she neared the music, she could discern other sounds: the tumbling of water and dove calls, gentle in the slight breeze. Her slippered foot stumbled over a rock, and she could hear it clatter against others, splashing. The wind picked up, brushing a lock of hair across her forehead, dissipating the mist before her. Flickering light beckoned her closer as she picked her way across a stream.

Motion caught her eye, and she saw the minstrel for the first time. His voice soft, he chanted a tale of war and betrayal. In contrast to his bloody story, a white dove in his hand cooed counterpoint to his words. She barely saw his musicians through the darkness behind him, the torchlight catching only their movement as they played the drum and lute. Walls rising steeply into the fog told her where she was, filling her heart with dread. She was outside the castle. Again. As if cued by her realization, the minstrel sang what she knew would be the last of his song. When he finished, he dropped his head, and the musicians paused in their playing.

Sharp strains came from the lute alone, eerie in the dark mistiness. Unease filled her heart, for she knew what was coming. She wanted to turn and flee, but her feet wouldn't move. The deep rolling of the drum caused her to flinch in apprehension.

Startled by a sudden, intense beat of the drum, the dove flew from the minstrel's hand. Her fearful eyes could not look away as the dove's path took it up into a clear blue sky. She heard the shrill cry of a hawk, felt the sickening impact and averted her eyes from the bloodied feathers floating through the air.

Another drumbeat. Another vision.

Sunlight and shadow, dust motes sailing upon invisible drafts, playful secrecy.

She waited impatiently, squatting beneath the table in her father's chambers. Her little sister should have found her by now. Just as she was about to climb from her hiding place, the sound of booted feet chased her underneath again. Wishing she'd never begun this game, she shrank back, watching several pairs of legs stomp into the room. The voices were quiet and serious, rough with concern, and her ears pricked up in curiosity.

"What have you learned, Angus?" her father asked.

"My liege, the Invader is closing on our southern borders. He's movin' fast, burnin' the farms behind him."

A younger voice, similar in timbre to the king's, cursed. "Why destroy perfectly good farmland?" he demanded in righteous anger. "Should he get too far past our borders, he'll need it to support his troops."

"Calm yourself, son," the king directed, moving toward his heir.

Waiting quietly under the table, she recognized her brother's boots. He fancied those silly flaps on the sides to help pull them on. She wanted to know who this Invader was and why he was being so dim, but if her father found her now, she'd be in real trouble. The voices continued above her, and she focused on them again.

"Send me, father! With the Third Army, I could lay waste to him!"

With reluctance, the king consulted his aide. "Angus?"

"Aye, Your Majesty. If we can get to him before he gets to the Wynsul River..."

"See?" the young man asked. "Please, father! I beg you."

In the following silence, she entertained herself with the notion of her strong older brother begging. She bit her tongue to keep from giggling.

"Go."

After a startled pause, the son dashed forward. "Thank you, father! I'll make sure that bastard never invades another kingdom!" He turned and clattered out of the room.

"Angus," the king said, "go with the crown prince. He'll have need of your wisdom."

"Aye, sire."

Another beat of the drum. Another vision.

A hoarse cry, shouts of dismay, footfalls and movement just out of sight.

At the sound of her mother's voice, she looked up from her studies. Hearing something in the hall, she ignored her tutor and dashed out to see what the ruckus was about. Several people stood about the hall. Puzzled, she stepped closer. Her mother was on the floor, hovering over something, hugging it to her breast and sobbing uncontrollably. Others around her either stood back in embarrassment or tried to comfort her. The king appeared, face stricken as he clearly saw what his daughter could not. One of his aides gasped in shock.

"It's your fault!" the hysterical woman spat at him. "Your fault!" Her voice faded into loud sobs.

Unable to stay away, fear and inquisitiveness filling her, she stepped closer. Others were in her way, blocking her view. She edged around them, peeking between. When she finally comprehended what she was seeing, tears welled up in her eyes. Her brother's boots were bloody.

Another beat of the drum, the tempo increasing.

Dead and dying, razed fields lifting acrid smoke into the sky, enclosed, surrounded.

Even at this distance, the stench made her nose twitch. Less than a mile away, burning fields gave evidence of the Invader's progression toward her home. Below her window, she could see increasing activity in the courtyard: the injured straggling in from the front lines, women and older children providing supplies to the overworked surgeons. The guards on the walls had been tripled in response to the threat, but half of them were walking wounded. She'd heard the orders given by her father's aides: in the event of a siege, all foodstuffs and potables were to be brought into the castle.

A lone rider approached from the battlefield, his horse galloping at full tilt. Reaching the castle, he nearly toppled his steed as he pulled it up short. Even at this distance, she could hear a captain's voice challenging him, could distinctly hear his response.

"The king is dead! The king is dead!"

Drumbeat.

Darkness, whispers, rustling noises. A hand across her mouth, smothering her, scaring her. Startled shriek, heart pumping.

"Hush, lass!" a servant's voice said. "It's time to rise and dress. The Invader's at the castle walls. We must get you and your family away!"

She hurriedly dressed, barely having enough time to grab a favorite doll as she was hustled from her room. In the hall, her mother clutched an infant brother, her sister stared wide-eyed at the small gathering of loyal guards and servants. She grabbed on to her younger sibling, felt the smaller girl tremble.

As they were herded from the castle, the ringing of metal on metal filled the courtyard.

"They've breached the walls!"

Drumbeat, relentless nightmare.

Flash of moonlight on water, gentle music of the horses' tack, muted whispers, arms wrapped about a servant as their mount swayed gently.

"There's a small boat ahead, Majesty," a voice drifted back.

The world suddenly turned to thunder as hooves pounded and armor rattled. Crying out in alarm, she clutched the servant before her as their steed leaped into a full gallop. Branches tugged at her clothes and hair. And then she was flying, landing with a grunt on a patch of peat as she tried to catch her breath.

Standing, alone, she listened to the horse's hooves racing away. In the near distance, she could hear fighting, angry curses, and her sister's cry. Terrified and frozen with indecision, she clutched her doll to her chest. The baby was shrieking in the dark, a man's scream mingling with the sound for just a moment before choking into silence. Unable to stay away despite her fright, she pushed through the foliage.

Bodies lay all around, evidence of the guards' attempts to save the royal family. On a small strip of sand next to the river, her mother was on her knees, clutching the screaming baby to her chest. Before her was a man in armor, holding a sword. Several other soldiers and horses were gathered around them; some of the remaining servants huddled in a small knot nearby. Her sister was nowhere to be seen.

The armored man pulled off his helmet. His air of command reminded her of her father, though he wasn't as handsome. An ugly scar ran across his face from the base of his nose to curve down and around his cheek. He was saying something, his voice so low that she couldn't make it out.

When the blade pierced her mother's chest, pinning the babe to it, her scream matched theirs.

Drumbeat.

Panting, heart thumping, crashing through the wilderness. Noises everywhere, the call of wild animals urging her on.

She knew the Invader and his soldiers were chasing her, tracking her down to kill her. She was royalty, and her life was forfeit. Since she was a toddler she'd been instructed that she lived for her people; her people were gone.

Bursting from behind a bush, she screamed silently at the armored figure barring her way. Moonlight flashed on the blade above her, and she cowered, afraid of the deathblow that was coming. Cuddling her doll to her chest, she heard only the scuffle, the jangle of armor, felt the ground tremble as a heavy body hit. Then a gentle touch fell on her shoulder, and she peered fearfully at her savior.

The minstrel smiled, a bloody dove in his hands. "Hush, child. You're safe now."

As she struggled with the familiar nightmare, barely surfacing into consciousness, she felt fingers caress her forehead.

"Shhh. It's just a bad dream," a familiar voice murmured. "You're safe now."

Sighing, she relaxed back into sleep.

Part 1

Furtive movement alerted her.

To her credit, her flinch to wakefulness was minor, causing hardly a sound. Her mind raced as she struggled to remember where she was. Cracking her eyelids a fraction, she surveyed her situation. Warmth was behind and beside her, evidence of her sleeping handmaiden. A root had dug its way into the small of her back; she'd been so exhausted when they'd stopped running, she hadn't realized it was there. Her cloak was wrapped about both of them, scarcely protecting against the chill of the early morning mist.

Steam rose from her mouth and she tried to keep her breathing even. There, the movement again — a rustling of cloth, just outside her vision. A twig snapped, sharp in the hush, and her heart fluttered in her throat. Unseen beneath the cloak, her hand grasped the ornamental dagger her father had gifted her on her last birthday. Despite her attempt to appear asleep, her dark eyes widened; she held her breath.

The bush to her left rattled — someone trying to get into the tiny clearing where the women were hiding. Unable to keep up the pretense, she threw off the cloak, pulling the dagger from its sheath. Her handmaiden, rousing at the sudden movement, looked wildly about, keeping her tongue at the warning gesture from her mistress.

A figure on all fours pushed slowly through the thick undergrowth. Gripping the hilt with white knuckles, hand shaking, she prepared to launch her attack. The figure raised its head; their eyes met.

"By the gods, Your Highness!" the man breathed. He used one grimy hand to tug at his forelock. "It's me! Hector!"

Terror quickly faded to elation, and the princess scrabbled forward to draw the servant in. "Hector! You survived!" Her hands were frantic on his shoulders, grasping at his tunic and pulling him, unable to believe he was still alive despite the tactile proof. "Mother? Prince Liam?"

Hector's weathered face sagged. "Nay, Your Highness. I saw the Invader run them through."

The heaviness in her chest threatening to overwhelm her, she drew away and sheathed her dagger.

"I'm sorry, Your Royal Highness," the man whispered.

She flinched at the added "Royal", an indication of her new status as Crown Princess. "Nay, Hector." Taking a deep breath to quell the need for tears, she looked at her two servants. "Call me Katerin. *Both* of you. If we're to survive this night, the Princess Sabine must not be mentioned."

The handmaiden, Ilia, made a soft noise in her throat and reached out to grasp the younger woman's shoulder.

Survival first. "Hector, did anyone see you escape?"

Hesitantly, he said, "I don't think so, Your...Katerin. The guards were busy with the royal family. Two of us slipped away, but Matteo was killed by a patrol after we'd gone less than a league."

Nodding, she looked up into the foliage. "Get some sleep, Hector. Ilia and I will remain on watch." With a sad smile, she leaned forward and touched his shoulder. "It's good to see you, my friend. I'm glad you stayed alive."

Hector's face twisted into a smile. "And I am greatly happy to see you, High...Katerin."

~~*~*~*

"Have you found her?"

Swallowing, the captain fought the urge to tug at the collar of his uniform. "Nay, we have not, sire." In a rush, he added, "All but one of the men have reported back. And he's not been seen or heard from in two days."

Thoughtful, the Invader stroked his bare chin and stared out over the city with muddy blue eyes. He held himself with the power and grace of a man half his age. His hair was turning gray with a vengeance, the rich mahogany color of youth fading away, and a scar marring his lower cheek drew his mouth into a permanent frown. He stood on a balcony, behind him the main chamber of the previous Dulce king — victim to the ordained destiny of the Invader, one of many who'd attempted to resist the inevitable. Below the Invader, tendrils of smoke still rose from outside the castle walls, smoldering remains of a long siege and ultimate success. He inhaled deeply, the acrid scent reminiscent of so many other battles in his long and bloody career.

"In which direction was my man riding before he disappeared?" he finally asked, voice gravelly from an old scar across his throat.

"Southwest, sire," the captain reported, hard put to refrain from wiping at the sweat on his face. "I've already taken the liberty of sending a full patrol in that direction."

"Good." The Invader turned, eyeing the guardsman. "Catch up to them. If you don't personally bring her head back, I'll take yours in its place. Is that understood?"

Ashen, the captain, nodded. "Aye, my liege," he whispered, swaying on weak knees. He flinched a bit when a hand waved at him.

"Get out." A worried frown crossed the Invader's face as he watched the man stumble out the door as though all manner of demon were upon him. Sardonically, he thought, *I suppose I'm close enough to that particular description.*

He approached a large oak table in the center of the room. Beneath a layer of expensive clear glass laid a map of the kingdom he'd just taken, and he regarded it with partial satisfaction. Hearing movement, he looked up and saw an aide standing at the door leading into the king's bedchambers. Frowning, the scar only making him look fiercer, he growled, "You said you'd take care of the royal family. I should send you out with my captain...and the *same* instructions."

The man bowed obsequiously. "My apologies, Your Royal Majesty," he said, voice oily from many years at court. "You'd be well within your right. I'm afraid my success would be limited; I'm not well versed in tracking errant princesses."

"Had you fulfilled your bargain, no one would need tracking. If I recall, you were to drug the royal family and get my men into the castle with a minimum of fuss." The Invader studied the aide, disgusted with the finery the man insisted on wearing. "You failed, Dominic."

"Aye, sire," the aide responded with another bow before stepping further into the room. "But had it not been for my assistance, you'd still be outside the walls. It's hardly my fault that Cook decided to have a go at the stew before it was served."

Turning away in distaste, the Invader picked up a goblet of wine from the table and sipped it. "What's done is done." He returned to the balcony and stared out over his kingdom. "Get out, Dominic. Pack your belongings and see my quartermaster for your reward before you leave."

The aide froze before a flash of anger crossed his face. He took an automatic step forward as he spoke. "That's not what you promised me. You said I'd remain as a member of your court."

"Yes," the Invader agreed, turning to glare at the dandy. "And you promised me the royal family and a good number of the guard would be drugged before you opened the gates. Too many of my men died as a result of your failure. Since you did not accomplish your end, I hardly need to hold up mine." He padded closer to Dominic, circling him, his manner that of a beast hunting. "You betrayed a king to whom you had sworn allegiance; did you think I would trust your oath of fealty to me?"

Dominic ground his teeth, but forced himself to remain prudently silent.

"You're a traitor now, and you'll be one in the future; you don't fool me." Stopping behind him, the Invader leaned close, voice soft. "Now get out, before I decide to add another head to my walls."

With a swallow, the aide turned and backed away. When he reached the door, Dominic intoned, "Your Majesty," and then stepped into relative safety.

The Invader sighed and resumed studying the map of his new acquisition — the fourth in his military career. He was now master of more land than all remaining realms put together. Sipping his wine, he recalled the witch who had set him on his path.

Fidgeting on the stool, young Prince Germaine peered at the strange designs on the witch's cards. He wasn't supposed to be here; his father would have a fit if he discovered his youngest son had visited a soothsayer. But when the teenager had ridden past the witch, he felt something call to him, and here he sat.

The decrepit woman cackled, rubbing stones together in her hands before casting them upon the cards. Leaning close to study them, she said, "You'll be a great warrior, a great king, young pup. You'll not be defeated in battle."

Germaine puzzled over that. "But I've two brothers before me in line for succession. How can I be king?"

"Never mind the present." The hag dismissed his statement with a wave of her wrinkled hand. "You will be king."

Leaning closer, dread and fear and intense yearning filling him, he asked, "Can you see my death? If I am never to be defeated in battle, how will I die?"

The witch clucked a bit, poking at this stone and that as she muttered to herself. "You will die by a sword, kingling. It will be wielded by the child of your enemy, one of royal blood who will avenge those you will have wronged."

Her prophecy had proven true. After his brothers had been killed in war, his father gasping his last at the end of an enemy spear, the Invader had stabilized his hereditary kingdom and begun his campaign of conquest across the map. Within the four kingdoms he'd taken, every person of royal blood had been slain. There'd been an instance or two of difficulty in expunging the existing royal line, but ultimately, he'd been successful.

"And I'll be successful now," he stated, finishing his wine.

~~*~*~*

Stepping into the courtyard, Dominic cuffed a page that inadvertently impeded his path. He smiled in grim satisfaction when the lad yelped and ducked away from a further beating. The physical attack did nothing to ease the deep anger in his heart. *Bastard! How dare he toss me off as so much rubbish?*

Dominic made his way across the crowded courtyard, ignoring the soldiers still in the process of sorting through the Invader's new wealth. "Wealth he wouldn't have if it weren't for *my* intervention."

"Eh? You say somethin'?" a passing guardsman asked, carefully balancing a large tapestry on one shoulder.

Startled, his anger deepening at his slip, Dominic growled, "Nothing for *your* ears."

The guardsman snorted derisively but held his tongue.

Without further encounters, Dominic arrived at his destination — a low door on the east wall. The hall he entered was dark with an aroma of coolness and death, the scent of musty stone mingling with a coppery tang. As he closed the thick door behind him, the rattle and activity of the courtyard faded away. Sighing in relief at the audible reprieve, Dominic moved silently through the hall. He sidestepped a drying pool of blood, thoughts intent on his abrupt dismissal. *Bastard would never have taken the castle without my help,* he grumbled.

Most of his life at court had been orchestrated toward attaining power. Dominic wasn't presumptuous enough to desire the throne. He was a realist; no one would follow a king who had more interest in the fashions of the day than in his people. But to be the man who had the king's ear...that was a worthy endeavor. Things had worked in Dominic's favor, and his career had flowered as he progressed along the path to become the king's personal aide. But it all shriveled away when he ran into the stone wall called Queen Mugaion Caesarin Elizabeth Dulce Annaatje.

To say the queen disliked Dominic was to make an understatement of grand proportions. He was never sure whether he'd done something that offended her, or if she had a distinct loathing for him for no other reason than that he existed. Dominic assumed the latter, for nothing he did or said seemed to alter the queen's distaste. Unfortunately for the ambitious man, Caesarin *also* had her husband's ear.

Dominic slipped into the small chambers he called home. Throwing open an oak wardrobe, he looked at his clothes in dismay. There was no way he could take all his belongings. He began sorting through the clothing as his frustrated musings continued.

Every attempt he'd made to get into the monarch's good graces had been met with resistance. Dominic soon realized that his hopes were destined to be unrealized, and he began searching for another way to attain his goal. Moving on to another kingdom was out of the question; Dominic's network of informants and hoodlums couldn't be moved. He either had to find another king and start from scratch, or remain and bring another to power. It had been a difficult decision, but with no other way of reaching King Frederick, only one avenue remained.

The Invader had been a hard man to make contact with. After the initial meeting, however, Dominic felt a renewed sense of purpose. His proposals and offers had been accepted, and a pact was made that would further his desires. The fact that the Dulce king and his bitch would die was only added incentive.

With a frustrated sigh, Dominic slammed the wardrobe closed. Everything would have to be replaced. Opening a trunk at the foot of his small bed, he pulled out a travel pack. A few pieces of jewelry, a couple of changes of clothing, and three small scrolls were all he could afford to take in the small space. Shouldering his bag, he took a final look at his furnishings. *I must take the bastard Invader down.* Another sigh escaped him, and he left the room.

Thanks to his having heard Ashen's report, he knew that somewhere a renegade princess was on the run from a usurper. *I wonder*, Dominic speculated. *What if I found her first?*

* ~ * ~ * ~ * ~ *

They kept to the forest, evading one patrol after another, with no chance to rest. The Invader was apparently not content with spilling most of the royal blood; he was obviously hunting for the last legitimate heir to the throne. Fortunately, Hector had served in the guard when he was younger. His experience was invaluable, as the need to hide their trail was tested again and again. A full day of travel had passed and Katerin was bone-weary. Now that night was upon them, the trio's pace had slowed to a crawl, and the smell of nearby wood smoke urged them to even greater caution.

Wrapped in the only cloak they had, the women waited in the shadows of a large elm while the ex-soldier scouted the source of the smoke. Stomach grumbling, the princess blushed in embarrassment. *Just what we need — to be betrayed by the noise from my belly.* Ilia heard the sound as well, and placed a hand on the young monarch's shoulder in a comforting gesture. Katerin's blush deepened, and she was happy that it was unnoticeable in the darkness.

Though the moon was full, clouds sent intermittent splashes of darkness upon an encampment in the hollow below them. The sight of Hector ducking back toward them through the undergrowth was a welcome one. He'd been gone for some time, and she had begun to worry.

Moving close enough for the women to see, Hector held a finger to his lips and urged them further into the forest. When they were far enough away from the encampment, he whispered, "It's a caravan of some sort, Katerin. Maybe merchants. I couldn't tell in the darkness." He pulled two sacks from under his shirt. "But here's some food and water from one of the wagons. We can get more before we leave." He pulled foodstuffs out of the sack: a half-round of cheese, a loaf of bread, and the roasted leg of some sort of animal.

Despite the ache in her belly, Katerin held her handmaiden back. "You stole it?" she asked, reprimand in her tone.

Drawing himself up to full height, Hector nodded. "Aye, Your Ladyship, I did." He frowned, peering intently into her dark eyes. "We don't have the crowns to pay for it. It'll hardly be missed, and I'll not have you starve out here in the wilderness! Your father would haunt me 'til the day I die."

Realizing the truth of his statement, she dropped her gaze. With a sigh and a nod, she gestured for Ilia to take the food. "You're right, Hector," she murmured. "We must survive at all costs." Glancing back down the hill, she vowed, "I promise to repay them...somehow."

Behind her, the servants looked at one another, worry lining their faces.

Much as she wanted to eat it all, Katerin knew to do so would be folly. As Ilia used the dagger to slice the cheese, the princess doled out a portion of meat, deciding to save the bread for later. Filling the sack with the remaining items, she tied it shut and patted it gently.

They made short work of their meager allotments, then shared the water skin among them. Acid burned in Katerin's stomach as it demanded more, her appetite scarcely whetted. With a sigh, she put the enticing smell of meat from her mind. "We need to find a place to sleep," she announced.

"Aye, Lady," Hector agreed, glancing around with a calculating gaze. Pointing away from the encampment below, he said, "P'rhaps we can follow this ridge here and see if there's a safe place."

Nodding, she picked up her skirts with one hand and the sack of food with the other. Beside her, Ilia gathered what few personal items they'd been able to scramble for during the attack. *A lifetime ago*, Katerin mourned.

As the women stood, Hector suddenly grabbed both of them about the waist and pulled them back. Hissing to silence their surprised gasps, he cupped a hand to his ear and pointed up the hillside. They distinctly heard a horse whicker nearby. Sudden terror filled

Katerin's heart as her servant waved at the encampment below, urging them toward it. As quietly as possible, the trio moved along the hillside. Behind them, they heard a muffled curse and the heavy thud of someone dismounting. At the edge of the forest, clouds still covered the moon above, and Hector chanced discovery by herding his charges across a cleared area and into the encampment itself.

Ducking behind a wagon, the princess then leaned against it, watching her one and only aging guardsman peer around the side of the wagon, back the way they'd come. Before her were several other wagons, their coloring indistinct in the dim light. Her eyes narrowed as she studied one. *Is that a design painted on the side?* Hector's hand on her arm refocused her attention.

With exaggerated movements, he urged them along the line of wagons until they came to the fourth. There, he stopped, holding his hands aloft to indicate they should wait. Stealthily, he eased around the wagon to have a look behind them.

The smell of food was so overpowering, it almost made Katerin swoon. She knew that this must be the wagon from which Hector had purloined their repast. Her stomach growling in demand, she grasped Ilia's hand for comfort and closed her eyes against faintness. Above them, clouds drifted aside and the moon illuminated the area.

"Bleedin' Sif!" came the soft curse.

Startled at hearing such language from her servant, she blinked.

Hector returned to the women, face visible in the moonlight, clearly concerned. Leaning his head close, he breathed, "Only one man. He's got our trail, and he's following." Glancing about, assessing the situation, he grabbed the princess's arm and pulled her toward the back of the wagon.

As he eased the wagon door ajar, the aromas that assailed her nearly made Katerin faint. Hector pushed her toward the opening, and she stumbled on her skirts as he forced her inside, her handmaiden following. Turning in the darkness, she saw Hector's silhouette against the moonlit encampment — the tense set of his shoulders, his hand reaching out.

"Give me the dagger, lady." He glanced backward at a noise. "Quickly! I'll try to draw him away!"

Katerin knew there was no other choice. She handed it to him. "Be careful, Hector," she insisted. "I need you now more than ever!"

"Aye, lady." Hector grinned. "I'll do my best. Now get back!"

She obeyed, darkness closing in as the wagon door was shut. With a thrill of fear, she heard the latch click into place. Groping about blindly, she found Ilia, and the pair sank to the floorboards. They heard cautious movement as someone in chain mail neared the wagon. Then quiet dragged on for what seemed like an eternity. Katerin felt her eyes widening as she tried to see in the pitch-black wagon, her ears nearly growing in length as she sought to hear. She held her handmaiden tightly, comforted by the arms wrapped about her. Then they heard a sudden blur of sound from some sort of skirmish just outside. The wagon thumped once, rocking at the impact of two bodies running into it, and the women were hard-pressed not to cry out in fear. Dogs nearby sounded an alarm as a man grunted in pain. Then there was ominous stillness, broken only by dogs barking in excitement.

Dread filling her heart when Hector did not reappear immediately to open the door, Katerin rose and pushed further into the wagon, pulling her handmaiden with her. Curling into a corner with Ilia, the princess drew her cloak over their heads and wrapped it tightly about them. Outside, voices were raised in sleepy question and irritation. The barking drew closer, and soon happily snuffling hounds were all about.

"Freya's tears, Daiki," somebody cursed, getting closer to the provision wagon, "your hounds raising a ruckus for a midnight snack? Thought you had 'em better trained than that."

Someone snorted in derision. "If you wouldn't sleep on watch, Tommaso—" He was interrupted by a gasp of surprise and another man's curse.

"Ros is not going to be happy with this," Tommaso commented. After a pause, he continued, "Both dead, and no good comes of that. What do you think they're doing here?"

Katerin bowed her head in mourning. *Poor Hector... All this death and destruction. And for what?*

"Don't know," Daiki answered. Another set of footsteps approached. "Habibah! Get Ros."

Further away, a woman answered. Only the men shuffling about as they waited disrupted the evening's stillness. After a few moments, other footsteps neared the wagon. "What's going on, Daiki?" The voice was low and gruff, filled with command.

"That, Ros."

"Kemplak's Hells!" Ros cursed. "Tommaso?"

"That's how we found 'em, Ros," the man responded, his tone a bit desperate. "I didn't hear or see nothing. I was on the other side of camp when it happened." A derisive snort came from one of those present.

"Well, we can't stay the night here. Someone will be looking for the guard. And who knows what people are waiting for this poor fellow. Tommaso, wake Martim. I want you two to clean up this mess.

Hide the bodies as best you can. Daiki, Habibah, lock up the dogs. We need to get water from the creek and clean up this blood before we move on." As Ros walked away, the orders continued. "We leave within the hour. Roust everyone!" A chorus of acknowledgment followed, and soon, the encampment buzzed with activity.

Even if Katerin and Ilia could have left the provision wagon, there'd be no way they would get far without detection. *And now we don't even have a weapon*, Katerin thought.

The wait was long, and the terror of the previous days was taking its toll. Katerin's eyelids drooped heavily, startled wide only when the wagon jerked into movement. Making a decision, she sat up, pulling the cloak away from her head.

"Your Highness?" Ilia asked softly.

"'Katerin' or 'lady', Ilia," she reminded her in the dark. She felt for the bag of food that Hector had stolen. "We'll be here a while, I think. It's high time we had more food, and some sleep. We're not getting out of this wagon without help."

"Aye, Lady."

The women split the bread and devoured the meat and the remainder of the cheese. Finally sated, Katerin leaned back, weariness washing over her. After two days of running, Katerin was exhausted. A full belly and the lazy swaying of the wagon didn't help matters. The gentle rocking of the wagon lulled her into sleep. Her slumber was sound, as was that of her handmaiden.

~~*~*~*

Bright sunlight spilled across her closed eyes, and Katerin jerked upright. Wincing, she raised her hand to block the unwelcome light, turning her head to one side. Beside her, Ilia pulled the cloak over her face.

"Well, what have we here?" a gruff voice asked in amusement. "A pair of sleeping mice?"

Memory crashed in on Katerin, and her heart thumped in fear. She lowered her hand, peering out the wagon door at a dark silhouette. Her handmaiden peeked over the edge of the cloak.

"Well?" the voice asked again.

Swallowing, Katerin cleared her throat. "My name is Katerin." She nodded at the woman beside her. "This is Ilia." Then she became silent, at a loss.

They heard the sound of running, and a small voice piped, "Da! Mum says she'll make cherry hotcakes for breakfast!"

"Hold, Wilm," the man ordered, looking over one shoulder. "Go get Ros."

"Aye, da." Small feet pelted away.

Children. There are children here, so these people can't be bad. Katerin pulled the cloak off her shoulders, preparing to rise and move toward the entrance.

"Hold there, girl," the man said, his attention back on the women. "We'll just wait until Ros gets here."

Katerin nodded. "Of course," she answered softly. Remembering the terror of the night, she recalled the sharp command in Ros' voice and the obvious respect of the others. She could feel Ilia trembling and reached over to pat her knee comfortingly, dark eyes warming with the promise to get them both out of this alive.

As they waited for the mysterious Ros, the sounds of people making camp drifted through the morning air. Men and women called back and forth cheerfully. Somewhere in the near distance, a man yelled. They heard the rumble of a tree being felled. Footsteps approached.

"What's the holdup, Willem? We've got hungry people to be fed."

The man at the entrance stepped back and to one side. "Looks like a pair of mice have crawled into the provisions," he said with a grin, nodding into the wagon.

Abruptly, Katerin realized that the new arrival was a woman. She wore a black tunic and breeches, the only color a splash of light blue from her under-tunic. Her curly golden hair was cut scandalously short; it gave her a roguish appearance that was reinforced by the sword strapped to her hip.

Eyes narrowed, the woman studied the stowaways. "Come out of there," she demanded, hand resting gently on her sword hilt.

Recognizing the voice as Ros', Katerin obeyed, helping Ilia to her feet. Making no sudden movements, she guided her handmaiden out of the wagon, wincing at the bright sunshine that assailed her eyes. Despite the circumstances, she sighed in happiness at finally being able to stand, and she surreptitiously stretched in pleasure. Eyeing the strangers before her, she subtly stepped in front of her handmaiden.

Ros raised an eyebrow. "I can only assume that you are the reason we had to leave in such haste last evening?" she asked, directing her question at Katerin. Her hazel eyes flickered up and down the smaller woman with disdain. "While you are beautiful, you hardly appear worth fighting over."

At first, Katerin was surprised; anger quickly followed. She'd been rousted from her bed in the dead of night, had watched her family and friends being slaughtered, and had been running for two days. It took a supreme effort to hold her tongue. She bit down fiercely on her cheek. *Simpleton!* At length, unable to remain silent, Katerin responded, her tone icy. "A dear friend is dead, and you've been inconvenienced. My deepest apologies."

A faint glimmer of amused understanding lit Ros' eyes; a corner of her mouth quirked, and she bowed her head. "Apology accepted."

Katerin's teeth ground together.

Looking at the man beside them, the blonde asked, "Sati is making breakfast this morning?"

"Aye. Wilm says it's to be cherry hotcakes."

"Good," Ros said with a chuckle. "The troupe needs the extra sweetness." Her eyes returned to the two bedraggled women before her. "At the very least, to make up for the night's unscheduled festivities."

"What of these two?"

With a calculating look, the woman studied the stowaways, ignoring Katerin's obvious hostility. After a thoughtful moment, she said, "Have Lucinda and Gemma get them cleaned up. I think they might have some clothes that will fit." Her gaze became less guarded. "When they're presentable, I'll see them at my wagon."

"Aye, Ros."

Still angry, though relieved that they were not in any immediate danger, Katerin let herself be escorted toward a tall, colorfully painted wagon. Holding Ilia's hand, she watched the encampment's proceedings with a calculating gaze.

Ten tall wagons were in the clearing, each with its own intricate decoration. Nearly twice that number of people of all sizes and colors were out and about, working with happy industriousness. It appeared that most of the wagons were traveling abodes — the inhabitants were setting up awnings, chairs, and tables outside of them. To one side of the clearing, several men were unrolling a vast length of canvas. Ros was among them, calling directions and lending a hand. From what Katerin could gather, she and Ilia had stumbled into a circus.

As they neared the wagon, a voluptuous redhead looked up from the colorful flowers she was arranging in a vase. "Ho, Willem! What have you there?" she asked, a welcome smile on her face.

"Katerin and Ilia," he responded, pointing to each in turn. "Ros said for you and Gemma to assist them. They need cleaning up and clothing."

Hands on hips, the woman nodded, looking the pair up and down. "Aye, that they do." Looking over one shoulder, she called,

"Gemma! We've guests!"

Katerin started when a shuttered window in the side of the wagon popped open. Another woman looked out, her hair and skin nut-brown. Solemn green eyes regarded them, and she nodded.

The redhead rubbed her hands together. "Well, let's get started then, shall we?" Waving her hands at their escort, she said, "Shoo, Willem. I think Gemma and I can handle these two dangerous creatures."

He chuckled. "Aye, I know you can, Lucinda. In the meanwhile, I'll be helping the men with the tent. Give a yell when they're ready."

"I will that." Lucinda remained where she was until he'd gotten out of earshot. Casting a conspiratorial look at her visitors, she winked. "Men! What they don't know about women could fill a book."

A smile crossed Katerin's face. *I think I'm going to like this one.*

"Let's have a look at you, eh?" the redhead insisted, waving the pair closer.

Part 2

Being clean again certainly feels wonderful, Katerin thought, tugging at the unfamiliar skirt. Gemma's garment had been a near-perfect fit for her, the waist and length being a size she could wear comfortably. The blouse belonged to Lucinda, however, the dark woman's bosom not being quite as small as Gemma's. With the pair declared fit for viewing, Willem returned to his escort duties. He led them toward one of the wagons. Beside her, Ilia kept pace in a gown borrowed from the redhead. A bit baggy in places, it still fit well enough.

Still busy with activity, the clearing looked much different than it had earlier. A large tent sprouted in the center, and men tied down the last of the thick supporting ropes. The wagons created a crescent around the main entrance, the painted side of each serving as an advertisement for the available acts. Pictures depicting brightly dressed buffoons, a lion tamer, graceful bodies flying through the air, and jugglers teased the eye. Instead of a painting, one wagon was barred, with a large animal curled up in one corner.

Katerin stopped her woolgathering and focused on a nearby wagon. Ros was relaxed before it, feet up on a stool, idly watching their approach. On a rough wooden table beside her were several familiar items. Ilia's gasp matched the princess's sudden recognition of the few things they'd been able to steal away from the castle. Instantly furious, Katerin marched forward, passing Willem to plant herself before the lounging woman, hands on her hips. "How *dare* you go through our personal belongings?" she growled.

"How dare *you* disrupt the lives of these people?" was the response. Ros stood, towering over the smaller woman. "Do you realize the danger you've put us in? Whoever those men were, one wore the insignia of the Invader. You can imagine he'll not be happy at the death of his personal guard."

Blinking in surprise, Katerin felt her anger fade. *She's right. It's not these poor people who are at fault.* She dropped her hands and gaze, properly chastised.

Taken aback by Katerin's sudden change of demeanor, the blonde sucked in a breath, quelling her irritation. "What's done is done," she finally said, sitting down. Waving to two other stools, she continued, "Please, sit. We must speak."

"Do you need me to stay, Ros?"

"No, Willem," the woman answered. "Though perhaps you could have Sati bring breakfast to these fine ladies?"

Willem smiled. "Aye, Ros. I'll do that," he agreed, walking away.

Waiting for the women to settle, Ros studied them. Once she had their attention, she said, "As you've no doubt gathered, my name is Ros, and I own this fine circus where you find yourselves. You've stowed away and stolen our food. The Invader is chasing you for gods know what reason, and two men are dead. Is there anything else I should know?"

With a sigh, Katerin shook her head. "Nay, I think not. That's more than enough."

"Then the next question is — what I should do with you." An interminable pause followed, the silence broken only by the people around them going about their business. Sighing heavily in irritation, Ros asked, "What do you think will happen to two women such as you if I send you away?"

Recalling the very unexpected recent events, Katerin raised her chin. "We'll be dead or worse inside a fortnight."

Mouth turned down, Ros agreed. "Aye. And it's the worse you should be worried about." She eyed them shrewdly. "Despite the pains in my arse you've become, I'll not have your deaths on my head."

Katerin ignored the flash of anger, instead considering her immediate future. *There's nothing left for me. My family is dead; another rules my people.* Looking at her handmaiden, she made a decision. "Ilia is a fabulous seamstress. I'm sure you could find use for her," she said, leaning forward on her stool in earnestness. "And should you have a lute about, she plays it very handily."

"I see. So you would have me hire your servant?"

"Aye." Katerin nodded. "She has a pleasant demeanor and is loyal to a fault. You could do no wrong in taking her on."

Ros crossed her arms, one hand stroking her chin in thought. "And what of you?"

Looking away, Katerin swallowed past a tight throat. "I shall be on my way."

"Your Highness!" the handmaiden whispered. "Nay!"

"Ilia!" Katerin snapped, cutting her off. She glared intently at her companion, warning her. "It's for the best." Returning her gaze to Ros, she searched the woman's face, hoping she hadn't caught the royal address.

Ros' face remained serious, her hazel eyes revealing nothing. Stifling a relieved sigh, Katerin continued, "What say you?"

Ros was slow to respond, eyeing them both in contemplation. With a reluctant nod, she said, "I've one open bunk right now. I'll hire Ilia at three coppers a week. She'll help with costuming, play the lute at showings, and learn to clown." To the servant, she continued, "You'll be sleeping in Lucinda and Gemma's wagon. They've an additional bunk, now that Tilly's gone off to have a babe."

Katerin felt a heavy weight lift from her shoulders. *At least Ilia will be safe now. She won't have to follow Hector beyond.* She refused to look at her handmaiden, hearing the gentle weeping, not wanting to be caught up by the emotion.

"And what of *your* qualifications?"

Surprised, she stared at the circus owner. "Me? I have no qualifications. Not for any task you would have here."

Ros sat forward, taking the smaller woman's hands in her own, studying them. "Aye, I can see that you're a stranger to hard work. Your hands are too fine for menial labor. Do you play any instruments? Sew? Cook?"

The remarks stung, and Katerin yanked her hands from the other woman's. "Nay. None of those." She rose to her feet. "I ask for your generosity in supplying me with one meal, and I'll be on my way."

A slow, impish smile crossed Ros' face as she stood as well. Her face took on a decidedly wicked appearance as her eyes roamed the smaller woman's body with lascivious familiarity. "I think not," she said. "I could...*use* a woman of your breeding."

It took a moment for Katerin to comprehend what the woman was insinuating. When she did, she blushed furiously. *She's a...a...a Sapphist!* she thought, shocked. Taking a step back, she said. "Nay. I'll be on my way." The princess turned, preparing to leave the clearing and her handmaiden behind, when Ros' next words froze her blood.

"Then take Ilia with you. She'll be of no use to me while she's pining away over your loss."

Katerin swallowed, staring blindly at the clearing and its occupants, weighing the choice of having another death on her head against prostituting herself to keep herself and Ilia alive. Hearing her handmaiden hastily rising to follow made the decision for her. She spun around, holding out one hand to still Ilia. Tentatively, she looked at the circus owner, heartened to see the leer had left her handsome face. "You have me at a disadvantage, madam." With a swallow, she drew herself up. "I'll stay."

Ros nodded slowly, an expression of grudging respect in her eyes. Gesturing to the table, she said, "Sort through your things. We've no other bunks; you'll be staying in my wagon." She looked to one side, waving a dark-complected woman forward. "And eat the breakfast Sati has made. We've a long day ahead of us. Rehearsal is this afternoon, and there is much to do." The woman strode away from them, dismissing their presence as she headed for the now-finished tent.

Watching her go, the princess bowed her head. *A Sapphist harlot and a death warrant on my head — what more could I ask for?* Reaching Ilia, she hugged the taller woman close. *At least my handmaiden will not die as well.*

* ~ * ~ * ~ * ~ *

Ros circled the tent, her practiced eye scanning the structure. Occasionally, she pulled on one of the thick ropes, checking its tautness. Despite her apparent attention to the task, Ros went over her conversation with the strangers. *The Invader's personal guard and an obvious man-at-arms are dead,* she mused sourly. *As if we've not enough trouble surviving in the midst of a war.* Ros kicked at a thick iron tent peg, grunting in satisfaction as it remained firmly in place.

During a normal season, the troupe would have spent some time in the Dulce kingdom. Ros had diverted them from their usual route when word of the Invader's activities reached them. *And now we've a blasted royal in our midst!* Growling to herself, Ros ducked beneath a flap of canvas, eyes slowly adjusting to the darkened interior. The lack of light reflected her attitude. Again she circled, pushing against poles, noting where more logs could be added for seating, ignoring a few of her people rigging the backstage area.

Ilia's use of Katerin's title was not lost on Ros, though she hadn't reacted. *A Dulce princess. And the Invader rabid as a wolf, no doubt.* Notorious for hunting down all heirs to every throne he stole, the Invader stopped at nothing to attain his goals. Neighboring realms, their leaders already nervous about the potential threat, would be doubly paranoid until the princess was found or an innocent substitute was executed in her place to appease the tyrant.

There was no denying that Ros' first thought had been to toss both women into the wild and hightail it away. The circus had the misfortune of having had occasional dealings with the Invader. She remembered well the terror of her childhood when a child with blonde hair and hazel eyes was the Invader's target. It was both fortunate and unfortunate that the child had been discovered, her head delivered to a displeased usurper. Thoughts of dealing with the Invader in any manner caused Ros a tremor of terror and hatred that rocked her to her core.

Sighing in frustration, she left the tent and stood in the main entrance, scanning the small encampment. She spotted the women in question; they had finished their breakfast and were returning to Lucinda and Gemma's wagon. *I cannot leave them behind.* Her hazel eyes lingered on the dark one; a mixture of sorrow, sympathy, and dull anger filled her heart. *Life's never easy, is it?*

* ~ * ~ * ~ * ~ *

Dominic awoke, shivering. With a curse, he pulled his cloak tighter and attempted to go back to sleep. Every pebble and root made its existence known by pressing into him. After an interminable time, the aide yielded to nature with utter gracelessness and rolled out of his makeshift bier. Quiet surrounded him; he heard only his heartbeat. His breath steamed in the chill gray of early morning.

As long as the Invader was in residence, remaining within the Dulce capital was out of the question. He had been roaming the countryside for two days, irritated apathy his constant companion. Still uncertain of his future, Dominic was reluctant to leave the area. *Better to be near. Just in case.* In case of exactly what, was a mystery.

With no fire to give away his tiny encampment to the roaming brigands who always seemed to multiply after a siege, breakfast was a distasteful affair. Dominic sniffed at the meat he'd taken from the castle larder, his suspicions confirmed by the faintly sweet odor. Grunting in disgust, he tossed the rotting mess into some nearby bushes and proceeded to nibble a crust of bread, his thoughts filled with sumptuous royal feasts. When he finished eating, Dominic brushed uselessly at his travel-stained clothing. Then he had an internal debate: *Move on or remain here for the day?* A check of his water bag solved the dilemma. Dominic hefted his pack onto his thin shoulders. By now, light cast a golden glow over the area, the sun finally breaching the eastern horizon. Regardless, the air was chill, and Dominic groused as he plodded along, holding his cloak tight about his neck. *That bastard will pay for this!* he promised himself.

Just how the Invader would be punished for his infraction, Dominic didn't know. He was painfully aware of his pitiful odds of finding the Princess Sabine. If experienced soldiers and trackers were having difficulty locating her, there'd be no way that he could.

The sound of running water interrupted his thoughts as he stumbled upon a tiny game path. He froze. Several moments passed before the insects and birds felt comfortable enough in his presence to continue their racket. Relieved, he turned right and followed the trail, searching for the source of the sound of babbling. A few strides away, the game trail opened up to reveal a small clearing with a creek. Dominic dropped his pack, retrieved his water bag, and, after a moment's consideration, removed his cloak. *Cold and filthy or cold and clean — one is preferable to the other.*

Shivering, he crouched upon the bank and began filling the bag. Task completed, he hissed as he splashed icy water on his face. In mid-scrub, Dominic froze again, peering between his fingers. Directly across from him, one of the small deer that lived in the forest nibbled at tender new growth. Mouth watering at the thought of fresh meat, his eyes lit up and he reached for his belt knife. The deer suddenly stiffened and raised its head, looking about with wary intensity. Once again Dominic stilled, mentally cursing whatever was disturbing his potential meal.

As if by magic, an arrow sprouted from the animal's ribs. Startled, Dominic fell backward onto his butt with a grunt, even as the deer leapt and crashed away into the forest. Before Dominic could do anything, he saw the archer pursuing his prey, rushing forward just inside the tree line, a flash of metal and green.

Dominic blinked. *That was one of the royal guard! They should all be dead!* Leaping to his feet, he barely had time to grab his pack and cloak as he chased the soldier. *Does the princess have a guardsman with her?*

* ~ * ~ * ~ * ~ *

After breakfast, Katerin and her handmaiden sorted through their meager possessions, collecting the few that belonged to Ilia. She returned the remainder to the carry sack and set the sack under the table. Katerin wasn't willing to set foot in the now-foreboding wagon where Ros lived until necessary.

At Ilia's new abode, Lucinda was openly pleased by the new additions to their troupe, as demonstrated by the affectionate hug she gave them both. "Here, now!" she exclaimed, leaning back to peer at them. "Why the long faces? Surely it's better to be here than where you were?" Seeing the women's reticence, she dismissed the question. "No, don't answer. You'll discover soon enough that Ros only bites when she's backed into a corner. Now go inside, Ilia, and Gemma will show you where to stow your things."

Only after receiving an encouraging nod from Katerin did the handmaiden obey. Silent and solemn as was her nature, Gemma waved Ilia into the wagon.

"Why does Gemma look so grave?" Katerin asked when they were out of earshot. "Why doesn't she speak?"

Lucinda's eyes became sad in reflection. "She's had a very difficult life for one so young. When Ros found her, she was near dead from her injuries." They watched her friend through the open window. "And her tongue had been cut out."

Katerin's hand flew to her mouth in shock. "The poor woman!"

"Aye," Lucinda agreed with a nod. "It's a good thing Ros found her when she did. Someone else might have left her for dead." With a gentle shake, she forced a smile onto her face. "Enough sadness! You're both here and alive — new sisters added to our family!"

Nodding reluctantly, Katerin forced a small smile. *Lucky me.* Ros' leering appraisal flashed through her mind, her low voice ringing in the princess' ears, and Katerin swallowed a sudden thrill of dread. To distract herself, she asked, "What do you do here?"

Lucinda's smile widened. "I dance." With a provocative look, she raised her hands over her head with feline grace, her belly undulating seductively. Seeing the other woman blush, she laughed merrily and dropped her stance. "I sing as well. And play the tambourine. But the men don't care of that."

Unsure what to say, Katerin murmured, "I can imagine they'd not."

"What can you do?" Lucinda asked in curiosity.

I can run from danger. I can get loyal servants killed. I can fade away in obscurity as a harlot. "Nothing," she said. "I've no skills that you talented people could use."

"Well, no worries there," Lucinda said, patting the smaller woman's shoulder. "I'm sure Ros can find something for you." She looked to the wagon as Ilia and Gemma stepped out of it, and so failed to see the troubled expression cross Katerin's face. "All done, then?"

Gemma nodded as the woman beside her looked at Katerin.

"Let's take you visiting then, shall we?" the redhead asked cheerfully. "I'll introduce you to the rest of our fine troupe."

"Certainly," Katerin said politely, nodding. "Lead on."

With happy excitement, Lucinda led the way toward another wagon.

* ~ * ~ * ~ * ~ *

The tour of the wagons was short, there being only a score of performers, but meeting them all at once was confusing...names and faces whirled about in Katerin's mind. She doubted she'd be able to remember one in three for the next fortnight. They were of all colors and sizes, old and young. Wilm was the baby at a tender four years,

Daiki the eldest at fifty-six, though he appeared hardly older than thirty.

As she entered the large tent, people inside were laughing and joking in the cool interior. Eyes adjusting from the direct sunlight, she saw Ros standing in the center, awaiting them. Several logs had been felled, trimmed and laid out in a rough circle. Outside the circle, more logs were placed in fairly neat lines.

"What are those for?" she asked Lucinda, pointing.

"Seating for our guests," she explained. "And the center is the boundary for our stage."

Ros gestured for the entertainers to settle down. Even little Wilm was in attendance, though the black-and-white monkey he played with was distracting him. Once everyone was assembled, their leader clapped to gain their attention. "You've all done wonderfully on short sleep. We're weary from our travels and toils, so there'll be no show tonight." Grinning at the applause and whistles, Ros ducked her tousled head in acceptance. "Rehearsal this afternoon, as usual, and we'll take the evening off." More cheering followed, interspersed with a few groans.

She should smile more often, Katerin mused. *It eases the stern lines of her face.*

Ros' expression turned serious. "I'm sure the reason why we left in such haste has reached your ears. I'll not lie to you: Two men are dead, each killing the other. We've enough problems without the added headaches of being caught up in a feud." She waved the two new arrivals forward. "Ilia...Katerin."

Startled by the candor the circus owner showed to her troupe, Katerin rose and stepped before the audience. Her handmaiden followed timidly, wringing her hands.

"You've probably already met both of them, if Lucinda's had her way," Ros said with a grin, standing between them and placing a hand on each woman's shoulder.

"Aye," a black man called from the rear of the gathering. "And when does Lucinda *not* have her way?" Laughter greeted his response.

The woman in question stood and whirled about, hands on her hips. In a scolding tone, she said, "You're just jealous, Usiku, because I haven't had my way with *you!*"

Katerin wasn't certain which was more disconcerting — the warm hand placed so proprietarily on her shoulder, or the bawdy humor of the crowd laughing and teasing one another in such a manner. She could feel her face heat up as she blushed.

"Be that as it may," Ros called out cheerfully, regaining the people's attention, "this is Ilia, and this is Katerin." She indicated each with a nod. "For whatever reason, they found their way into our cook wagon. I've decided to keep them on. Ilia will be our seamstress, and she can play the lute. She'll also train with Gemma and Minkhat as a buffoon."

"Can you do the Rapath Swing?" a swarthy man questioned Ilia.

Ilia half-shrugged and shook her head, uncertain what it was.

"For now, it's not necessary," Ros interrupted. "Should she decide to remain longer, she'll have the opportunity to learn." Indicating Katerin beside her, she said, "And I've hired Katerin as my personal attendant."

Guffaws of laughter rippled through the small crowd, several of the men making colorful remarks. One or two women joined in or glared in feigned anger at the raucous comments. Katerin stared at her toes in embarrassment, feeling the initial flush suffuse every inch of her skin. The fact that the circus owner didn't rebut any of the comments didn't help.

Chuckling at some of the observations, Ros held up her hand to gain their attention once more. "Again, be that as it may..." her voice trailed off at the laughter, "we now have two more mouths to feed. And a potential danger." Her face became solemn. "As far as anyone need know, these women have been with us since we stopped at Aimsbury near a month ago. Understood?" There was a general rumble of agreement.

"Good." Her hazel eyes scanned her people with practiced ease, making contact with each individual, calculating. "We're in this together — have been for many a year. I trust you with my life, as you trust me with yours. Trust me in this."

"Aye, Ros!" a woman called. "We're better together than apart. You've said so yourself. We'll stand by your decision." Several others loudly voiced their approval.

With a slight bow, Ros said, "Thank you, Sati." A smile returned to her face. "Rehearsal after lunch. Eat light, and until then, enjoy the morning."

The performers dispersed, chattering at their good fortune. Katerin attempted to join them, but the hand on her shoulder tightened.

"Stay," Ros ordered.

Swallowing the bile in her throat, the brunette fought anger and fear as she nodded reluctantly. She watched as Ilia was urged to follow the rest, giving her a false smile of encouragement. When they were alone, Katerin was relieved when the hand fell away.

"I'll not lie to you, either," Ros said. She walked away, turning to straddle the first log she came to. "May I speak frankly, Lady?"

Katerin blinked, surprised by the clear gaze directed at her. "Certainly," she answered softly.

"I may be a Sapphist, but I do not condone rape." Seeing Katerin's blush, she looked away. "You'll be as safe in my bed as you would in your mother's arms."

Flustered, Katerin took a few moments to respond. "I...thank you."

"The Invader's not someone to play lightly, however," Ros continued, still not looking at Katerin. "I'll get you away from his clutches, and you can stay as long as you wish, but you must make the decision when to leave my troupe." With that she rose, dusting wood chips off her breeches. "Lunch is promptly at midday. As I said, eat light. We work hard at rehearsals."

Puzzled yet intrigued, Katerin watched her stride out of the tent.

Part 3

Ros certainly didn't speak in jest, Katerin thought, wiping a sweaty brow on the sleeve of her blouse. She watched as half a dozen members of the troupe performed feats on what they called Standing Poles. Two tall poles stood in the center of the stage, a series of ropes holding them upright in their bases. On each pole were three of the buffoons, and they leapt and bounced from one to another, passing by mere breaths. At one point, Katerin could only gasp as the performers levered their bodies parallel to the ground, using only their arms.

Ros clapped. "No, no!"

Everyone paused, all eyes and ears focused on Ros. Those on the poles shifted their stances, locking their feet and arms around the wood and giving her their attention.

Stepping into the ring, Ros continued, "Minkhat, your timing is off. Is your shoulder still paining you?"

"Some, I'll admit, Ros," said the man who had asked Ilia about the Rapath Swing. He rolled one shoulder with a wince. "I can still have a go."

Ros' tone and face brooked no argument. "No. Pain means it's not healed. Hop down; we don't want you to do further damage."

Mildly disgruntled, Minkhat did as he was ordered, pushing away from the pole, flipping into a backward somersault and landing easily on his feet, though he had been suspended several body lengths above the ground.

"Katerin, are you at all versed in the healing arts?"

Startled at being called upon, Katerin blinked in response. At the irritated look she received, she quickly spoke up. "Aye, a bit."

"Good. Have Sameer show you where our herbal supplies are, and see to Minkhat's shoulder." Dismissing her new charge, Ros returned her attention to the performers. "Let's start from the top. Gemma, Sati, close up the gap, and we'll try it with five people."

Sameer, the troupe's only dwarf, put down the length of rope he'd been repairing. Climbing off a log, he ambled awkwardly toward Katerin. "This way," he ordered, his voice surprisingly mellow compared with his craggy appearance. Katerin followed him, Minkhat trailing both of them slightly. Bright sunlight met the trio as they emerged, the muggy warmth of the tent chased away by a mild breeze. Sighing, Katerin wiped the sweat from her forehead, enjoying the cooling wind.

When they arrived at the cook wagon, Sameer clambered up the three steps and struggled with the latch. Katerin watched for long moments, growing concerned as she watched him fumble with the simple mechanism. He was obviously not quite tall or strong enough to open it with ease. Glancing over her shoulder, she saw Minkhat gazing idly back at her. He would offer no assistance.

Vexed, Katerin tsked. *What was Ros thinking? The little fellow can't do this!* She stepped forward to intercede but felt a hand wrap about her upper arm and pull her back. Whipping her head about, her black eyes fearful and frustrated, she saw Minkhat holding a finger to his lips and shaking his head. As her heart slowed, she heard the latch finally give way, followed by the dwarf's lusty sigh of satisfaction.

"There we go," he said, a wide smile creasing his face as the door swung open. In moments, he was inside the wagon, shoving boxes and rough sacks aside as he rummaged about.

Minkhat released her, pulled up a nearby stool and sat down. Still uncertain, Katerin kept her expression neutral as Sameer found what he was looking for. Wood grated on wood as he pushed a medium-sized chest toward the door. Opening the lid, he waved at it with a flourish and bowed. "All of our healing supplies — at your disposal, Lady Katerin."

Despite her irritation that the dwarf was forced to work so much harder than a normal man, Katerin smiled, dropping into a curtsy. "Thank you, kind sir." His answering chuckle caused her smile to widen.

Sameer climbed down the steps. "That's all we have. We've not had anyone skilled in the healing arts for some time. If you need anything else or would like to restock what we have, let Ros know," he chattered. "She'll purchase what we need at the next village."

"Thank you for your assistance, Sameer," Katerin said. "I shall go over what you have."

Minkhat finally spoke. "Thanks, Sammie," he said with a wave and a mocking grin.

The dwarf's eyes flashed in feigned anger. "That's 'Sameer' to *you*, 'Minkie'." With a final wave at the pair, he returned to the tent.

When he was far enough away, Katerin turned and glared at the man on the stool. "Why wouldn't you let me help him? He was obviously unsuited to the task. It would have been far easier for me to do it myself."

Holding his hands up defensively and leaning backward, Minkhat said, "Because he'd have been insufferable for the remainder of the day. And you," he continued, pointing at her, "would have made an enemy."

Katerin blinked, trying to comprehend. Finally she murmured, "I don't understand."

"Obviously," the man muttered. At her sharp glance, he smiled. "No, I mean no insult, Katerin." Warm brown eyes studied her. "You've not spent much time with commoners, have you?"

Swallowing, Katerin looked away, not wanting to give the man any more information than he could discern on his own.

"No matter. Let me tell you the way of it with people such as Sameer." Minkhat's eyes became unfocused with thought. "You spoke truly that he wasn't suited to the task at hand, but do you believe he'd enjoy being treated like a child his entire life? Would you?"

"What?" Surprise lit Katerin's eyes. She'd not thought of it in those terms. "Certainly not." She considered Sameer, wondering how life would be for a commoner of that stature, and what her life would have been like had she been in his place. To be looked down upon as being less, regardless of intelligence or skill — it would be a tedious existence indeed. *And to forever be denied the opportunity to prove myself...*

Seeing her comprehension, the man smiled. "You understand how he would be insufferable for the remainder of the day?"

Katerin grinned sheepishly. "Aye. I can."

"And how you've brightened his day considerably with your acceptance?"

"Again, aye." She bowed her head slightly. "Thank you for the lesson. I'll not forget it."

Minkhat raised an eyebrow, keenly studying her until he realized she was amused rather than annoyed. "You're welcome," he responded, nodding.

"Now turn about on that stool and take off your shirt," the woman ordered in a matter-of-fact tone. Obediently, he did as he was told.

* ~ * ~ * ~ * ~ *

From the welcome shade of her awning, Ros watched her troupe in the waning light of afternoon. She'd long since removed her black over-tunic, rolled the pale blue shirtsleeves up to the elbow, and opened the neck lacings. Her long legs were propped up on the stool before her, feet crossed at the ankles, and she held a rolled-up parchment in one hand.

Supper was being served, and her people were clustered about the central cook fire, chattering and laughing. Despite Minkhat's stubborn injury, the decent rehearsal that afternoon merited cheerfulness. He had reported that Katerin had been gentle and knowledgeable in her treatment of his shoulder.

Ros' hazel eyes lighted on the new arrivals, studying them. Ilia, the less gregarious of the two, remained quite uneasy. Her smile was hesitant, her movements gentle and understated. She seemed to have been a gangly youth, all elbows and feet, her adult form still awkward and clumsy. Katerin, on the other hand, appeared to be dealing well with the heady mix of the performers, treating each with pleasantness. Watching Katerin's face melt into a laugh at something Ilia said, Ros' lips twitched to match it. *Aye, she's a beauty. I'll give her that. It's too bad she's...* Shaking her windswept head, Ros banished the thought. *Enough of that! You've got much more on your trencher to deal with.*

Hips swaying as she walked, Lucinda neared the wagon. Ros grinned and waved her forward.

"And how are you this fine afternoon, handsome Ros?" she asked with a flirtatious wink.

"Much better with a beautiful woman such as yourself here to brighten my day."

Snorting, Lucinda settled onto a chair without invitation. "You've a silver tongue, for certain. Your da taught you well."

Ros grinned. "Aye, he did at that." More laughter from the fire drew her attention.

Lucinda glanced over her shoulder, a shrewd gleam in her eye as she noted what held the circus owner's interest. "So, that's the way of it then?"

"What?" Ros' brow creased for an instant as she made the connection. "No! The woman's a beauty, I'll give her that, but hardly the type for the likes of me."

Lucinda leaned forward and cupped Ros' cheek. "Oh, love, we both know the true nature of the likes of you." On impulse, she rose and planted a kiss on Ros' lips. Then she straightened, a saucy smile on her own lips. "Now cheer up. No need to be so glum. Come to the fire with me."

Ros smiled. "Soon. You go ahead." She raised her hands in surrender at the piercing stare. "I *promise*."

"All right, then," Lucinda said, smoothing her skirt. "I'll hold you to it." She turned to leave.

"One thing, Luci."

"Another kiss?"

"Your kisses are always welcome, but no." Ros chuckled as the redhead's lower lip stuck out. "What did you do with their clothing?"

"It's been set aside for cleaning and mending," Lucinda said. "There's some fine fabric there, I'm telling you."

Ros sighed, knowing the economical ways of her people were necessary for survival. "Much as I hate to do it, the clothes need to be destroyed. I don't want the Invader's men to have a clue, should they track the women to us."

Regret colored Lucinda's voice. "Aye. I understand. I'll see that it's done."

"Thank you."

"But don't think I'll not hold you to your promise anyway, young scalawag." Lucinda waved a warning finger at Ros. "I'll send Abdullah over here to cart you to the fire, chair and all."

Ros laughed. "I'll be there! I swear it!"

"Best be." Lucinda's stern expression melted into a grin as she sashayed away.

Sighing, Ros watched her go and considered her next step. She'd already begun integrating Kat and Ilia into her troupe, ensuring that the score of people would insist they were from Aimsbury. All evidence of their previous stations would be destroyed. Now she had to get Ilia firmly established with the buffoonery and lute, so that her experience would lend respectability to the lie. Katerin was going to be tougher. Perhaps she'd allow her hair to be cut, to aid in her disguise.

Ros' stomach rumbled. *Aye, perhaps, but not now.* Slapping the rolled parchment against her leg, she dropped her feet from the stool and rose. Negligently, she tossed the parchment onto a nearby table; it unfurled to show a portrayal of a woman with fire billowing from her mouth. *Supper first — a night of enjoyment with my family. Tomorrow's another day and another show.* Ros left the shade beside her wagon, striding toward the fire and food, smiling and returning the salutations of her friends.

* ~ * ~ * ~ * ~ *

When she finally returned to the owner's wagon, its darkness greeted Katerin. She'd waited as long as possible, drawing performers out in conversation as she stalled the inevitable. The fact that Ros had told her she'd be safe didn't ease her heart. The obvious weariness of her handmaiden ultimately decided the issue, Ilia unwilling to leave her mistress' side. With a gentle smile, Katerin urged Ilia to bed, walking her part of the way there and watching until she was safely inside her wagon.

Katerin inhaled the night air deeply and turned to scan the encampment. She could see only Abdullah, a hulking beast who played the circus strongman, on first watch at the fire. He sang quietly as he poked at the fire, his voice a sweet alto that contrasted oddly with his size. Everyone else had gone to bed. Her gaze reached Ros' wagon and her heart thumped. Ros had left the fire long before, and the wagon was dark. Not wanting to step foot inside when she'd had the opportunity earlier, Katerin hadn't seen the interior; now she'd be a stumbling fool. *I'll probably trip and break something*, she mused. A thought occurred to her and the worried expression on her face faded. *I'll just sleep out here on a chair.*

Pleased by her idea, she stepped closer to the shadows of the awning. Katerin's eyes widened, and she gasped in shock at the dark form seated there. "Ros!" Patting her chest, she said, "You scared ten years out of me."

"My apologies, Lady," Ros murmured, rising to her feet. "I have an unfortunate tendency to brood, as my family will attest." She yawned, politely covering her mouth. "Are you ready to retire?"

Katerin swallowed, her heart beating double-time. She tried to stutter an answer, but her tongue betrayed her.

Amused, Ros raised an eyebrow. "Come with me, Lady. I'll not ravish you yet."

The cutting tone lit Katerin's anger. Before she knew it, she had stepped forward to glare up at the older woman. "You'll not ravish me at *all*!"

A wicked smile grew on Ros' face. "True," she said with a nod. "Not until you ask it of me."

Gasping at the audacity, Katerin could only bluster at the woman's gall.

Ros, her smile turning genuine, wondered how many shades of red the smaller woman could turn, wishing it were light enough for her to see properly. Rather than remain outside the entire night, she stepped closer to Katerin, towering over her, her face returning to seriousness. "I've told you, Lady, I do not condone rape."

The words were ice water on Katerin's indignation, leaving her gaping in the aftermath.

Relaxing her aggressive stance, Ros stepped back, studying the shocked brunette before her. "Come, Katerin," she said, brushing past and opening the wagon door. "Bring your things, and we'll find a place for them."

Left standing alone, Katerin collected herself, dulled anger and uncertainty warring within her. She could hear Ros rummaging about inside the wagon, and she shivered in the cool air. Moving to the table, she located the sack that she and Ilia had carried for so many fright-filled leagues. Katerin sighed, face somber, and squared her shoulders before approaching the wagon door.

The interior was lit by a hooded lantern. Gathering her skirts, Katerin stepped up inside. It was cramped and cluttered, as was to be expected. On the right side, a row of cupboards took up the entire wall. To the left was the shuttered window; a small table and two chairs sat below it. The bed against the far end, decorated by a quilted blanket, looked soft and comfortable.

Regardless of the situation, Katerin's body ached for that bed. The mere sight of it brought her bone-deep weariness to the fore, and she swayed with the sudden rush of exhaustion.

Digging in the cupboards, Ros pulled a handful of items out of one and stuffed them into another. "You can put your things here, Katerin," she said, stepping back in the cramped space to allow the smaller woman access.

Quelling the fear that rose at the close proximity, Katerin slipped past Ros and stashed her bag. She closed the cupboard quickly and spun around, not liking having her back turned to Ros. At the blonde's knowing smile, she blushed but raised a challenging eyebrow.

Ros' smile widened, and she bowed slightly in acknowledgment. "If you'd like, I can step outside while you change for bed?" she asked gallantly. Opening another cupboard, she pulled out an oversized shirt. "You can wear this until we've had time to outfit you." Not waiting for an answer, Ros turned and stepped out of the wagon, closing the door behind her.

Katerin blinked, holding the shirt in one hand. She didn't know what to make of Ros — honest and honorable one moment, a cad the next. *Best get changed quickly, then. No telling when she'll decide to pop back in.* She turned her back to the door — lest her knight in rusting armor decided to peek at her attributes — and removed the blouse she'd borrowed from Lucinda. Pulling the shirt over her head and smoothing it down, she could see that it dropped to mid-thigh, and she felt a bit easier. When she was finished changing, Katerin folded the clothing and looked about the wagon. Shrugging, she opened her cupboard and placed the items inside, adding her shoes to the pile. There was a knock on the door just as she closed the cupboard.

"Are you decent, Lady?"

Swallowing against the familiar thrill of fear, she called, "Aye, I am."

Ros stepped inside, eyes flickering over her charge. She noted the embarrassed blush but chose to ignore it. "If you'd like to get into bed..." she said, beginning to remove her over-tunic. "You can sleep on either side; I've no preference."

Katerin paled as she turned to look at the bed. If she slept on the inside, against the wall, she'd be trapped. On the other hand, sleeping on the outside would mean that Ros would have to climb over her. Katerin chewed her upper lip in consternation. When she glanced over her shoulder, she saw that Ros was naked from the waist up and untying the drawstring on her breeches. *Gods!* She jumped into the bed and scooting as far away as possible. *Does she have no modesty?*

Aware of the other woman's discomfort, Ros couldn't help but smile as she kicked off her boots and breeches. She paused long enough to blow out the lantern and open the shutters a bit before climbing under the covers herself. Sighing in pleasure, she stretched and settled comfortably on her back. Beside her, she could feel the waves of tension radiating from the other woman. "Good night, Katerin. May your dreams be sweet."

Dark eyes wide in the darkness, Katerin listened to the fluttering of her heart, Ros' naked nearness agitating her to no end. "Good night," she finally whispered. She nearly jumped out of her skin when the woman moved in the bed, quelling her fear when she realized that Ros was simply rolling over onto her side. For some reason, having Ros' back to her helped her relax. Despite the panic, her body eased into the mattress. Well fed and warm for the first time in days, weariness overtaking her, Katerin drifted off to sleep.

~~*~*~*

Cold sweat, chattering teeth, thunder and jolt of hooves. Warning yell, clash of metal, screams.

With a shuddering gasp, Liam awoke, struggling to get to his feet. Sharp pain lanced through him, and a strangled gasp came from his over-dry throat as he fell back, writhing in agony.

"By the gods, he's awake!" a voice exclaimed. A thump and assorted other noises followed. "Get that witch in here!"

Uncertain of his fate or surroundings, Liam opened his eyes, relief flowing through him as he recognized the face above his. He tried to speak, but nothing would come.

"Hush, my liege. You're as dry as sand. Be still while I get water."

Nodding weakly, he shut his eyes, hearing the trickle of liquid being poured. Someone helped him sit partway up and handed him a wooden mug. The water was ambrosia to his parched throat, and he greedily drank what little was given him.

"That's enough for now," Dominic said, pulling the cup away, "until the witch has a look at you. You've given Ian and me a scare,

Majesty. I'd rather not take any chances."

Majesty? My liege? It took two tries before Liam was able to voice his question. "My brother?"

Dominic's face became somber. "No, Majesty. Of the royal family, only you have survived. The rest of them have gone to the afterworld."

Before Liam could form a response, a door opened, and another person hovered over him, face craggy and gray, toothless mouth drawn down.

"How do you feel, lad?" the old woman asked. She pulled back blankets to peer at his chest, ignoring Dominic's burst of protest.

"Keep a civil tongue, witch! This is your king!"

Grimacing, the old woman glared at the interruption. "Nay. He's a lad, and one that should count himself lucky to be breathing 't all."

The squabbling made Liam's head ache, and he raised his hand, shocked by how heavy it felt. "Please don't fight. It's all right, Dominic. She means no disrespect."

Dominic's eyes narrowed in warning at the witch and then softened as he looked at the teenager. "Aye, Majesty. As you wish."

With much muttering, the woman examined her patient. Surprisingly, her touch was gentle, causing little pain as she removed the bandages from Liam's chest.

In an attempt to distract him, Dominic leaned closer. "You're a very lucky young man, my liege. Had the Invader's blade been a finger span off, you'd be in the afterworld as well."

"How long has—" Gasping at the sudden sharp pain in his chest, Liam ground his teeth. "How long has it been?"

Dominic left off glaring at the witch to answer. Face sad, he said, "Four days, Majesty. Your guard, Ian, was knocked unconscious and left for dead. When he woke, he found you still breathing."

Try as he might, Liam couldn't remember the cause of his pain. There had been war; his family had fled the Invader. "I don't recall."

"And doubtful you would, lad," the witch stated with a grin. "You'd been spitted like a pig for feast. If'n your man hadn't found me, you'd be feedin' the ravens now." Finished with her ministrations, she laid a clean cloth over the wound. "You need to drink this, lad."

A stinking cup was held to his lips, and he recoiled.

"Drink it, Majesty," Dominic urged. "Your kingdom needs you whole and hale." Watching the young man obey, he smiled. "When you're well, we'll begin the task of returning you to your rightful place." Prince Liam Dulce Caesar Alfric, heir to the Dulce throne, drifted off to sleep as Dominic held his hand.

* ~ * ~ * ~ * ~ *

Waking was a slow process. Katerin's muscles were languid from sleep. The urge to stretch was too much for her, so she followed her body's demands. Sighing, she luxuriated in the feeling before opening her dark eyes. Vague light filtered through the cracked shutter, reminding her where she was and what had happened. Dread filled her heart, and she searched for the cause.

Ros was nowhere to be seen — the blankets on that side of the bed tossed to one side, a hollow on the pillow where she'd laid her head. Katerin heard the restrained movements of the camp just awakening and the low voices of people talking quietly while others slept. Rising from the bed, Katerin breathed a sigh of relief. *You're being a ninny! Ros hasn't hurt you in any way.* She moved to the shutters and peeked through the crack. The circus owner sat by the fire, talking with some of her troupe, reaching over to tousle Wilm's hair. It presented a very familial picture, and a smile crossed her face as she watched. *Cad or no, she has a wonderful way with her people.*

Reminded of Ros' less-than-proper remarks and looks, Katerin stepped away from the window. "Time to get dressed," she murmured, "before Ros comes looking." She opened her cupboard and pulled out the borrowed clothing. In moments, she was dressed, tucking the blouse into her skirt. Katerin looked back inside and removed her shoes and the sack. Settling on the bed, she rummaged among her meager belongings and removed a brush. After some time, her hair gleamed. She pulled it back, tying it into a knot before returning the brush to the sack.

Katerin paused, her fingers finding her doll within the sack and caressing its flaxen hair. It had been silly, grabbing Isabella the night of the attack. *I should have grabbed food. Or another weapon.* Thumb running along the doll's porcelain cheek, she pushed away the need to cry. Clearing her throat against the lump, she said, "Now's not the time." Briskly, she closed the sack and returned it to the cupboard. Sniffing and blinking against stinging tears, she slipped on her shoes and purposefully made her way to the door.

Sunlight had yet to make its way into the clearing; only the tops of the trees were aglow. That hadn't stopped a good number of the performers from waking, however, and the site was abuzz with activity. A few people sat around the fire, drinking tea and watching one of the men stirring a pot; others puttered about their wagons, doing any number of odds-and-ends chores.

As Katerin approached Ilia's wagon, she received several calls of greeting. She smiled and waved to each person in turn, her heart warmed by the honest welcome. Upon her arrival, she found her handmaiden throwing two balls in the air as she concentrated on Gemma, who was juggling three. "Good morning, Ilia."

Startled, the woman caught one ball but dropped the other as she whirled to curtsy. "Morning, Lady," she murmured, looking at the ground in deference.

Horrified, Katerin rushed forward. "Nay, nay, Ilia!" she said, grabbing her by the shoulders, forcing the bowed head upward. "You mustn't curtsy any longer, or we'll never survive the coming weeks." She looked at Gemma, who watched them curiously.

Ilia gasped, chagrined. She almost curtsied once more but stopped herself. "I'm sorry, Lady!" she exclaimed, blushing.

Pulling the handmaiden into her arms, Katerin held her close. "Nay. You've no need to apologize. I surprised you." Feeling the need to gloss over the incident, to protect them both, she released Ilia and stepped back. "And what are you doing this fine morning?"

"Learning to juggle, though I fear I'm making a mess of things," Ilia said, face tinting.

Gemma shook her head vigorously, giving a thumbs-up signal. In one hand she held the three balls she'd been tossing as she stooped to pick up the ball Ilia had dropped. Throwing it to the woman, she began juggling again, nodding at Ilia to resume.

Katerin stepped back. "I believe Gemma thinks you're doing a fine job, Ilia," she soothed. "I'll see about breakfast while you continue your lesson."

"Aye, Lady," the handmaiden responded, already distracted as she concentrated on the buffoon's movements. Her hands twitched in mirrored reaction before she began tossing her two balls back and forth.

Attention diverted from her, Katerin eased away, lest she disturb the lesson once more. Looking about the clearing, she found there was nowhere to go but the fire. With a resigned sigh, she neared the central gathering place of the circus, hoping the others would keep Ros distracted and deter further discourteous remarks.

"Good morning, Lady," Ros welcomed in a smooth tone.

Perhaps she only imagined it, but Katerin thought she detected a note of mocking humor. Raising her chin in cool defiance, she said, "Good morning, Ros." Smiling at the others, she greeted them with more warmth. That they appeared amused by her obvious slight of Ros didn't faze her, aside from a blush.

The man who'd been stirring the pot waved a wooden spoon at her. "Would you like some breakfast, Katerin?"

She tried to recall the dark young man's name, to no avail. Her eyes reflected her embarrassment as she stammered, "Very much, thank you..."

"Amar," he supplied with a chuckle. He scooped porridge into a bowl and handed it to her.

Accepting it, Katerin made a small curtsy. "Thank you, Amar." She grinned.

"Eat well this morning, Katerin. We've a busy day ahead," Ros interrupted. To the others, she asked, "Who has the midday meal today?"

"T'would be Gemma, if I don't miss my guess," Lucinda announced, looking up from a shirt she was mending.

Calling to the juggling woman, Ros said, "Remember, Gemma, we work today. Make the meal light and easy to carry."

Gemma nodded, her eyes never leaving the balls she juggled.

Begging the question, Katerin looked about the fire.

"We'll be eating afoot today," a woman with skin as dark as night explained. "Once breakfast is complete and we're preparing for our pageant, Gemma will fix our midday meal."

"Aye," a blond man agreed. "And we'll pack it with and eat when hungry until the show's over and our guests go back to their homes." He leaned forward with a ready smile. "Be sure to get plenty. It'll be a long day."

Ros interjected, "But then, Cristof eats like he's never had enough. Which is why we make him last in line for meals." As everyone laughed, including the blond, she added, "Else there'd be nothing left for the rest of us."

Unable to do aught but laugh with the others, Katerin watched as the blond patted his belly, his skinny form contrasting the gluttonous look on his face.

Clapping her hands, Ros gained the attention of her troupe. "Time to prepare!" she called, her voice reaching everyone in the clearing. "We leave at midday for the township of Hodsin, down the road. Gemma, the fire's yours. Ilia, you'll need to stick close to Minkhat and Sameer for the remainder of the morning. Habibah and Katerin, I need to speak with you at my wagon when you've finished eating. And Habibah, bring your scissors."

The black woman nodded. "Aye. I'll go get them now."

Rising from her stool, Ros smiled at her troupe. "Today we give our guests the best show ever!"

A rousing cheer went up as the clearing became industrious. Ros, her manner that of a proud and indulgent parent, watched over the troupe before striding to her wagon. Caught up in the excitement, Katerin watched her go, puzzling over what motivated Ros.

Part 4

Katerin scratched her scalp, wishing it didn't itch so much. At Ros' request, Habibah had cut her waist-length hair, the dark mass now only reaching to her shoulders. With its sheer weight no longer hanging, gentle breezes teased her hair, causing a relentless tickling. Her nose also itched, but she refused to scratch it, not wanting to smear the makeup that Lucinda had applied so diligently. Turning in her seat, she looked at the remainder of the troupe.

Four wagons trailed Ros', each with an assortment of colorfully dressed people. A vague grumble came from the nearest one, the circus' tiger pacing about her cage in reaction to the excitement. Cristof was the driver of that particular wagon, the cat being his. The horses, their manes neatly combed and braided, wore feathered headdresses. A few people remained at the encampment, finishing last-minute preparations for the show. Ilia was there, lending a hand with final costume stitching and practicing the lute for her first performance.

Despite the circumstances, Katerin's heart fluttered at the impending presentation, and she was hard put not to fidget. Being among commoners was an education in itself. Seeing how an entertainer lived and worked interested her far more than regal propriety allowed

Beside her, Ros clucked at the horses and held the reins. Occasionally, she glanced at her charge, lip curled in amusement at Katerin's barely contained anticipation.

As they broke through the trees, a small valley of farmland opened before them. Homesteads, small dark knots in the distance, sprinkled the green patchwork. The road stretched out before them, bearing directly toward a large cluster of buildings.

Ros pulled up her steeds, tying their reins around the brake. "Come, Katerin," she said before disappearing over the side of the wagon.

Gulping, Katerin obeyed, stopping long enough to peer down the suddenly very tall traveling wagon. She saw the circus owner looking up, her impatience flashing, and Katerin lifted her chin in response. Gingerly, she eased herself over the side, her feet finding the rungs that would carry her back to the ground. By the time she had planted herself firmly on the dusty road, everyone else had gathered around Ros at the back of her wagon. Katerin drifted closer.

"Hodsin is up ahead," Ros was saying. "Daiki, release the dogs and have Minkhat help with the hoops. Martim, Tommaso, Cristof, Willem, and Katerin will drive the wagons. Sameer and Abdullah, pass out treats and make it fun. Gemma, Minkhat, Usiku and Sati, do some tumbles and the like. Wilm will stay with the monkey. Have I forgotten anyone?" Everyone looked at one another, murmuring understanding.

With a nod, Ros continued. "Fantastic. Hodsin was a godsend last season when we came through. Rumor has it they've done twice as well with the crops this year. Make it good, and we'll have food on our table for a fortnight." With a final scan of her people, she grinned rakishly. "Let's have at it, then." The performers parted, babbling excitedly, each person bent to the task at hand.

Chewing her lower lip, Katerin edged closer to Ros. "I've not driven a wagon before," she murmured, blushing at her inability.

"No matter, Katerin," Ros answered in a distracted tone as she pulled on soft black leather gloves. "Just hold the reins and keep them from being tangled. You'll not need any experience for it; the horses have been well trained." When Katerin still hesitated, Ros' eyes fixed upon her. Her voice warmed and she grinned slightly. "No worries, lass. I'll be holding their bridles down below. These big lummoxes don't spook easily."

Coloring further at Ros' attempt to ease her mind, Katerin said, "Aye. No worries." Swallowing hard, she turned without another word and climbed the rungs up the wagon. Katerin untied the reins and stared at the mess of leather in her hands.

To give the newcomer a bit more time to collect herself, Ros made a final check of the wagons and people, stopping here and there as needed to adjust costume or placement. When she was satisfied that all was well, she returned, looking up to see that Katerin had finally figured out which rein went where. "Ready?" she asked softly as she took the lead horse's bridle.

Katerin inhaled deeply, bolstering her courage as she nodded.

Ros craned her neck to look down the procession. "Let's go!" she called, tugging on the steed to get him started.

All in all, handling the wagon wasn't as difficult as Katerin had thought. True to Ros' word, the mounts stayed steady despite their improperly trained driver. Katerin simply held the straps of leather loosely as the circus owner led the team.

Hodsin woke to the new arrivals as the wagons passed the first low buildings. Children called in excitement and ran toward the center of the village, announcing their visitors. A pair of wandering geese honked in displeasure at nearly being trampled. The adult inhabitants left their homes and businesses to trail along with the circus, grinning in welcome at the pleasant interruption of their day, and a fine procession arrived at the town square. People stood aside as the troupe circled about a time or two, showing off the richly painted wagons — and themselves — before stopping.

"Township of Hodsin!" Ros called, her voice ringing through the square. She raised her arms and stepped forward; all eyes were upon her smile. "Let it be known that tonight — *tonight!* — a performance beyond your wildest imaginations shall occur not two leagues east of this spot!" Ros stamped her boot to punctuate her sentence. "You are invited to join us, to witness spectacular acts that will tease your fancy and bedazzle your mind!" Turning to the wagons, Ros waved her people forward.

Startled out of her reverie, Katerin blinked, chagrined that she'd been staring so openly at Ros' short presentation. The energy fairly crackled about the circus owner. Glancing around, she saw the others climbing down from the wagons and moving toward Ros. She scrambled to follow suit. Unsure what to do, she opted to stand at the head of the team, gently holding a bridle as she watched.

"Witness just a sampling of what we have to offer," Ros finished, bowing elegantly and stepping back.

Daiki and Minkhat surged forward, four small dogs yapping at their heels. The buffoon held two medium-size hoops in his hand. At the dog trainer's instruction, the animals leapt through the hoops in an intricate pattern. In response, the people clapped, laughing when one dog appeared to take a liking to Minkhat, jumping up to bounce off his chest and through a hoop.

While this occurred, neither entertainers nor audience were idle. Some people drifted toward Cristof, who regaled them with horrific tales of how many men his tiger had killed. At one point, he rapped the cage with a cane; the cat snarled and growled in response, scaring the living daylights out of the youngsters. Wilm wandered about the crowd, the monkey on his shoulder, answering questions about the animal and allowing children to pet it. The boy's mother, Sati, was chased around the crowd by Gemma, their behavior ludicrous in the extreme as they ran circles about people and generally created lighthearted havoc. Usiku, his midnight-dark skin sporting a patchwork of colorful paint, studied an old man's clothing closely, half-undressing the fellow in his inspection.

When the dogs finished their exhibition, Daiki called them back, tossing each of them a treat before taking the hoops from his assistant. Freed from aiding the trainer, Minkhat leapt into the air with a whoop, doing a back flip before joining Gemma in chasing Sati.

Taking their cue, Tommaso and Martim stalked forward and glanced confidently about the clearing. After sizing up the crowd, they looked at each other, nodded and began their act. Tommaso squatted down, holding very still as Martim placed a huge hand on his head. In seconds, the audience gasped as the second man levered his body up until he was standing, one-handed, on his partner's head.

Katerin watched in awe, as she'd done in rehearsal the day before, while the two men practiced what they referred to as "hand to hand". Out of the corner of her eye, she saw movement that drew her away from the act: Sameer and Abdullah handing out candy. She couldn't help but giggle at them, one tiny and the other massive, as they played off their size to perform their task. Abdullah would squat down, allowing the dwarf to clamber up his muscled body. Sameer, now eye to eye with an average-size woman, would flirt outrageously with her as he handed her one of the many sweets he carried in a satchel on his shoulder. At another point, he circled a man who appeared to be the tallest one in the audience, and his craggy face screwed into a scowl of consternation. Tugging on Abdullah's pants leg, he made some comment. In response, the large performer picked Sameer up by the back of his shirt and dangled him before the tall man's face.

"What do *you* do?"

Surprised at being approached, Katerin looked down to a girl of about eight. "Me?" Her mind raced as she tried to come up with an answer, dark eyes casting about as she searched her thoughts.

"This is my assistant, Kat," Ros responded as she stepped near and knelt down.

The girl giggled, glancing back at two of her friends, who were edging closer. Pointing up at Katerin, she said, "She's not a cat! And what does she assist with?"

Relieved by the interruption, Katerin was nonetheless wary of the circus owner's answer. After the innuendo yesterday, there was simply too much that Ros could say to answer the girl's question.

Also picking up the potential, Ros looked up at the princess, her grin impish. "Well," she said, returning her attention to the child, "Kat is her name. And she helps me with my magic."

"Are you magic?" the girl asked, eyes wide, all thought of Katerin gone. Her friends, interest piqued, pushed closer.

"Aye." The woman nodded solemnly. "Let me show you."

Katerin watched Ros entertain the trio with sleight-of-hand for a few moments, rolling a coin along the backs of her fingers, making it disappear and reappear once more. Despite her desire to keep away from the blonde, Katerin, intrigued by the conversation, felt a small smile forming as she watched Ros teach the girls a simple trick. *How can she be so sweet and so vulgar at the same time?*

When the children had mastered the disappearing coin act, Ros appeared to pull pieces of hard candy out of their ears and presented the candy to them, smiling and commending their magical abilities. As the children scampered off to their parents, she rose, winked at Katerin, and returned to the center of the square. Tommaso and Martim also finished their act, waving at the scattered applause as they backed away.

"Township of Hodsin! What you have seen here is but an insignificant offering. Tonight, you will witness wonders that only the courts of kings and emperors have seen." Ros turned in place, eyes raking everyone present with a mixture of mystery and glee. "You will be able to see aerial feats of daring, magic, juggling, and much, much more!"

"Do ye still breathe fire, lass?" a woman called from the audience.

Ros turned and bowed, a grin on her face. "Aye, I do. And I've yet to lose an eyebrow from it."

Laughing, another spoke. "And do you still have dancers?" He wiggled his eyebrows as a friend guffawed and thumped him on the back.

"Aye!" Ros answered. "Lucinda and Habibah are preparing for your...entertainment even as we speak." She smiled at the murmur of anticipation. Bringing things to a close, she bowed with an elegant flourish and stepped back, her troupe taking her cue and boarding their transportation. "Join us tonight, good folk of Hodsin. We will be awaiting you."

Katerin hustled up the wagon steps, Ros in close pursuit. Settling on the seat, Ros grabbed the reins, quickly untangling them. As the horses began the trek back through town, she murmured through smiling lips, "Smile! Wave at them, Katerin."

Doing as she was ordered, Katerin watched as the people drifted along with them, excited children running alongside until they reached the edge of town. From there, the troupe continued on unescorted. When the wagon was around a bend in the road and out of the townspeople's sight, Katerin dropped her arm and faced forward again.

"That went well," Ros said. "I expect we'll get quite the turnout tonight."

Heartened by the attempt at conversation, Katerin asked, "Is it like that in every town?"

"No. Not always. During good years, we receive good bounty. In bad... Well, suffice it to say that when the crops suffer, so do we. People are less willing to be kindhearted." After a thoughtful pause, she said, "It's been a good year so far, and we've only just begun the season. Any extra foodstuffs we receive will go into the stores for the winter."

Conversation halted for a few moments, the only sound being the steady clop-clop of hooves on the road. "What happens now?" Katerin asked.

"Now? We return to camp, prepare to greet our guests, and put on the best show ever."

* ~ * ~ * ~ * ~ *

Tending the fire pits was a filthy job. Katerin, a smudge of dark ash decorating her right cheek, added more kindling to the iron brazier. As the flame caught and held, she adjusted the mirror, directing the light toward the makeshift stage. Keeping low, she moved to the next pot to repeat her actions. A dozen braziers circled the center of the tent, providing illumination for the performers. It fell to Katerin and Ilia, the least skilled of the troupe, to keep them blazing. Currently, the dark young woman worked alone, as her handmaiden was needed to play the lute for an upcoming act.

Around her, the crowd burst into laughter. Glancing at the cleared center, she saw Usiku pulling what appeared to be a long string of colorful cloth out of his breeches. That the material turned out to be several small clothes tied together only made the audience laugh harder. An exaggerated look of embarrassment when he finally peeked into his breeches forced a chuckle from Katerin. She smothered it and returned to stoking the small fire before her.

Scattered around the edges of the tent were torches to light the way for those who wanted to come and go, though not many people used the opportunity. It appeared that the entire population of the valley was present, torchlight reflecting no fewer than fifty people enjoying the show. This was the troupe's third performance in as many days, the word of their presence leaping through the small community and its surrounding countryside. Ros had been correct in her assessment of the bounty; the cook wagon now held several additional pounds of wheat and corn, three salted hams, two dozen eggs, and an assortment of drying herbs. There had been promises of two casks of beer and a handful of roasting hens, should the troupe decide to stay for another day.

Katerin scooted to the next brazier, wiping sweat from her forehead, smearing even more ash on her delicate features. Around her, the audience roared and clapped as Gemma pulled Usiku's breeches down to his ankles, revealing a monstrous leaf guarding his manhood. Grabbing up his drawers, the man gave chase, his buttocks flashing as he stumbled after his companion.

When the clowns were out of sight, Ros strode to the center of the tent, a barely suppressed expression of somber excitement upon her face. Instinctively, the people hushed, some even leaning forward in anticipation. Katerin became mesmerized once again, an unsettling habit she'd developed over the past three days of watching the woman.

"In the deepest, darkest jungles of Mohsir lurks a beast so vicious, so horrible, that the natives of the region liken it to a demon," she said, her rough voice pitched low. As Ros spoke, music began to build somewhere behind her. "Many have seen it; few have survived to tell their woeful tale. One man — a great and noble hunter — braved the depths of that jungle, searching for the Mohsir Demon."

When Ros looked pointedly at Katerin, an embarrassed flush crossed the princess' face as she realized she'd missed her cue. Thanking the gods for the darkness, she hastily adjusted the mirror before her until the light washed across Cristof, waiting to one side.

Satisfied that things were back on schedule, Ros continued weaving her story, circling around and making eye contact with her audience. Behind her, Cristof acted out the tale. "Upon finding the beast's lair, he gathered his weapons. His goal was to capture this horrible animal, and so he built a cage of bamboo and vines."

A bizarre wooden contraption was trundled out, pushed by Minkhat and Willem. Made of elm and rope, the cage was created out of leftover branches stripped from the tent poles. In the flickering light, it looked rustic enough for the troupe's purpose. Minkhat and Willem rolled out two barrels, placing them in the center of the stage near the flimsy cage before disappearing into the dark.

"Armed only with a whip and a stave, the great hunter prepared to lure the beast into the open. What follows is a reenactment of that fateful contest," Ros finished, moving out of the central area.

Cristof pulled the whip from his belt and let it fly, the crack causing the audience to gasp. A low growl came from the darkness behind the stage, causing a woman in the audience to squeak in fear. Katerin, her attention no longer diverted by the circus owner's presence, bent to her task. She had seen the "Mohsir Demon" lying on her back to receive a tummy rub from young Wilm, so the act was less than astounding. Ilia soon reappeared, her lute no longer needed, and the pair of them fell back into the mindless drudgery. Lost in her thoughts, Katerin didn't notice the new arrivals.

Ros, however, did. From her vantage point, she saw three men slip through the main entrance and begin scanning the crowd. Although they weren't causing a disturbance, Ros had no doubt who they were looking for. Catching Abdullah and Willem's eyes, she nodded toward the entry. The three troupe members converged on the obvious soldiers.

"I'm glad you could join us," Ros said, her voice nearly a whisper so as not to disturb the nearest villagers. "Perhaps you and your men would like to sit? The show is not quite half-finished."

The apparent leader looked her up and down. "No," he responded. "We'll stand." With a nod at his comrades, he sent them to look through the audience.

With great skill, Ros refrained from scowling at the unwelcome visitor. "I'm the owner of this circus. Is there something I can help you with?"

Eyes narrowing as his interest was piqued, the soldier asked, "How long have you been in this area?"

His tone brooked no demurral, and Ros was hard put not to respond in kind. "I'm not at liberty to answer your questions right now. As I said, we're halfway through our performance." She gestured behind her to the stage, where Cristof had his tiger balancing precariously upon one of the barrels. "This act is nearly over, and I must introduce the next."

"You'll answer what questions I put to you when I ask them," the soldier growled, taking a step forward.

Holding up her hand to forestall her companions from coming to her aid, Ros raked her eyes over the man before her, her face stern. "Do not forget yourself, Captain. I doubt the queen of Dellenri would appreciate hearing about the Invader's soldiers rousting citizens within her borders." Before he could respond, Ros continued smoothly, "I will be most happy to answer any questions you have when this performance is over. Feel free to post your men as guards. After our guests have left, we will speak."

Studying her closely, searching for any sign of subterfuge, the captain nodded stiffly. With a jerk of his head, he recalled his men, and the trio stepped outside.

Turning away, Ros sighed in frustration. *The question is, did they track us, or stumble upon us during a sweep?* She gauged how far along Cristof was in his act, not surprised to find that the ending had long since passed and that he was improvising. The crowd appeared to be getting restless, instinctively knowing something had changed.

"Now what, Ros?" Willem asked.

Ros sighed again and adjusted her sleeve. "Let's get this finished. We've got a far more important performance tonight. Inform the others." She barely heard their responses as she strode toward the stage to introduce the next act.

* ~ * ~ * ~ * ~ *

All too soon, the routines were over. Standing at center stage, Ros looked out over the audience, catching the telltale glint of torchlight on chain mail, and gave her closing speech. A cheer met her invitation for everyone to return the next afternoon for one final show. Bounding forward to accept their accolades, the entertainers bowed and waved before dashing out of sight into the darkness.

Katerin and Ilia lit torches around the stage, giving the guests better illumination on their way out. About them, the hubbub of a satisfied crowd rose and fell.

Normally, after everyone had left, their next chore would be to put out the torches and make certain the braziers were extinguished before going to bed. Sameer had come 'round earlier, however, to inform them they had unwanted guests and that there'd been a change of plan. Looking toward the main entrance at the three guardsmen, Katerin felt fear flutter in her throat.

"Katerin."

Flinching in surprise, she turned to find Sati standing there, remnants of clown makeup smearing her face.

Reaching out, Sati laid a calming hand on Katerin's forearm. "I'm sorry I startled you," she said softly. "Ros sent me."

Katerin placed her hand over the older woman's. "It's all right. What did Ros need from Ilia and me?" she asked, smiling in reassurance at her handmaiden.

Sati nodded at the shy blonde before returning her gaze to Katerin. "We've been through similar situations. Ilia, you're to clean up and go to your wagon. The soldiers will want to know who sleeps where."

Swallowing heavily, Katerin felt her heart sink as she realized where the charade was heading. "Me as well?" she asked, forcing her voice to remain steady.

Sati smiled in sympathy. Squeezing the smaller woman's arm, she said, "Aye. Though Ros says you're not to clean up first." She reached up with her free hand to muss Katerin's recently shorn hair. "She says to act the simpleton and follow her lead."

Nodding, the princess raised her chin, giving the impression of a lamb being led to slaughter. *A simpleton who warms the Sapphist owner's bed.*

A scowl crossed Sati's face and she squeezed Katerin's arm again. "Stop that! Ros would never hurt you or take advantage."

Katerin bowed her head in shame. "Forgive me," she murmured. "You're absolutely correct."

"Let it go, Kat. We've no time to discuss it." Glancing around at the now-empty tent, Sati released her arm. "Come. Let's see how good an actor you are."

As she followed, Katerin mused that she was royalty. *Acting is in my blood.* Reaching out, she grasped Ilia's hand, giving it a gentle squeeze as they stepped out into the evening. Certain that the pair would follow orders, Sati left them at the entrance, joining her small family at their wagon.

"Milady?" Ilia whispered, eyes large as she spotted the guardsmen walking through the encampment with Ros.

"Do as Sati said, Ilia. All will be well. Remember, you and I joined the troupe a month ago." With an encouraging nod, Katerin released the woman's hand. In sudden inspiration, she leaned over and whispered, "Pretend that one of the guardsmen is young Malcolm."

Ilia blushed, dropping her gaze at the memory of a certain smith's apprentice who'd been sweet on her. "Aye, Milady," she said. At Katerin's urging, she grabbed up her skirts and left to join Gemma and Lucinda at their wagon.

Katerin watched her until she reached her destination. Scanning the encampment, she saw that Ros had almost completed a full circle and had only three more wagons to go before her own. "Best get on with it, then," Katerin said under her breath. Aware of the soldiers' watchful eyes, she ducked her head and allowed her shoulders to slump. Her steps became a shuffle as she went to Ros' wagon. Once there, she settled upon the stool on which Ros propped her feet. She didn't have to wait long.

"And here is my wagon," Ros said, leading the Invader's trio.

"Who's this?" the captain grunted, looking down at the woman seated on a low stool.

"Kat! Stand up and greet our guests!" the circus owner insisted, pushing past the guard and dragging Katerin to her feet.

Startled, Katerin jumped at the sudden strong grip on her arm. Biting her tongue against the immediate irritated response, she opted to keep her head down, masking an angry flush. "Good evening," she mumbled, giving the soldiers an awkward curtsy.

Apparently satisfied, Ros released the younger woman's arm, rubbing it gently. "Aye, much better." Turning to the captain, she grinned ruefully. "Please excuse her. She's not had much experience with proper etiquette."

The captain eyed the smaller woman in speculation. Ordering his men to search the wagon with a nod of his head, he returned his attention to Katerin. "How long have you been here?" he asked the filthy woman.

The uncomfortable silence was broken only by the sounds of Ros' wagon being searched. Finally, Katerin shrugged one shoulder. "I don't know, sir. A long time."

"She's a bit simple," Ros explained in an undertone, finger circling the air beside her ear. "I picked her up in Aimsbury at the same time as Ilia."

Ignoring Ros, the captain reached out and tilted Katerin's face up. "Here, girl, let's have a look at you." His touch was not unkind as he turned her face this way and that, squinting at her ash-covered features by the light of a nearby lantern.

Katerin's dark eyes were fearful as they met his. Although her royal training insisted she hold his gaze, she knew better. Allowing her trepidation to show, she chewed her lip, attempting to stare at the ground during his inspection.

The two soldiers interrupted him as they returned from their search. "Anything?" he asked.

"No, sir," one responded, scanning the blonde woman's length. "Only one bed. A few changes of clothing for this one, though nothing but a shift for the other."

Pursing his lips, the captain turned his attention to Ros, an eyebrow lifting in question.

With a wave at Katerin's dirty appearance, Ros said, "That's hardly surprising, is it? Her job is to take care of the braziers during performances. I'd be a fool to waste money on more for her. She'd soil it within minutes." She continued, with an ingenious grin, "Besides, her other...attributes are what I keep her for, and clothing isn't necessary."

It took a moment for the comment to sink in. While one soldier was able to keep a straight face, the other burst into a wicked guffaw before he could stifle himself. The captain's eyes narrowed, his expression turning cold. His grasp on the small woman's chin tightened, and he leaned forward to stare at her. "Is this true?" he grated. "Do you share this...woman's bed?"

His weathered face filled her vision, and Katerin forced herself to look at him. *Gods! Now what do I do?* Realizing that the situation precluded Ros from helping her, she went with her instincts. A sweet smile crossed her lips, and she said, "Aye, sir. I keeps her warm at nights."

Releasing her and stepping backward, the captain sneered at Ros. "Sapphist bitch."

Ros' smile turned feral as she moved smoothly between the man and woman. "Aye, that I am. Not only a Sapphist, but a bitch as well. You'd do well to remember that." Her tone was not quite a threat, and she made no move to reach for the sword hanging from her hip.

After staring at her in disgust for another moment, the captain waved his soldiers off. "What we're looking for is not here," he pronounced. "Let's go." Without another word, he turned on his heel and strode out of the camp.

There was a long, breathless pause as everyone watched them go. Near the tent entrance, the three soldiers mounted their large warhorses. With a final, derisive backward glance, the captain kicked his steed into a gallop. The thunder of hooves faded into the distance.

Katerin, still standing behind Ros, stared at the woman, relief washing over her so thickly that she wondered whether she'd faint. Ros reached up to scratch her tousled hair, trailing her hand down to rub the nape of her neck. A sudden desire washed over Katerin — a yearning to ease the burden on those shoulders — and she almost leaned forward before she caught herself. Staring at the ground in mild confusion, she balled her hands into fists. Chuckling caught her attention, and Katerin looked up as the circus owner turned.

"*That*," Ros insisted, "was priceless!" Without thought, she grabbed the woman into a hug, spinning her around. "You've outdone yourself, Kat! You've missed your calling!" She set Katerin back onto her feet, chortling.

Flustered, equal parts embarrassed and pleased, Katerin allowed a small grin to cross her face. "Thank you."

As the rest of the troupe approached, laughing and talking excitedly in relief, Katerin could still smell the circus owner's scent and feel the strong arms about her, and her skin tingled in response. *What is this?* Before she could analyze the strangeness, Ilia distracted her with an embrace.

* ~ * ~ * ~ * ~ *

It was late, most of the performers having gone to their beds in exhaustion long ago. Ros, seated at the small table in her wagon with a hooded lantern illuminating her work, looked up from the book she scribbled in, diverted from last-minute accounts by a noise. The sound came from the bed to her right, where Katerin slept. Puzzled, Ros adjusted the lantern, allowing the light to sweep across the sleeping form. The woman moaned and tossed her head, her expression pained.

Another bad dream. Ros rose and settled on her side of the bed, reaching out to gently caress the dark bangs.

As Katerin struggled with the nightmare, barely coming to consciousness, she felt fingers caressing her forehead. "Shhh. It's just a bad dream," a familiar voice murmured. "You're safe now." Sighing, Katerin relaxed back into sleep.

Though Katerin no longer thrashed, Ros remained in place, enjoying the rare unguarded moment. Katerin was more likely to be pensive or angry in her presence than anything else. *Probably for the best*, she thought, drawing the backs of her fingers across Katerin's cheek. *It would be easy to fall for a beauty like this.*

Reluctantly, Ros forced herself away from the bed and back to the table. Unable to concentrate on the books, she sighed and closed them, vowing to do the accounting before the afternoon show. Blowing out the lantern, she stood and stretched, restless despite the exhausting events of the day. She knew from experience that sleep would not be forthcoming. Rather than toss and turn, possibly waking Katerin, she stepped out of the wagon.

The night air was brisk, and Ros inhaled deeply, finding the scent of new growth invigorating. Daiki, who sat first watch, noted her presence. He nodded at Ros as he walked a patrol around the encampment, receiving a wave in return. Ros settled into her chair and propped her feet on the stool. Her thoughts were as dark as the night sky, and she let herself peruse them fully.

Having the Invader's men roust them, although expected, still caused her a wave of disgust. Ros was quite surprised she'd handled herself as well as she had. The captain never noticed the thin film of sweat on her brow or the quaver in her voice. Breathing in and out deeply, she tried to release some of the residual fear.

Her response wasn't that far-fetched. The Invader had sent his men searching once before, when Ros was a mere child. Her da had talked those men out of carting away his daughter, but he'd barely succeeded. The child they searched for was apparently found elsewhere a week later; the blonde girl was beheaded, and the grisly remains presented to the new monarch. It had been a terrifying time for young Ros and the circus.

Old emotions wrapped about Ros — a familiar rotting blanket of disgust, fear, and regret. She knew that sooner or later, the Invader would get desperate. It was well known that he killed everyone of royal blood to ensure his claim to the stolen thrones. If his men didn't bring the Dulce survivor to him in good time, chances were that other heads would roll. How many women with black hair and eyes would die before he was satisfied? The future deaths weighed on Ros almost as heavily as the past one did.

Part 5

The Invader sat tall in his saddle as he toured his new acquisition. His armor had been repaired and cleaned of all signs of war, the metal chain glittering in the sunlight. Surrounding him, six of his guard kept vigilant eyes on his person. About them lay evidence of heavy fighting. Dried pools of rusty brown stained the cobblestones where men had been wounded or killed. Destroyed awnings, doors, and windows marred the homes and businesses from which residents had been routed; streets were littered with broken furniture and trampled foodstuffs. Only the rattle of horses' hooves echoed off the walls, the near-silence eerie under the brilliant sun and deep blue sky.

The clatter of an unshod pony interrupted the procession, the guards studying their surroundings with suspicion as the Invader halted. A horse rounded the corner behind them at breakneck speed, a scribe clinging to the animal's saddle, eyes frantic. The horse slid to a stop on the cobblestones, squealing at its rider's inexpert handling. Oblivious to the armed men preparing to draw steel, the scribe scrambled down from his mount, sickened relief evident on his face as he stumbled forward. "My liege! There's news!"

Waving off his men, the Invader turned his horse and waited for the skinny fellow to catch up to him. "What news, Phineas?"

"Your patrol has returned, Your Majesty!" Phineas puffed, face red as he tried to catch his breath.

The Invader's eyes sharpened as he leaned forward. "Did they find the princess?" he asked.

The scribe abruptly stiffened, remembering the fate of those who brought bad news. Bowing deeply, he said to the paved ground, "Nay, Your Majesty. They were unsuccessful."

Drawing himself up, the Invader growled. *Are they all such fools that a little girl can best my finest trackers?* He had no doubt there were others assisting Sabine. When he discovered who they were, he planned to eviscerate them. Slowly. He glared down at the cowering scribe, rather pleased his reputation still held strong. It had been years since he'd last lost his temper and killed those around him in a fit of pique. "Phineas," he said, his voice cracking.

The scribe jumped, knuckling his forehead. "Aye, Your Majesty?"

He choked on the words.

"Return to the castle. Tell my patrol to report to me personally at the market square."

"Aye, Your Majesty!" Phineas dashed off before his liege could have a homicidal change of heart. The pony shied away, forcing him to caper after it to catch the reins. Clambering into the saddle, the scribe sat in an indecorous heap as he hauled the animal around and kicked it back the way he had come.

Turning his horse, the Invader resumed the journey, his men following. He could almost smell the wariness about them now as they watched for traps — and watched him as well, wondering whether he'd become violent. *Let them watch. They'll see soon enough.*

Many years had passed since the last blueblood had escaped his initial clutches. It had taken a week before the child was found hiding in a millhouse. That time, two of his men had been executed for their failure. The Invader wondered how many would pass the veil this time.

The streets were no longer silent. As the group neared the market square, a dull whisper of sound grew and expanded. Voices, hundreds of them, talking, yelling, sobbing, came together in a crescendo that washed over the Invader as he led his men into a near-riot.

Every man, woman, and child still alive in the aftermath of the siege huddled in the square. A cordon of the Invader's men kept them penned, a row of sergeants and captains pacing outside the human corral, yelling encouragement to the soldiers. At one end of the square stood a makeshift scaffold, tall enough for all to see, a dozen nooses swaying in the warm spring breeze. A hush fell over the crowd as the Invader circled, making for the scaffold. By the time he and his men arrived there, the only sounds were children crying and the occasional wail of a wounded man.

Two wagons created a platform, where the Invader halted and dismounted. In three strides, he stepped onto the wagons and looked out over the gathered people, ignoring the glares and occasional curses yelled his way. For the most part, his audience was demoralized, no one willing to risk further death by angering him. *Now to keep it so.*

The Invader waved to one side, and several people were herded up to the scaffold. Each wore the tattered remnants of finery — silks and satins, torn and filthy from many days in the dungeons. Several had obviously suffered beatings; their faces and arms were bruised and cut. Only two women stumbled forward, both looking far worse than their male counterparts. As they took their places before the nooses, the ropes were dragged down and tightened around their necks.

When the victims were properly outfitted for their demise, the Invader nodded to one of his men. Without any pronounced judgment, the executioner walked down the line, shoving each of the twelve condemned people off the platform to strangle slowly before their people.

Screams of protest erupted from the crowd as the dying twitched and struggled against their bonds, unable to stop the inevitable. When the people surged forward, it took all the strength of the Invader's men to keep them captive; additional troops rushed forward to hold the line. The Invader remained silent, watching dispassionately until the twelve died in their final seizures, their muscles going lax and the stink of their released bowels tainting the already-charged air.

The Invader scanned the now-mourning people, sensing more despair than fury among them. His silent attention gathered the mob, hushed it, kept its heart beating fast and thready in trepidation. Finally, the Invader pointed at the string of corpses. "Those were your nobles," he called, his gruff voice echoing off surrounding walls. "They died because they chose the wrong side of this war!"

A trio of horsemen entered the square, making slow progress around the gathering as the Invader continued to speak.

"As will you, if you do the same! You know who I am! You know what I'm capable of!" His eyes studied the crowd. "If any one of you harbors a dissident, I will have ten executed!"

Low murmurs of muted anger and fear rumbled through the audience. The riders arrived at the platform and dismounted. The Invader turned to look down at his patrol, grim understanding narrowing his eyes as they refused to meet his gaze. "Did you find her?"

The captain, a craggy fellow, fell to his knee. "No, Your Majesty. We tracked her to a large camp but lost the trail. We found two merchant caravans and a circus in our sweeps; she was with none of them."

Nodding, jaw muscles flexing, the Invader looked over the gathered people, not seeing them. "You failed."

His swallow audible, the captain nodded. "Aye, my liege."

"Cut them down," the Invader said to the executioner, waving at the bodies. As his orders were being carried out, he gestured to another soldier. "Hold them."

The three guards shouted in surprise as their fellows pounced. A scuffle ensued, but they were soon brought under control and disarmed. With further instruction, the executioner added more rope to the scaffold, and the trio were wrestled up to their destiny.

"If *anyone* fails to obey my rule, this will be the ultimate price!" The Invader gave a curt nod to the executioner, who promptly tossed the guards to their deaths.

Not even babes in arms dared to interrupt the proceedings.

* ~ * ~ * ~ * ~ *

Liam pushed the spoon away with a deep sigh. "Enough, Dominic." He winced as he adjusted himself, a sharp pain pulsing through his chest as he eased an ache in his back.

"You've hardly touched your broth," the aide said, still holding the wooden utensil.

"I'm *sick* of broth," Liam growled, fuming at the quaver in his voice. "I'm sick of not being able to feed myself, of being stuck in this godsforsaken cottage while my family remains unavenged!"

Used to the youth's sickbed tantrums by this point, Dominic, turned away, setting the bowl to one side. "That's to be expected, Majesty," he said, reminding the teenager of his title. "You've been ailing for a month. But if you don't take care of yourself and regain your strength, vengeance will be moot."

Liam signed. "I know, Dom," he said, lightening his tone. "I'm sorry. I know you're taking a great risk to keep me alive and well."

"You've been lucky. The witch's healing talents have kept you safe from fever. But if you do not eat, you'll be susceptible." He studied the youth. "Your people need you strong, my liege."

Nodding, Liam pursed his lips. With considerable lack of enthusiasm, he said, "Let's have more of that broth, then, and you can tell me of the Invader's doings."

Pleased, Dominic retrieved the bowl and scooped another spoonful into Liam's mouth. "The Invader returned to his capital of Lusthor two weeks past. He should already be sitting on his throne, counting the monies he's made here."

"Who oversees Dulce, then?"

"A steward from Barentcia named Fetah. Also, an entire regiment of men has remained to keep the peace."

Liam swallowed more soup, not quite grimacing at the sickeningly familiar taste. "You've kept very quiet about his actions, Dom," he said. "Certainly our people aren't happy with the way of things."

"I didn't want to vex you, Majesty." Dominic feigned chagrin as he studied the bowl in his hands. "Your health is far too important."

Snorting, Liam scowled at another stab of burning pain through his chest. "If I am to be king, I need to be kept informed of my enemy's actions."

So the young pup finally decides to claim his birthright. The aide looked up, pinning Liam with a fierce gaze. "And *will* you be king, my liege?"

The youth blinked, startled by the question. Undoubtedly, he would be king. Wouldn't he? His eyes narrowed in thought, broth and man forgotten as he puzzled over the issue. He was barely a man, only fourteen years old, and the Invader thought him dead. By all reports, the usurper had personally run Liam through. It would be an easy enough task to walk away, once he was healed. He imagined what his life would be like if he chose to let things be. Would he be able to find a vocation, perhaps marry a pretty girl someday and have children? With his dark hair and eyes, he was certain his children would be similar in appearance. *Children.*

His memory flashed on his younger brother, Aiden, a sweet boy who adored Liam through all his short life. He was dead now — murdered for the blood running through his veins. Then there was Sabine, older than Liam, beautiful and intelligent. Their father had only recently begun the search for a likely husband. Now she was married to Death, moldering in an unmarked grave somewhere east of the city.

Bertram, eldest and heir to the throne, was quick to anger and just as quick to apologize for his temper. Liam remembered the joy of being lifted by those strong arms and set astride a warhorse when he was no more than three or four. He idolized Bertram as much as Aiden idolized him.

He thought of his father, his light brown hair a rarity in a family of brunettes, strong and just, equal parts kindness and steel. His queen, Liam's mother, was dark of hair and eye like all her children; she was never too busy with the intrigues of court to dote on her offspring.

His jaw flexed as he fought tears of mourning and anger. He realized the illusion of his "choice". There was only one alternative open to him. Liam's black eyes, stern as his father's had been, stared at Dominic. "Of course I'll be king," he stated. "I'll personally grind the Invader under my boots."

The aide smothered a thrill of victory in his heart. Leaning forward, his manner as solemn as Liam's, he said, "And I will stand by you to see it done."

They stared at each other, the unspoken pact blossoming between them. Liam fought off more tears, these of relief at knowing he was not alone in his quest.

Dominic chuckled inwardly. The trap had been sprung upon the inexperienced lad. As befitted a man of his lower station, he sat back, turning away to allow the crown prince an opportunity to collect himself."

Liam inhaled through his nose, lifting his chin to gather himself. His injury made him weak, not only in body, but also in mind. Soon, his emotions would not run so close to the surface. Until then, he'd leave things in the hands of his trusted man, Dominic, and the guard, Ian. Under control, he raised an eyebrow at the man seated beside him. "Tell me of the Invader's actions since he killed my family."

Nodding, Dominic returned to feeding the youth. "Once he had control of Dulce, he ordered the city sacked. Though it's been a month, there are still many buildings damaged from the looting. I expect it will be a hungry winter this year."

"What of the nobles? Do you think any will support me in a fight?"

"Some, perhaps," the aide said, shrugging. "There aren't that many left these days, and those that are have firmly established themselves in the Invader's graces."

Liam frowned. "Not that many left? What happened to them?"

Dominic looked as if he'd tasted something sour. "Several of your father's staunchest supporters were arrested and held in the dungeons. They were tortured and beaten for any information they might have." He sighed and glanced away.

Despite the pain, Liam sat up, intent on getting answers. "What happened?"

The aide's eyes flickered to and away from the lad, playing him. "They were murdered, Majesty; strung up to suffocate in front of the people of Dulce. They were examples of what he would do to them if any disobeyed his rule."

Liam relaxed back into his pillows with a slight exhalation. "Suffocated?"

"Aye, my liege." Dominic appeared to be troubled. "It was a very slow and painful death."

Seeing the executions in his mind's eye, Liam felt more than the querulous anger of a cripple. It was fury, strong and clean, pulsing through his heart and reaching every inch of his body. His family had been hunted down and slain; even the nobles of his court were killed in a manner most foul. Suffocation was a punishment reserved for only the most heinous of crimes. The only wrongdoing on the part of any of the dead was standing by their king and country.

"I want all the information you can get on the Invader's people, Dom," he ordered. "And find a Siffian priest who can be trusted to anoint me. If I'm to rule my people, I need to be their king instead of a crown prince."

Dominic's face melted into a smile at Liam's royal tone. He stood and bowed formally. "Yes, Your Majesty! I'll see it done!"

Liam nodded. "Go. Send Ian in to finish feeding me."

"As you wish, my liege!" The aide set the bowl on a nearby table and backed out of the room, showing the youth the deference due his future title. As soon as the door closed, he leaned his forehead against the cool wood and sighed in relief. It was finally time to begin.

~~*~*~*

Katerin picked her way along a stony creek bed toward the river. The musical trickle of water her only escort, it was soothing to her soul. Behind her, the gentle murmur of the performers at camp faded away, leaving her with only her thoughts.

Solitude was a rare commodity among the circus people, whose gregarious natures seemed to preclude anyone from needing to be alone — except for Ros, who indulged in her brooding late at night when everyone else was asleep. Once the tent stood tall in some clearing or other, Katerin made it a habit to explore the immediate vicinity, to be alone. If any of the others found it odd, no one said so to her. Accustomed to the circus owner's foibles, they had little problem understanding hers.

The creek opened up before her, its stony bank meeting a small spit of sand. There, the running water became sluggish, a thick expanse of subdued blue flanked by towering trees of all varieties. Katerin eased her way along the shore, fascinated by the footprints she left behind on the virgin soil.

Inhaling deeply, she located a fallen log and sat down. It was cooler by the water, a welcome respite from the heat of early summer. The circus had come far in its travels these past two months, well away from her homeland in the north. Katerin was glad her hair was short; its previous length would have stifled her here. She could hardly imagine what high summer would bring.

Some time passed as Katerin allowed herself to *be* — not thinking, not feeling, not doing. While she sat still, her eyes remained restless, tracking the movements of nature around her. Tree limbs caressed a breeze, dancing with invisible partners, showing off their green finery. Distinct plops in the river heralded the occasional fish surfacing for a snack, the ripples swept away before they could reach shore. Interesting conglomerations of debris floated past, chasing the ripples with slow majesty.

A flash of white near the creek caught her eye, and she swiveled her head to see Ilia following her path. Katerin felt a pang in her heart. She and Ilia rarely spent time together anymore; their duties in the circus ate away every spare moment. Watching her handmaiden walk across the rocks with ease, it struck Katerin that Ilia had changed. The woman had always been rather hesitant and clumsy in her service. And here she walked with grace and ease over difficult ground. A smile of wonder crossed her lips. *It appears the gawky flower has finally bloomed. Intriguing that it took a circus to do such a thing.*

Ilia noticed Katerin. She smiled and waved, coming closer. "I thought I saw you come this way."

"You were right." Katerin patted the log beside her in invitation, trying to recall the last time Ilia had slipped and referred to by her title or as "lady", but she failed to pinpoint an answer. "It's been quite some time since we've talked. How are you?"

"Well enough." Ilia sat beside her former monarch. "I've mastered juggling six items at once. Gemma says she'll incorporate me into her act soon."

Katerin bumped shoulders with Ilia. "That's fantastic! Congratulations!"

The old Ilia flashed to the fore as she blushed red to the roots of her hair and ducked her eyes. "Thank you, Kat."

"It's well deserved. You've done a commendable job here." Katerin stopped before the woman became abashed by the praise, turning her attention to the meandering river.

Saved from further embarrassment, Ilia did the same, collecting herself. Several moments later, her voice a murmur barely louder than the river's, she asked, "Do you miss them?" Katerin glanced sharply at the woman's profile. "I do," Ilia continued, not waiting for a response. "Some days, it's all I can think of — whether they're still alive, where they've gone." She shrugged slightly. "Other days, I imagine they're safe and well in hiding."

Clearing her throat, Katerin asked, "Who?"

Ilia sighed deeply. "My parents, my sister."

Frowning, not wanting to visit this shared past, Katerin nevertheless knew that Ilia needed to talk about it. "Your father was...a minor noble, yes?"

"Aye. He was only a Lord. He had a small steading in Resso Valley." Ilia turned to Katerin, blue eyes flashing a combination of bleak resignation and the slightest hint of hope. "Do you think they lived?"

Katerin pulled Ilia's hands into hers, mustering an expression of confidence. "I'm certain of it, Ilia. The Invader would not trouble himself with a minor lord. If your family submits to his rule, they should yet live."

Relief colored Ilia's face, and she dropped her gaze, slumping her shoulders.

Tears stung Katerin's eyes — tears of rage that she had no hope in this respect, tears of jealousy that Ilia's parents had no doubt survived the upheaval, tears of self-pity. Ultimately, the strongest tears were those of sorrow.

Ilia looked up, seeing the barely contained emotion on Katerin's face. "Oh, Kat," she said softly. Releasing Katerin's hands, she pulled the woman to her, embracing her. "I'm so sorry."

The sudden compassion broke down the final barriers, and Katerin sobbed, relaxing into the arms holding her. Her heart, throat, and face felt so hot, she thought she'd burst into flame. Perversely, she welcomed the combustion, believing such pain would be clean and temporary compared with what she felt now. It didn't happen, however, and she was resigned to a thick pool of grief threatening to drown her as surely as the river before her could.

Eventually, the need for tears abated, leaving Katerin with a hollow in her chest. Wiping her face, she sniffled and pulled away, face flushed. "I'm sorry, Ilia. I didn't mean to lose control." She felt a hand gently brush the bangs over her forehead, and she looked at the handmaiden, startled. The sensation was so familiar, yet Katerin knew that Ilia had never done such a thing.

"We all need to cry upon occasion, Kat," Ilia said, her face kind. "Even royal princesses."

Katerin shook off the oddness, focusing on her words. "I suppose. Though I was taught from an early age to suppress my emotions among the people. They want someone to look up to in times of crisis, not a blubbering idiot." She sniffed once more and scrubbed at her tear-stained face.

"I don't mean to be blunt, Kat, but you really aren't a princess any longer." Ilia's blue eyes shone with concern. "Unless you plan on taking back your throne?"

Blinking, Katerin eyed her companion. "I honestly hadn't thought of it," she said. Her hands fell into her lap to fidget as she stared out over the river. "And who would follow me? I'm a woman. My best hope of defeating the Invader would be to marry a wealthy and powerful man who would raise an army." She shrugged, returning her gaze to Ilia. "I'm not ready to subjugate myself to a husband, no matter the reason."

Ilia nodded slowly. "It is freeing, being here, isn't it?" she asked. Inhaling, she continued, her expression one of satisfaction. "Had I remained at court, my days would be overseen by your matrons. My father would find a likely man for me to marry, someone to further my station in life. Eventually, I'd be wed and have children to perpetuate our line."

She waved off thoughts of her potential future, the gesture holding an elegance it never had before. Katerin was once again amazed by the subtle changes in her companion.

"Yet here I am. In a *circus*, no less!" Ilia laughed. "When I was a child, I used to entertain fantasies of running off to travel. I never expected it to come true." She sobered. "I know what happened in Dulce is a tragedy, a perversion, but I cannot help but feel a measure of happiness that it caused my coming here."

The blonde apparently expected a response, and Katerin nodded. "I find being here intriguing as well."

"Do you plan on staying?" Ilia asked, studying her intently.

"I honestly don't know. It's something that hasn't even occurred to me."

Ilia sighed and looked over the river, a slight smile on her lips. "I think I'd like to stay."

Katerin felt a twinge of what could only be jealousy, this last connection with her past fading away to abandon her for a future as a performer. *Ninny! What's stopping you from doing the same?* The thought took her by surprise, and she could only murmur something in response.

"I'd best be returning," Ilia said, standing. "Gemma and I plan on working on our act this afternoon during rehearsal. If Ros likes it, she may give us a position on the stage!"

Bemused, Katerin stood as well, slipping her arm through her handmaiden's. "That would be grand, wouldn't it?"

As Ilia excitedly explained the intricate details of her act, the two wandered back the way they had come.

Part 6

Katerin sighed and closed the ledger, carefully sealing the precious jar of ink. In an effort to make herself useful to Ros, she'd taken over the books a few weeks after her arrival. It was preferable to feeling like an extra wheel on a wagon. The troupe had more than enough supplies to make it through the remainder of the season, and it was only midsummer. Preserving what they had would take them past winter and into next spring. Katerin wondered whether she could talk Ros into staying put for a day or two — just long enough to put up some of the goods for the future.

She stood and stretched a bit, working a kink out of her lower back, then blew out the lantern and stepped out of the wagon, looking up at the night sky. Stars sparkled back at her, the same ones that had always been there through her childhood, sometimes the only constant she felt that she had. Dropping her gaze, she saw a good portion of the troupe gathered around the fire for the usual impromptu bardic session. Katerin smiled and approached.

Abdullah was singing a song about love, incongruous coming from such a giant of a man. The dwarf Sameer and Gemma played a lute and tambourine, respectively, in accompaniment. Habibah, her black skin flashing in the firelight, danced seductively in front of her husband, the dog trainer. One or two others sat about them, tapping feet and nodding heads to the beat.

Katerin slid easily into the gathering, taking the seat offered by Minkhat, who scooted aside to make room. As she allowed the song to wash over her, Katerin scanned the faces, noting Ros was not among them. The song ended and Habibah finished with a flourish, dropping into Daiki's lap and kissing him thoroughly. Katerin looked away, skin reddening as the others around her erupted into cheers and hoots. When the clamor died down, she asked, "Where's Ros?"

"Off brooding somewhere, no doubt," Amar said with a laugh.

"Aye, she does that well enough." Sameer boosted himself off the stool he sat upon and waddled closer to the fire, tossing another log into the flames. "She was born to suffer the darkness."

Frowning, Katerin asked, "Has she always been so?"

Minkhat, staring into the fire, said, "Aye. She has as long as I've known her, and that's been some time."

"How long *have* you known her?" Katerin asked, curious.

Daiki looked around his wife. "I've known her since she was a child. Abdullah and Sameer were raised with the Adamsson Circus too."

"Aye," the big man agreed in a smooth tenor. "But I was already a young man when she came along."

Sameer returned to his stool. "Ros has always held a piece of herself away from us. I think that's why she wanders off so often. Like you, Kat."

The comparison surprised Katerin, and she blinked at the dwarf.

"True enough," Habibah said from her husband's lap. She absently caressed Daiki's hair. "The current runs strong and deep in that one."

"What was she like? As a child, I mean," Katerin said. She blushed at the smiles sent her way, knowing what the others thought of her relationship with Ros. Heavy speculation among the troupe had the pair pegged as lovers — if not in deed, most definitely in heart. Katerin didn't disavow the notion, but found the thought very unsettling.

"Always underfoot," Sameer said with a good-natured grumble that earned a round of laughter.

Amar nodded. "I've heard the tales. She always found some sort of mischief to get into."

"Aye. Remember the lion tamer?" Daiki asked, his usually solemn face crinkled in fond nostalgia.

Sameer barked a laugh, spurred by memory as the others joined him. "I remember! The trainer, Yvonne, was apoplectic!" Seeing Katerin's puzzled smile, the dwarf explained. "When our Ros was but a youngster, she decided that the lion traveling with us should be freed. One morning, the trainer came out to find the cage open and her lion long gone."

"Oh, I've heard that one!" Minkhat said. "The nearby village was up in arms about a lion stalking the premises. Everyone had seen her in the show and assumed she was a wild and dangerous animal."

"Aye! She only wanted to be fed her breakfast, but no one knew that," Daiki said. "It took quite a bit of fast talking on Griffith's part to save the lion from being killed."

"Griffith? Ros' da?" Katerin asked.

Minkhat nodded.

"When the dust settled," Sameer continued, "we were invited to leave and never come back."

"It was then that someone noticed Ros was nowhere to be

found," Daiki said.

"Took a lot of searching before she was located hiding in a tree near the tent," Abdullah said. "She knew she was in deep trouble."

Daiki snorted.

"What happened to the lion tamer?" Amar asked, as enchanted by the tale as Katerin was.

"Yvonne quit in a huff, especially when she decided Ros' punishment would never fit the crime. Took her lion and left." Daiki hugged his wife close. "I hear she ended up working with large animals in a city somewhere in Barentcia."

Mystified, Katerin leaned forward, elbows on her knees. "What kind of punishment did Ros get?"

"A thorough talking-to by her da, for one," Sameer said. "And forced to apologize formally to Yvonne."

Katerin could see why the lion tamer would find such a reparation inadequate. She frowned in thought, wondering why the child had gotten off so lightly.

Daiki, sensing her confusion, spoke. "You had to understand Ros as a child, Kat. To admit a wrong and apologize was quite a hardship for her. She hated with a passion to be wrong. Still does."

Nodding, Katerin thought the explanation made sense. From experience, she knew that it was difficult to admit wrongdoing. Of course, her training as a royal had much to do with her point of view. A king or queen could not rule if he or she admitted to being wrong. She'd been taught to apologize for anything necessary to appease the other party, but never to admit she'd been in error. Katerin returned to the conversation. "What other things did she do?"

Warming to the topic, the group began to fill Katerin's ears with all manner of willful behavior on the part of their friend and leader.

Outside the firelight, Ros watched and listened. A half-smile of memory curved her lips as she recalled the incidents being discussed. Her eyes were on Katerin, however, watching the woman's responses.

On Lucinda's suggestion, Katerin had taken to pulling her hair into two tails on either side of her head. What resulted was a much younger looking woman, the hair bound high enough to create what looked like ears. Because almost everyone called her Kat, it furthered her disguise. No royal in his or her right mind would appear to be so common. *Or adorable.*

The range of emotions on Katerin's face fascinated Ros. Here, away from Ros' presence, Katerin's expression was open and caring, her laughter easy despite the darkness just behind her eyes. When the circus owner spent any time around her, Katerin's eyes became guarded and her manner wary. It had become a game with Ros to tease the woman, pricking the defensive maneuver until she received a laugh, a puzzled look, or even a flash of anger. In sleep, Katerin's muscles relaxed, leaving her looking sweet and peaceful. The nightmares always chased away that peace.

Squatting, Ros continued to watch her family, smile fading. They'd been fortunate so far. No further word regarding the Invader's search had reached them. Either some luckless soul had been substituted, or the hunt hadn't extended as far as the circus. Ros wasn't sure which she hoped for.

A fresh bust of laughter brought the smile back to her lips, and she watched Katerin's dark eyes dance as Minkhat regaled them with a story — something about a hurried leavetaking from an inn because of someone or other's angry husband. The princess blushed, her skin glowing bright against the fire, when she realized that Ros had been the one doing the fleeing. Ros' smile grew as she watched the consternation. Life with the circus had been exciting, no doubt of that. She counted herself lucky to be among these wonderful and giving people. Her eyes still on Katerin, she had to wonder: *And what will become of you? Now that you've found us, will you stay?*

* ~ * ~ * ~ * ~ *

Giving the stew pot another good stir, Katerin sat down and returned to the bowl of snap beans. Late afternoon sunlight filtered through the trees along the western side of the clearing. Around her, some of the troupe finished putting the final touches on the tent, raising colorful pennants high overhead; others kept themselves occupied with chores at their wagons, mending costumes, or practicing their acts. Young Wilm ran about the clearing, Daiki's dogs chasing his heels and yapping excitedly.

In the past three months, Katerin had actually come to enjoy her turn at cooking, something she'd never thought she had a talent for. She couldn't recall visiting the palace kitchens as a child; the chances of her discovering an aptitude would have dwindled to nothing, had things remained the same. *Had things remained the same, my family would be alive, and I would be wed to a man of my father's choosing.* Although the latter prospect held little appeal for her, seeing her parents and siblings whole and happy would have been well worth the cost of her maidenhood. It was moot, however. The Invader had done his bloody work, and presumably still searched for her.

Considering the threat of discovery, Katerin preferred to work in the background with the circus, despite Lucinda's constant prodding to teach her to dance. Katerin flushed at the concept, having heard the hoots and hollers of excited men as they watched Habibah and Lucinda during the show. Even if she hadn't been a fugitive, performing on the stage as a dancer was out of the question. The very idea of those men watching her with naked lust caused her to shiver.

So she remained working the braziers during performances, taking extra cooking duties, updating the ledgers as the circus received payment, even helping with stitching upon occasion, though she was still clumsy with a needle. Oddly enough, while Ros continued to press Ilia to become further involved, she did not approach Katerin. The thought chased a frown across her face as she snapped beans in half. *Does Ros think I am less able?*

As though her thoughts had called the circus owner out, Katerin looked up to see Ros inspecting the tent. Normally dressed in black, Ros had stripped down to an emerald green under-tunic — one that Katerin noted brought out that particular shade in her hazel eyes. Ros circled the construction, tugging on thick ropes, her tanned forearms flexing. Usiku said something as she passed and she flashed him a grin, Katerin mirroring her amusement despite not hearing the comment.

When Ros ducked inside to continue her examination, Katerin blinked and shook her head, staring down at the snap bean she held in her motionless hands. She broke the bean in half sharply, enjoying the crack. Even after three months, Ros' presence caused her to forget everything. *Which is probably why she doesn't push to have you join an act. You can't even get the lighting right on a given evening because you're enamored of her.* Katerin finished the beans with ruthless single-mindedness. With a sigh, she set the basket aside and rose to check on the stew.

Ilia and Gemma practiced by their wagon, various items flying through the air between them in a maddening blur of motion. It seemed that Ilia had found a position here. For that, Katerin was happy, though it shared a place in her heart with the melancholy of loss. The very nature of her predicament meant she'd be alone forever — no family, no friends, a wall of secrets thicker than any castle's dividing her from a normal life.

But what was normal, anyway? Here, the people stood by one another, as close as family — probably closer than blood. In Dulce, people surrounded her, but none had been friends. They'd been courtiers, servants, and ladies-in-waiting. None were there out of desire for friendship or love. At least with the circus, Katerin could find companionship — joyful people with whom to share her life and heart.

As she'd said to Ilia several weeks earlier, the thought of marrying a powerful man to regain the Dulce throne held no attraction for her. Katerin stirred the stew, wondering whether such feelings made her a bad person. She'd been raised to sacrifice herself for her people. Subjugating herself to a man would definitely be a penance. Still, she didn't know that such a man existed — one who was powerful enough to stand against the Invader. That monster had taken four kingdoms thus far in his lifetime, and would continue on his ambitious path until he died. Although the notion of defeating the Invader gave her bitter enjoyment, it would not bring her family or her kingdom back. What was done, was done.

"Whatever's in that pot smells delicious."

Startled, Katerin almost dropped the spoon into the concoction as she glanced up at the interruption. Hazel eyes and a wicked grin flashed at her. Swallowing, she lifted her chin regally. "Thank you."

If anything, Ros' smile grew as she settled onto one of the many stools scattered around the fire. "Mind if I have a taste?"

Katerin's mouth opened and closed, and she stared down at the wooden utensil in her hand. "Uh...of course not." She dipped out a bit of stew and took it to the circus owner, cupping her hand beneath the spoon to keep it from dripping on her clothes.

Ros leaned forward, allowing Katerin to feed her, gently taking a mouthful. The stew was hot, singeing her mouth and tongue, but she dutifully ate the offering. "Perfect," she declared.

Shaking herself away from the fascinating view of Ros' lips, Katerin put some distance between them, moving around the fire. "Thank you." Having heard many tales over the passing months, she knew Ros' reputation with women was a thing of legend among the others. Aside from the occasional lewd insinuation, however, Ros always treated her with respect. It didn't make Katerin any less uncomfortable.

Obviously amused by the stiff response, Ros rested her elbows on her knees and watched Katerin.

Katerin tasted the stew, trying not to think of Ros' lips touching the same spoon. Ignoring her audience, she decided the mix needed a hint of rosemary and proceeded to crush some of the dried herb into the pot. Once finished, she tidied up her workspace, needing something to do to keep from fidgeting. Finally, the only option available was to store the beans she'd snapped earlier. She couldn't leave the stew, however, and was unwilling to ask Ros to do her the favor. At a loss, she sat down and stared at the flames, forcing her hands to be still.

Ros tilted her head, amazed by how much her presence bothered the young woman. Rather than feeling remorse, however, curiosity spurred her on. Her da would have said that it was the imp in her, always testing, always teasing. He would have been right.

The dark eyes across from her flickered from the flame to her own. Ros felt a shiver of triumph, and she winked at Katerin, enjoying the reddening skin as the brunette dropped her gaze again.

Around them, conversation faded as Katerin refused to look at Ros. Tension mounted around the fire, seeming to keep people away, though suppertime was fast approaching. Finally, unable to stand it, Katerin glared at Ros, further infuriated by the smug grin on the woman's face. "What are you looking at?"

Ros straightened, placing her hands on her thighs. "I'm looking at you."

Not having expected a straightforward answer, Katerin blushed, her irritation fading into confusion.

Her objective obtained, Ros chuckled and stood. "If supper is ready, I'll tell the others."

Katerin swallowed. "Yes, it's ready."

Circling the fire, Ros passed behind Katerin, leaning down to whisper, "I've not heard you ask yet."

Head rising in shock, Katerin recalled the first night she'd spent with Ros, again heard her say, *"I'll not ravish you yet. Not until you ask it of me."* She rose to her feet in a flurry, spinning around to give the rogue a piece of her mind, only to find that Ros had already sauntered away.

Katerin gritted her teeth, lips thinning as she glanced around the clearing. Should she speak now, she'd have to raise her voice. Everyone within earshot would know exactly what was said and why. Grumbling, she turned back to the fire and flounced onto her stool. "That woman will be the death of me!"

She refused to ponder the sensation of Ros' warm breath against her ear or the strange tightening in her belly at Ros' nearness.

~~*~*~*

Her right arm was asleep.

Ros stretched, half-awake, wondering why such was the case. Something weighed her down, however, and she frowned. Cracking open an eye, she concentrated on her surroundings, and waking memory slowly filtered through her sleep-fogged brain.

It was still dark, not even a hint of dawn peeking through the crack of the partially open shutter. Ros remembered going to bed, a faint smile curving her lips as she recalled how angry Katerin had been at her jest before supper. The flash of those black eyes made

Katerin's irritation well worth the cost, and Ros had been quite smug. But what was on her arm now?

She inhaled deeply, stopping midbreath as something tickled her nose. Mumbling, she reached up to scratch it with her free hand, confused to find hair so close to her face. Ros jerked back, her arm remaining pinned in place. Katerin murmured in her sleep and shifted, resettling herself on her makeshift pillow.

Fully awake, Ros realized the smaller woman's head rested on her upper arm, which tingled as blood pumped through previously blocked arteries. They both lay on their sides, the warmth along Ros' body not a blanket, but Katerin's back. The traitorous right arm in question was curled around Katerin's neck, the right hand settled just beneath Katerin's left arm.

Ros swallowed. She could feel the gentle swell of Katerin's breast beneath her palm through the vicious pins and needles attacking her. If she shifted only a little, she'd be cupping Katerin, brushing against the woman's nipple. Forcing herself to stillness, Ros closed her eyes against the rush of arousal twisting in her belly.

As always, Ros slept nude, her skin now snuggled cozily against Katerin's sleep shift. Nerve endings came alive along her thighs where they nestled with Katerin's bare legs. It felt as though the shift had hitched upward during the night, the cloth settling somewhere around Katerin's hips. In her mind's eye, Ros could almost see the dark patch of hair peeking from beneath the shift.

She inhaled deeply, bracing herself to do the decent thing and pull the shift back down. Unable to help herself, however, she found her hand caressing her sleeping companion's neck, baring the skin as she pulled the hair away. Leaning her head closer, Ros rested her nose on Katerin's skin, breathing in her scent. Her hand paused on Katerin's shoulder and squeezed gently before sliding down her arm. She froze when the woman in her arms sighed and stretched, revealing more of her neck in unconscious invitation. Ros wasn't certain whether the gods were gifting her or teasing her.

She swallowed hard again and continued her action, drawing her hand along Katerin's waist. It stalled there, her libido reminding her of the flat belly only a few finger lengths away. *And a little farther from that — another flash of vision.* Ros let out a soft whisper of a moan, nuzzling Katerin's neck before forcing herself onward.

The shift had indeed ridden up the brunette's hip. Her posterior was firmly cupped by Ros' lap, and Ros realized that the skin touching her upper thighs wasn't Katerin's legs. She bit back a groan and tugged the hem of the shift along. When the clothing firmly covered Katerin to mid-thigh, Ros let out an aggrieved sigh. Now to get herself out of this mess before the smaller woman woke. Ros had no delusions regarding her bedmate's thoughts about what happened during the night. If she were to catch herself in such a compromising situation, Katerin would be extremely embarrassed first, and completely impossible to live with after.

She rolled onto her back, her flesh regretting the loss of Katerin's warmth. She forced her right hand away from Katerin's breast, resisting the urge to brush against the tempting nipple. Pulling sideways, she attempted to slide her arm out from under the dark head. She was partially successful; Katerin groaned in protest and turned. Ros used the movement to release her arm completely and ducked out of bed in a flash. She stood in the center of the wagon, the evening chill pricking her aroused body. Shivering, Ros located her clothing and dressed. So as not to wake Katerin, she eased quietly out of the wagon.

Tommaso sat at the fire, peering into the darkness at her approach. "Ros?"

"Aye." Ros entered the light and sat nearby. "Who follows you?"

"Gemma. As soon as the Eastern star touches the tips of those trees."

Ros looked overhead, noting the star in question. "I'm not sleepy. Go on to bed, and I'll wake her."

"You sure?"

Grinning, Ros picked up a stick and played in the fire. "Go, before I change my mind."

Tommaso needed no further encouragement. "Night, Ros."

"Good night."

As soon as he was away from the fire, Ros inhaled and yawned. She scrubbed her face with one hand and looked around the fire. A pot of water waited to be boiled for tea. Dropping her stick into the flames, she proceeded to put the pot close to the heat and settled back down on a stool.

She stared into the flames as she considered what to do with Katerin. It wasn't as if the woman were a hardship. Despite the occasional lighting mishaps at the shows, Katerin excelled at everything Ros asked of her. She'd even taken over the books on her own when she realized Ros' handwriting wasn't as tidy as hers. If it hadn't been for the threat of the Invader, Ros would have long since pushed Katerin to join some of the buffoonery and acrobatic acts. Katerin had the grace of her upbringing so deeply instilled in her, Ros had no doubt that she'd do extremely well with many of the physical aspects of their calling. *But gods be damned! I don't think I can sleep much longer in the same bed with her!*

Unfortunately, there weren't many other possibilities. Every other bed was occupied. Truth be told, Ros' only other option was to have Ilia swap living quarters — not something she wanted to consider. She pondered the issue until bubbling from the pot drew her attention. Finding a thick cloth, she pulled the water away from the flames and poured it into a relatively clean mug. In no time, she had tea steeping.

What she needed, she finally decided, was to bed a woman. Katerin's beauty was dazzling, and Ros admitted to being drawn to her, but it had been a long time since Ros had tupped a woman. Her body demanded the attention. Nodding to herself, she held the steaming mug. They were near the city of Yorvik; perhaps only a day's travel away. It would be a simple thing to declare a rest there for a day or two, convert a bit of their supplies into coin, and allow the troupe to spend a little silver. The season had been a bountiful one and would no doubt continue to be so. There'd be no loss of revenue from the small holiday.

That decided, Ros sighed and drank her tea. *After I take care of this itch, things will be better.*

Part 7

Katerin chose to ride with Ros this fine day, making sure to bring along a shawl and a large floppy hat to protect herself from the late-summer sun. Behind them, Yorvik faded into the distance as they drove the wagons toward another village and another show.

Upon their arrival at Yorvik two days earlier, half the troupe — Ros among them — had divvied up their share of the excess goods and entered the city for some needed entertainment. A few had remained at camp to keep things safe until the first group returned to relieve their companions. Although Katerin was eager to see a city marketplace, she had chosen to stay at camp, uncertain how far the Invader's search had spread. At least she had been able to enjoy a quiet afternoon of reading.

The evening had held interesting chatter as the first of her companions returned, bringing with them a keg of rum, some sweet cakes, and much laughter. At a market stall, Ilia had found hair combs decorated with carved wooden cats and purchased two as a gift for Katerin, who wore them now, as they traveled, to keep her dark bangs out of her eyes.

She watched the countryside as they trundled past, fields of wheat and corn standing tall, the occasional farmstead in the distance. There was quite a lot of traffic as people passed them on their way to the city, forcing the circus wagons to stay close to one side of the road.

Katerin surreptitiously studied her companion's profile. Since Ros' return, she'd seemed different — less caustic, more relaxed. Her smile had been a lazy one, and Katerin couldn't help but wonder what sort of thing would put such an expression on her handsome face. "Did you have fun in Yorvik?"

"Aye, I did," Ros said, smiling.

"You never mentioned what you did," Katerin said, raising an eyebrow. "I know what everyone else was doing in the city. What of you?"

"Oh, a little of this, a tad of that."

Realizing that more response was not forthcoming, Katerin turned away to look at the passing countryside. "Fine. Be that way," she said with a sniff.

Ros' smile grew, and she wisely kept her tongue.

Several moments of silence passed, broken only by the clopping of the horses ahead of them. Despite her vague irritation, Katerin noted the quiet was a comfortable one, marveling that she felt so at ease with the circus owner. Finally, she turned back. "How much longer will we be on the road? Or do we work through winter?"

Accepting the change of topic, Ros said, "I figure we've about a month, maybe two before harvest. Once that rolls around, we do best to quit for the season. Everyone is far too busy attending to their crops to come to our shows. It gives us time to reach our winter quarters."

"Quarters? We don't stay in the wagons?"

Ros barked out a laugh. "No, Kat! We don't winter in the wagons! Even entertainers enjoy the comforts of a fireplace and a well-stocked larder."

Blushing, Katerin looked away, wishing that she'd not exposed her ignorance.

Ros capitulated. "I'm sorry, Katerin. I shouldn't have laughed at you." Seeing her apology was accepted, she smiled. "We've a place south of here called the Compound. I'd say about half of us will stay there. The others will move on to other homesteads in surrounding villages."

Katerin frowned, staring at her lap. She wondered where she would go.

Sensing her thoughts, Ros said, "You're more than welcome at the Compound — you and Ilia both. With a bit of shuffling, there are beds for all."

Peering at Ros with a tentative smile, Katerin said, "Thank you. That's very kind."

Ros shrugged. "You've worked hard this season, regardless of your beginnings. As I said, you can stay with us until you decide to leave."

Katerin didn't want to think of her beginnings with the troupe. Changing the subject, she asked, "How long have you been in charge of the circus?"

Scanning the horizon in thought, Ros said, "Six seasons, I think."

"And your da? Is he at the Compound?"

The good humor faded from Ros' face. "No. He passed the veil four years ago. I'd spent the last two seasons running things for him."

Her own loss being so recent, Katerin felt sympathetic tears sting her eyes. She touched Ros' shoulder. "I'm sorry."

Ros grinned weakly in response. "Thank you." She shrugged slightly, regaining her equilibrium. "He died doing what he loved, directing at center stage in the middle of a show. Not many can lay claim to that."

"True enough."

"This circus was his life's blood."

Katerin remembered what Sameer had said about Ros' darkness. "And you? Is it your life's blood?"

Surprised by the question, Ros frowned in thought. "I'm not certain. I do enjoy what I receive — the smiles and laughter, the gasps of surprise, the joy of children as they see something they thought impossible occurring right before them." She grinned at the woman beside her. "Life's blood or not, it's well worth the reward to someone like me."

Someone like me. Katerin found the phrase odd but ignored the words. "I like the pageants most of all, I think," she said, smiling softly in memory. "It's quite a lot of fun to rouse a village from their drudgery. Very exciting."

Silence surrounded them. Clearing her throat, Ros said, "You know, if you choose to stay, you might consider spending the winter practicing with Sati and Sameer. I think you'd make a good buffoon."

Katerin stared at her. "Me?"

Ros chuckled. "Aye, you. I've noticed you move with precision and grace, good skills to have in tumbling and the like. You fare well enough with the lighting during shows. I think you'd do a fine job."

Blinking, Katerin wondered what happened to the rogue who had so recently lived in Ros' skin. Here she had thought her work poor, only to discover Ros had other ideas. "You really think I could be a buffoon?"

"Well, you'd have to laugh at my jokes instead of throw things at me, but I think you'd do well."

Katerin finally realized Ros was poking fun at her. With a grudging smile, she slapped the blonde's arm. "You."

Ros' unrepentant smile flashed back at her. "Me."

Katerin laughed. "It's a thought. I'll seriously consider it."

"Do that. I think you'd be a fine asset to the circus."

They continued along, each wrapped in her own thoughts.

* ~ * ~ * ~ * ~ *

Katerin discovered that constant travel was not always beneficial. In some village or other, she contracted a nasty head cold, complete with clogged nose, fever, and chills. On Ros' orders, she remained in bed when they stopped early in the morning. Lucinda made her tea to help with the congestion, and she slept fitfully. When she awoke, the wagon shutters were slightly open to allow fresh air in and bright sunlight outside indicated that it was midafternoon. She felt almost hollow, as if her entire body was in the process of pausing between one cough and sneeze to the next. Surprisingly, the usual sounds of camp were muted. Yawning, she puzzled over the strangeness, finally deciding Ros must have ordered the pageant into the next village, leaving her behind. She pouted at missing her favorite aspect of the circus, her nose feeling stuffed and empty at the same time.

"How is she, then?"

Katerin rolled over, yawning again from the herbs in Lucinda's tea.

"Sleeping soundly," the redhead said just outside the window, her voice lowered so as not to disturb her charge. "She's a luckless soul for getting so sick. I'm glad it hasn't spread to the rest of us."

"Aye, as am I," a man said. Katerin identified him as Usiku. There was a rustle of movement, and she figured he'd sat down to visit with Lucinda.

"Who do you think will do the lights tonight?" Martim asked.

"I expect we'll go back to shifts while Kat's ill."

"Ugh," Usiku grumped. "I dislike the braziers immensely. No matter how hard you try to keep it off, the soot gets everywhere."

Lucinda laughed, her tone deep and musical. "Well, darlin', it's not like it shows against your skin as well as it does on ours," she said, referring to his midnight complexion. The men joined her mirth, Katerin smiling inside the wagon.

Silence followed, an easy one born of many years of living and performing together. Katerin's eyes closed of their own accord, and she yawned a third time. She heard more movement, a stool scraping the ground and the flutter of cloth.

"There, I'm finished," Lucinda said, satisfaction in her tone. "What do you think?"

Martim whistled as Usiku said, "Very nice, Luci. Are you going to wear that tonight?"

"I've a mind to."

Chuckling, Martim said, "You'll give some old geezer chest pains for sure."

"And some young geezer other pains altogether," Usiku added.

Lucinda's voice was full of mirth. "Can I help it if my beauty is painful?"

Even as she blushed, Katerin snickered to herself in bed. She found it much easier to see humor in the bawdy remarks when she wasn't in the presence of those speaking them. She'd been with the circus long enough to understand much of the innuendo that was bandied about. Lucinda must finally have completed her new outfit. Ilia had told Katerin the material was so diaphanous, it left absolutely nothing to the imagination.

"I'm off to put this away for the time being," Lucinda said. "Will one of you stay a bit until I return? I don't want to leave Kat alone."

"Aye, I'll stay."

"And me."

"Good. Here's water for tea. The herbs are already measured into this mug. I shan't be but a few moments."

The men voiced their understanding and became silent until she'd gone. "So. What do you think?"

"About what?" Usiku asked.

"Them."

"Ah!" There was a pause before Usiku said, "I don't know. Sometimes, I think aye, other times, no."

Martim sounded a bit dejected. "I know. I've two silver pieces riding on this with Tommaso."

"What's the wager?"

"That they are and have been since Yorvik."

Katerin frowned as she attempted to puzzle out the cryptic remarks.

"You truly think so?" Usiku asked, surprised.

"Aye! They've been much happier together since our visit there. You can't deny that."

"Well, aye, but—"

Martim scoffed. "Please! When was the last time Kat was angry with Ros over some trivial thing?"

Katerin blinked. *He's talking about me.*

Usiku hummed. "It's been a bit, true."

"And you know how Ros gets when she's tupped someone. Everyone knew she'd been bedded."

"Aye. But are you sure it was Kat and not at a Yorvik brothel? No one knows where Ros went or what she did in the city."

There was a pause, and Katerin could almost see Martim's frown. Her thoughts were sluggish, no doubt from the herbs, and it was difficult for her to make sense of the conversation. *Ros? And me? And what does "tupped" mean?*

"I can't say it wasn't at a brothel, true," Martim said, grudging agreement in his tone. "But if such were the case, why has Kat been treating her different?"

"It *has* been four months. She was bound to get tired of fencing with Ros sooner or later. Besides, we both know Ros has a silver tongue. It just took a bit longer to get through Kat's prickles."

Chuckling, Martim said, "Aye, she's prickly enough when she wants to be."

"Especially with Ros."

The men enjoyed a good laugh as Katerin rolled onto her back and stared at the wagon ceiling. She ignored the continued conversation regarding Ros' tongue and its imagined uses, having heard similar tales of the circus owner's reputation many nights around the fire.

So they thought she and Ros were...what was it? *Tupping?* It had to be something Sapphists did; otherwise, Katerin would have heard of it before. And if it was something like that, Martim thought she and Ros were lovers.

Katerin felt her body heat up at the thought and wondered whether her fever was returning. She kicked off her blankets, strangely unconcerned about the speculation going on just a few feet away. She'd known that the others wondered whether she and Ros were sharing more than just sleeping space; the full extent of the debate had gone much further than she'd assumed, however.

It was true that Ros had left off teasing her so badly in recent days. She'd been almost pleasant upon occasion. Katerin blushed as she remembered wondering what caused the lazy smile on Ros' face in Yorvik. Intrigued despite her discomfort, she also remembered wishing she could be the one to cause such an expression.

Katerin rolled onto her side and buried her face in the sheets. She couldn't help but giggle at the thought of Martim and Tommaso wagering on such a thing. There was certainly no way it would ever occur. Katerin knew she was not a Sapphist, and even if she were, Ros would be the last woman she'd bed.

Why?

The thought brought her up short, and she pulled the sheet off her face, all humor gone. She'd been drawn to Ros from the first, finding her handsome and sweet. Even the roguish smile beckoned Katerin, the hazel eyes sparkling at some ribald jest or other. Ros was infuriating and alluring at the same time. She moved with powerful grace, her mantle of leadership resting easily upon her shoulders. The decisions she made for her family were well-considered and profitable to all.

Katerin could see that lazy smile again. She'd become somewhat used to Ros' nakedness in bed, but now she wondered: What did Ros' skin feel like? Was her hair as rough and wild as it seemed, or was it as soft as her own? Another wave of warmth swept over her.

"I'll not ravish you yet. Not until you ask it of me."

She's a cad, she reminded herself. *Irritating, smug, impossible to live with.* The list of Ros' detractions was as long as Katerin's arm. She harrumphed and flopped onto her back once more. Even if she were interested in pursuing a woman, Ros would *not* be the lucky one.

"Here, now!" Lucinda said sharply upon her return. "There must be something else to discuss than this!"

Martim laughed. "We were only wondering if they've gone ahead and done the deed or not."

Lucinda clucked. "And did you think for a moment that Kat might have wakened to hear you?" The sudden loud hush gave her the answer.

Katerin, expecting an interruption, quickly closed her eyes and schooled her features to relax. Sure enough, the creak of the shutter being moved reached her ears as Lucinda peeked in on her.

Several moments passed before the shutter moved again, and Lucinda said, "There, now, you've both been lucky. Can you imagine what Ros would say if she'd heard half of what you were talking about?"

"Sorry, Luci," Martim said.

"Shoo, now, both of you! The rest should be back any time."

Katerin listened to the men get up and leave, sighing in relief. It was already embarrassing to hear such tales about Ros; she could imagine the agony of having to acknowledge the conversation she'd just heard. With much to think about, she rolled away from the window and faced the wall.

~~*~*~*

With great effort, Liam reached the mug of water on the nearby table and brought it to his lips. Drinking deeply, he sighed and relaxed, cradling the cup in his hands.

His surroundings had changed from week to week since the witch had given him leave to travel. Today, he was in a house somewhere inside the capital. From what he could gather, it was in a poorer section — not that he could be certain. After the Invader had finished his foul work, most of the city appeared poor and unkempt.

At least the mattress didn't smell moldy like the one in the last hovel. Here, the linens held interesting stains, but were soft and clean — a definite improvement. The furniture consisted of a bed, small table, and a chair, all sturdy and well taken care of. This surprised the prince, as he'd heard the Invader had sacked the city following his victory. After listening to many complaints, Ian had shoved the bed close to the window on the promise Liam wouldn't be too careless and reveal himself.

Despite the constant movement, Liam rarely saw anyone but Dominic or Ian, his personal guard. The aide explained it would be easier for whomever owned these places to deny seeing the crown prince if they simply hadn't. Liam thought the precaution silly, but could hardly complain at this point. Still bedridden, he could sit up and feed himself, but not much else. Everything about the rebellion remained in Dominic's well-organized hands.

The teenager sat up a bit, grunting under his breath at the stinging pain in his chest as he adjusted the pillows behind him. All things considered, the witch had saved his life. Soon, he expected to get out of bed, even if it was simply to hobble around to the other side and get back under the covers. He'd be damned if he would remain an invalid any longer than necessary.

He could hear laughter outside the window. Boredom breeding curiosity, he reached the edge of the shutter and eased it open a crack. The heat of summer pelted him, sweat beading on his forehead and upper lip in an instant. Liam inhaled deeply of the fresh air as he looked down into the street.

A handful of boys kicked a tattered ball back and forth, enjoying a grand game, dodging pedestrians, horses, and the occasional cart. They wore rags, as most did these days, regardless of social standing, and their hair was long and shaggy. They whooped and hollered, celebrating life through their mere existence.

Liam peered through the cracked shutter, smiling in fond memory.

His sister, Sabine, stuck her tongue out at him, kicking the ball to one of the many pages who trained in the castle. Her black hair in an unruly braid, she impatiently tucked an escaped strand behind her ear as her team of children attempted to score points in the game. Only four years older than her brother, she hovered at the stage between growing up and remaining a child.

Barely six, Liam ordered his team to intercept, and a vicious battle ensued. Soon, the game wasn't about the ball or the score. In no time, the group of children fell together in wrestling matches. Laughing until his ribs ached, Liam yielded to his sister's superior tickling skills.

He could almost feel her lips as she kissed him on the cheek, freckles standing out against her flushed skin.

Another memory, another kiss.

Young Aiden, still smelling of babyhood, kissed his older brother's cheek, leaving dampness behind. His chubby arms wrapped tightly around Liam's neck — a reward for Liam's taking him riding on a "real" horse instead of his fat, tame pony.

Liam's chest hurt from a sharp stab of pain that had nothing to do with the wound inflicted by the Invader. "Ian!"

The guard outside the door immediately stepped inside. "Aye, my liege?"

"Sit and speak with me."

Ian bowed and sat on the only chair.

"Where's Dominic?" Liam asked, securing the shutter once more.

"I don't know, Majesty," the guard said. "Off preparing for your return, I'm guessing." He scratched his untrimmed reddish beard and sighed. "He's got a lot of contacts, that one. I don't doubt he knows everything going on hereabouts."

Settling back onto his pillows, Liam nodded. "We'll need all the help we can get to pull this off."

"Aye, true enough, my liege."

"Ian..." He suddenly found the rough edge of his blanket to be extremely interesting. "I want you to tell me what happened that night." He looked up to see a flash of discomfort. "I have to know, Ian. My injury...it was severe enough to play with my mind."

The guard sighed and nodded, his gray eyes sad. "Aye, I understand. My cousin was once hit on the head and couldn't remember anything but the day before."

Liam nodded. "I remember hearing of father's death and that Bertram still led our men in battle, and then word of our meal being poisoned just before the Invader got through the gates. We fled through the tunnels, yes?"

"Aye, my liege. We did."

The memories were murky, but Liam could almost make out his mother holding Aiden, leading the way. Behind him came Sabine and her handmaiden, protected by the last of the guards. He barely recalled escaping the castle walls before everything went dark. "What happened? We ran for the river. How did the Invader overtake us?"

"His witch must have told him our plans, my liege," Ian said. "Nothing else makes sense. A squad of his men came up behind us through the tunnel. I think they overtook Princess Sabine, or she became separated. I don't know."

Liam swallowed, the story feeling familiar though no pictures came to mind. "What then?"

Ian lifted his shoulders. "They continued to give chase, but we outdistanced them once we got to the horses. It didn't matter. The Invader was waiting at the boats when we arrived."

"Wait!" Liam leaned forward, ignoring the pain, dark eyes intent on his man. "He *knew* where we were going?"

"Aye, Majesty. That's why I think his pet witch cast a spell to divine our plans. How else would he have known to leave the castle for the river? Those tunnels are as old as your family; only the king and queen knew of them until that night."

Liam frowned in thought, eyes once more dropping to the edge of the covers as he fidgeted. The only witch he knew was the hag who had saved his life. Although rumor had it that the old witch women could cast various spells and the like, Liam had never really believed such a thing. *Was it a witch? The chef fell into a drugged sleep while he tasted dinner. The Invader entered the castle through gates that should have remained closed to him. Was it spell...or traitor?* Looking back at Ian, he gestured to him to continue.

The guard grunted. "It was a hell of a battle, begging Your Majesty's pardon." He reddened in apology for his language. "The servants who had been sent ahead were already dead by the time we arrived; the boats sunk. We were pinned between them for some time."

As the other man's voice trailed off, Liam recognized the slumped set of his shoulders. "It's not your fault, Ian. You did your best. Our only insurmountable barrier was the Invader's foreknowledge of our plans."

"Aye, my liege," the guard agreed, not convinced.

Liam braced himself. "What happened when they finally overtook us?"

Ian pursed his lips, reluctance in every line. "After we were subdued, the Invader removed his helm and shield. He spouted some dung about his destiny and murdered your mother and little Aiden."

Though his memory of the matter was dark, Liam could hear their death screams, and he shuddered, revulsion coloring his face and his stomach threatening to heave. "Go on," he choked. His guard appeared to be concerned for him, and the teenager's voice grew hoarser. "I need to hear this, Ian. Tell me!"

Swallowing, Ian nodded. "He asked you where your sister was, and you told him you'd never tell, though we knew she'd disappeared just after we'd left the tunnel. A few of us made a go of fighting off him and his men. I saw two escape. I think it was Hector and Matteo, but I can't be sure." He sighed, his gray eyes shining with pride and unshed tears. "Our resistance was crushed, and you spat on him." He stopped.

"And he ran me through."

"Aye, Majesty." Ian's voice was barely a whisper.

Liam shivered, his nightmare scream echoing. "What of the rest of you?"

"Well, Jassup went plumb crazy after that. He broke away and got a sword, threatening to behead the Invader hisself before all the gods. There were only four of us left alive, but we had a go at it." Ian blushed. "I guess I got knocked out in the melee. Had a wound on my leg that wasn't mortal, but plenty of blood on my clothes. I'm thinking they reckoned I was dead."

Nodding, Liam relaxed and closed his eyes. "As myself."

"Aye. When I woke, I was aiming to give you and your family a proper burial — maybe backtrack to see what became of Princess Sabine." His young face broke into an astonished grin. "But you were alive, Majesty! I nearly died of surprise! I knew I had to get you to safety."

Liam smiled sadly and held out a hand. Taking Ian's in his, he said, "And that you did. For that, you have my everlasting gratitude, Ian."

The guard blushed, almost toeing the floor in consternation.

"When this is over, Ian, you'll be the captain of the King's Guard."

Ian looked up, mouth opening and closing, his eyebrows arched.

Liam chuckled, wanting to laugh outright at the man's consternation but knowing that it would hurt like the dickens. "Shut your mouth, Captain. A bug will fly inside." He muffled another laugh at the audible click. "Thank you, my friend."

Ian squeezed back. "I hear and obey, Your Majesty."

Part 8

Ros woke from being slapped. Startled, she surged out of bed, looking wildly about the wagon for her attacker. No one was there. Confused, she rubbed her eyes and warily turned in a circle. A moan from the bed drew her attention, and she heard Katerin mutter in her sleep before throwing herself to one side. *The nightmare again.*

It had been some time since Katerin had suffered one so strong; Ros thought the illness might be exacerbating things. She slumped back onto the bed and blew out a breath, quelling her rapid heartbeat. Beside her, Katerin continued to toss and turn. Though her nerves still shook, Ros stretched out on the bed and whispered to the sick woman, "Shhh, it's just a bad dream. You're safe now." Her fingers found Katerin's forehead, brushing the bangs aside to soothe away the nightmare.

Her usual attempts didn't work. Katerin cried out as she batted at the hand. Ros scowled in sympathy, wishing she could do something to ease Katerin. No doubt the herbs the woman had been given so she could sleep through the night confounded the issue. Feeling helpless, Ros nevertheless continued to murmur encouraging words.

Katerin spoke people's names, fighting against whatever darkness held her. The only name Ros recognized was Ilia — something about leading Ilia and Hector to their deaths. Katerin called out to her parents and little Aiden, wanting to know whether Liam still lived.

Realizing no amount of comforting would help the thrashing woman, Ros took hold of Katerin's shoulder and shook her. "Wake up, Kat!"

Katerin became even more incensed by the touch, shouting, "No! No! Leave me be! I don't *want* it! I'm no threat!" She abruptly shot up in bed, fighting Ros' hands as she sobbed hysterically.

"Katerin!" Ros pulled back. "Katerin! It's a nightmare! You're safe! You're awake now!" Several moments passed as Ros continued to speak to the distraught woman. Katerin's weeping became less frantic, her weariness removing any control she might have had as she continued to cry. Once completely awake, she threw herself into Ros' arms. Ros sighed in relief, rocking the smaller woman as she continued to speak gentle words, caressing the dark head.

"Ros?" a low voice asked just outside the window.

"It's all right, Willem," Ros said. "Just a nightmare. Probably brought on by her illness."

"Call if you need anything."

"I will." She heard his footsteps move away from the wagon as she returned her full attention to the woman in her arms. Closing her eyes, she sighed and laid her cheek on Katerin's head, swaying back and forth as Katerin released her fear and anger.

She was so lost in the embrace, it took Ros some time to realize that Katerin had stopped crying. The brunette remained in her arms, however, soaking in the closeness between them. Not wishing to disturb her, Ros sighed, knowing it would be necessary anyway. "Feeling better?" she whispered.

Katerin sniffled and nodded. She fumbled for the handkerchief she'd kept at hand since her illness began and wiped her face. Her nose felt twice as stuffed as it had before, forcing her to breathe through her mouth. "I'm all right."

Ros made no move to release her, Katerin apparently being comfortable enough to remain where she was. "Would you like to speak of it?" Ros asked. "I find that sometimes, it makes a nightmare less terrifying."

Katerin stiffened in Ros' arms "No. I don't think so."

Wisely, Ros only nodded agreement; she was surprised she still held Katerin in her arms. The nightmare had been much more upsetting than usual. Ros had a fair idea of the subject as well and wondered how to bring the younger woman to trust her enough to speak about the matter. "You've no worries, Kat. We'll keep you safe and sound, I promise."

"I know" came the muffled response.

Ros reckoned that the main reason behind Katerin's aloofness toward her came from her past, something Katerin was unwilling to share. The longer it took for Katerin to open up, the more strength her nightmares would gain. Only by facing her past and accepting her role in it would she be allowed any freedom from her fears. And accepting meant confessing her true past to those closest to her.

Ros sighed and gave Katerin a hug, knowing her next words would shatter the moment. "You and Ilia must have had a very difficult time before you took refuge in our cook wagon." She could feel the woman in her arms draw herself up, though she still didn't disengage.

"Yes. We did."

Nodding, Ros brushed soft black hair behind an ear. "Was the man who was killed that night named Hector?"

Katerin pushed away, staring down at her lap. "Why do you ask?"

"Because you spoke his name with Ilia's."

Katerin glanced sharply up at her bedmate, dark eyes flashing. "I *spoke* of him?"

Ros nodded. "Aye. You did." She reached out and wiped an errant tear off Katerin's face, surprised when the other woman didn't pull away.

"What...what else did I say?" Katerin asked, her voice almost a whisper. She swallowed, unable to look away from Ros.

"You said that you were leading them to their deaths."

Katerin reacted as though the words were physical and flinched away from Ros' touch. She scooted away, drawing her knees up to hug them and leaning against the wall of the wagon.

Ros frowned, wishing there was an easier way to exorcise Katerin's demons. "Who are little Aiden and Liam?"

Again Katerin flinched, as though she were expecting a blow on her shoulders. She dropped her forehead to her knees, shivering.

"Kat?"

Choking on the words, Katerin said, "My brothers."

Forcing herself to continue, Ros nodded. "I thought as much. You cared for them deeply, I know."

"Do you?"

Ros regarded the sad black eyes. "Aye, I do. You said as much in your sleep."

Katerin looked away, her eyes glassy in the vague moonlight filtering into the wagon. In a dull monotone, she asked, "What else?"

Deciding she'd pushed enough, Ros gently ran her fingers along Katerin's forearm. "Who torments you, Kat? Who rides the pale horse you're so afraid of?"

The answer was there, lying between them in blood and armor, muddy blue eyes grim with dissatisfaction at being thwarted, a sword held sharp and ready for the final heir. They both knew it, but one of them had to admit it to the other.

"No one."

Ros almost heard the lock snick shut on Katerin's fears. The eyes that regarded her now were cool and calm, only a hint of the scared woman left behind. Impressed despite her concern, Ros nodded. *She's so much stronger than she lets on.*

Abruptly, Katerin's regal attitude fled as she blushed and turned away.

Puzzled, Ros suddenly realized she was still naked and had been through the entire exchange. Forcing herself not to chuckle, she eased back under the sheets, tugging on the ones on Katerin's side. Taking the hint, Katerin crawled back under them, allowing Ros to cover her. "Sleep, Kat. You're safe here."

Regardless of the harrowing nightmare and upset, Katerin yawned in answer, settling down. "Thank you, Ros."

Ros smiled. "You're welcome, Katerin."

~~*~*~*

Rehearsal over for the day, Katerin wiped her brow with an arm as she stepped out of the tent. A cool breeze met her, and she paused to drink it into her lungs. The other members of the circus passed by, intent on enjoying a free evening before tomorrow's pageant.

The clearing looked much like every other in which they'd camped in these past four months. Katerin expected the locals to descend upon them from a nearby village for several days' worth of shows. When the shows were finished, the troupe would pack up and move on, leaving behind the fallen logs they'd used for tent poles and seating. Those who lived here would collect most of the wood later in the season, splitting and setting it aside for next year.

Katerin cocked her head as she looked at the surrounding forest. Something seemed different. She blinked in surprise, noting the leaves beginning to turn colors. *Harvest is nearly here.* She remembered Ros' words about this time of year — how farmers became too busy with their crops to worry about entertainment.

She continued across the clearing with no destination in mind. Frowning, she steered away from the wagon she shared with Ros, making a circuit of the camp as she pondered. It had been much cooler at night lately. Soon, the performers would split up and go their separate ways, if she didn't miss her guess. Ros had invited her and Ilia to join those bound for the Compound, but Katerin hadn't discussed it with her former handmaiden.

"I suppose it's high time, isn't it?" she asked herself. "We've less and less time to make a decision."

Passing between wagons, Katerin glanced at the central fire, her eyes connecting with Ros' instantly. Her skin reddened and she looked away, knowing Ros smirked at her avoidance. Katerin continued on her path.

Since the night of her brutal nightmare, Katerin's feelings for Ros had taken a dramatic turn. She supposed it had something to do with the discussion between Martim and Usiku that she'd overheard. All she could recall of that night was Ros holding her as she wept, a warm cloud of safety surrounding her. Upon realizing Ros' unclothed state, Katerin had felt a strangeness flush through her body, an odd twisting in her abdomen, and a desire to feel the golden skin against her own once more.

Many a morning since, she'd wakened to find herself wrapped in a firm embrace. It didn't seem to matter whether nightmares plagued her sleep or not. So far, Katerin was fortunate enough to wake first, giving her the necessary time to extricate herself from Ros' arms. She didn't know how long she'd be that lucky, however, or what Ros' response would be.

The first time or two it occurred, Katerin had been half-terrified that Ros had instigated such physical closeness in her sleep. Truth be told, Katerin also felt a rush of fierce loyalty for the woman, regardless of her Sapphist tendencies — an odd emotion, considering Katerin's distaste for such things. Soon, however, she noticed a pattern: Invariably, she woke draped across Ros, *not* the other way around. Katerin sighed and shivered, wrapping her arms around herself.

"Kat! Where are you going with such a frown on your face?"

The frown in question faded away as Katerin waved at Lucinda. Seated on a chair at her wagon, the redhead relaxed with a mug. She gestured for Katerin to come forward, using a foot to pull another chair out from the table. "Sit! Tell me what troubles you on this glorious day when we've no work to do and no show to perform."

Katerin grinned and settled into the chair. "No troubles," she said.

Lucinda raised an eyebrow in suspicion. "A beautiful face like yours, as sour as it was? At the least, you were mighty deep in thought." She interrupted herself, looking at the window above her. "Gemma! Ilia! We've a guest at our humble wagon! Bring out more cups!"

Blushing, Katerin made to leave. "No, really, I was just walking." A hand covered hers, and she looked into Lucinda's laughing eyes.

"Stay, Kat. Your companionship is appreciated."

Slowly, Katerin sank back into her chair. "All right."

"You hold yourself away from us far too often, you know," Lucinda continued, pulling her hand away. Behind her, Gemma and Ilia stepped out of the wagon, mugs in hand. "I think you've been consorting with our illustrious leader far too much, letting her moodiness rub off, as it were."

Considering her most recent thoughts, Katerin felt her skin redden afresh. She dropped her gaze as Ilia placed a cup before her.

"Here. Stand close," Lucinda said.

As Lucinda's bunkmates crowded the table, Katerin looked up to see a crafty expression on the woman's face. Pursing her lips, she puzzled over the actions as Lucinda pulled out a wineskin. Katerin's dark eyes widened in surprise as a liberal amount of liquid poured into each mug.

"Now keep your lips shut," Lucinda said, grinning. "If Tommaso or Minkhat knew what I had here, they'd be crazed men in search of a drop. I swear they'd pester me 'til there was none left!" She plugged the skin and stashed it under a pile of sewing, the two other women backing away and sitting down.

Katerin's mouth worked, but no words came out. Eyes wide, she looked around the table at the smug women. Gemma straddled her chair much like a man, forearm on the back. Ilia grinned and wiggled her eyebrows, surprising Katerin no end. *What happened to the shy handmaiden I used to know?*

"To deep thoughts and a splendid season."

Automatically echoing the toast, Katerin sipped the wine, her eyebrows rising high as she realized the quality of the beverage.

"Aye," Lucinda said with a knowledgeable look. "Now you take my meaning."

"Yes, I do."

Lucinda shifted, getting comfortable. "You didn't answer my question, Kat. Why the long face?"

A shadow crossed Ilia's expression, and she scooted her chair closer, receiving a thankful look from Katerin.

"I spoke with Ros a while back about the winter season." Katerin lifted one shoulder, staring at her mug. "I just happened to notice the leaves beginning to turn today, that's all."

Gemma nodded in understanding as Lucinda cocked her head. Ilia looked startled, glancing away to see the change with her own eyes.

"The end of a season is always a sad one, no matter how much fun we had or the promise of future enjoyment," Lucinda said. "Is that what has you sad now, Kat?"

Feeling the fool, Katerin nodded nevertheless.

Lucinda lifted her mug. "To the end of the road: may it also be the beginning." The women drank, their mood somber.

Ilia seemed lost, long fingers fiddling with her cup, her expression wary. Katerin could sympathize. Apparently, Ilia hadn't realized the troupe would winter somewhere until spring.

"Here, now," Lucinda said, leaning forward, a concerned look in her eye. "Neither of you has any worries! Certainly, if you've talked to Ros, you've a place to stay?"

"You mean we don't stay together?" Ilia asked, paling under the full import of the discussion.

Gemma shook her tawny head.

Not wanting to stress her companion further, Katerin said, "Ilia, we've been offered a place at the Compound. Several of the performers stay there."

Ilia's blue eyes scanned the women around her. "But not you?" she asked Gemma. Her friend's smile was sad, her eyes reflecting a wistfulness that made her seem years younger.

"Gemma and I stay at my brother's place. It's a few days' ride away from the Compound," Lucinda said. "You're more than welcome, Ilia. And you, Kat. We've only the one room, but we could make it nice and cozy."

Katerin's eyes watered at the generous offer. She wiped away the tears with a smile. "Thank you. That's very sweet." The thought of being away from Ros for such a time, however, made her chest ache. Irrationally, she felt safe with the circus owner, as if nothing the Invader did could touch her while she was with Ros.

"'Tis only fair. You and Ilia are family now. I realize your coming to us was...less than pleasant for you," Lucinda said delicately. "But Ilia's made tremendous progress. Isn't that right, Gemma?"

The small woman smiled and nodded, holding up her mug in silent toast to the blushing young woman beside her.

Continuing, Lucinda said, "And I've heard Ros talk of your fine hand with the books. She'd most certainly regret returning to deciphering her scribbles if you weren't about."

The words dragged out of her, but Katerin couldn't help herself. "She says she wants me to winter with Sati so I can train as a buffoon."

Ilia took Katerin's hand. "That's wonderful, Kat! I think you'll do it a fantastic service!"

"Hear, hear!" Lucinda said, raising her mug again. "To our new family members, Kat and Ilia!"

Katerin diligently emptied her mug, surprised there was so little in it. Before she could refuse, the wineskin appeared in Lucinda's hands, and another healthy dollop poured into her cup. It had been some time since Katerin had more than a sip of wine at a royal function. She felt a bit flushed, a warm happiness effusing her. Ilia apparently felt the same way; her pale skin sported a healthy tint.

"So if you're to train with Sati, you'll be going to the Compound for certain?"

"Yes, I think so," Katerin said, rubbing the tips of her fingers together. They felt oddly numb. "Who else stays at the Compound?"

"It changes some years," Lucinda said with a shrug. "The talk I've heard this season is that Willem and Sati will be there. Cristof's brother stayed behind this year, as did Sameer's wife."

Gemma clasped her arms as though she were cradling something. "Aye," Lucinda agreed. "Florin should have birthed the baby by now."

Katerin blinked as she tried to picture the dwarf with a tiny wife and an even smaller baby.

Oblivious, Lucinda kept talking. "Em and Phizo and Joseph stayed behind as well." She leaned forward and dropped her voice conspiratorially. "Em helped Griffith raise Ros. If you'll be needing future fodder for teasing her, Em's the one to speak with."

Snickering, Katerin drank her wine, an evil grin crossing her face. It would be good to turn the tables when it came to making jibes.

"I believe that's everyone going there this winter. What about you, Gemma? Hear tell of anybody else?"

Gemma shook her head, waggling her hand.

"Aye, true enough," Lucinda said. "If there's one thing true about us, it's change. Between now and then, it might be different."

Part 9

"Charity? Charity?"

"Out of my way, old man," a soldier growled, pushing the vagabond aside.

As the column continued to march past, the peasant shuffled backward, cartwheeling his arms in an attempt to remain on his feet. Other people, already crowded back to make room for the Invader's troops, tried to avoid the filthy man, to no avail. Strident voices raised in complaint as the beggar fell, one hand on his chest and the other scrabbling at the people surrounding him. Butt thumping firmly on the ground, he began coughing, leaning forward in obvious pain. Not wanting to contract whatever ailment the old man had, people cleared the immediate area.

Soon, the soldiers were past, and the marketplace resumed its normal activity — or what passed for normal these days. Since the Invader had usurped the throne, artisans were in little or no demand, the people searching for more practical things. Food held a high value, what with half the surrounding farmsteads having been burned out during the siege. Many people came together to barter what they had to spare for what they didn't have any of.

Finally finished with his coughing spasm, the beggar struggled to his feet. He held his chest and limped along, occasionally asking for coin from passersby. Ducking into an alley, he splashed through puddles left from the late fall rain. *It'll snow soon. Make things more difficult.* At a door, he paused and rapped softly.

After some time, a peephole opened, and someone peered out at him. "Who wields the axe?"

"Liam." The vagabond pulled his hood back just enough for the autumn sun to illuminate his features.

After a muffled curse, the peephole slammed shut and the door flew open. A tall man, dark of hair and wearing a stylish mustache, stepped into the alley to usher his guest inside. After a quick glance to see whether they were being watched, he stepped back inside and bolted the heavy wooden door. He turned to glare at the man before him.

"Thanks for the welcome, Dominic," the beggar said with a

smile, pulling the grimy robe off his body. His clothing was homespun but clean, his face reflecting his true age — barely a man. Black eyes sparkled at the aide's discomfiture.

Dominic's nose wrinkled. "Your Royal Majesty," he intoned. "You shouldn't be out in the streets like this. You're putting yourself in danger." With thumb and forefinger, he took the proffered robe and dropped it on the floor by the entrance.

"Aye, Dominic," the "old" man agreed. Another coughing spasm came over him, and he bent double, holding his chest with one hand. His hair shone blue-black in the nearby firelight.

Galvanized, the aide helped his guest sit before the fire, rummaging for a cup of water to ease his sovereign's throat. When Liam had regained his breath and had a drink, he said, "And that's another reason. Your lungs aren't strong enough. You should be abed until you're completely healed from your wound."

"Aye. I suppose it's true, Dom. But I've about had it with being bedridden while you gather my army for me. If I am to be king, I need to begin acting as one." Liam inhaled shakily, relieved when the coughing didn't resume. He idly rubbed his chest, feeling the now-familiar scar tissue beneath his fingers.

The aide refilled his liege's cup before sitting down beside him. Twirling his mustache in agitation, he asked, "What of your guard? You shouldn't be alone! The people might not enjoy the Invader's rule, but your only protection is that you're believed dead. Some of your fine people would be happy to turn you in for the reward." *I've got to make the royal bratling see reason! Last thing I need is for him to be discovered...him and me.*

"Aye, Dominic. I'm aware of that," Liam said, rolling his eyes. "Ian should have already found my note and be hot on my trail. He'll be here before nightfall, I'm certain." He glanced sidelong at the aide. "When's the last time you were bedridden for months, eh? I'm sick to death of lazing about!"

Inhaling deeply, the older man reined in his anger. "I understand, Your Royal Majesty. I was fourteen myself once." A grim smile crossed his face at the prince's expression. "Aye, believe it or no, I was. Sometimes, it's easy to forget what a young man sees."

Liam nodded grudgingly. The pair were silent for a few moments. "What of the Resistance?" Liam finally asked, his voice soft.

It would be better to have him here where I can watch him. What's the saying? Keep your friends close and your enemies closer? Warming to his subject, Dominic answered, "We've had a few losses, but all is going as planned."

* ~ * ~ * ~ * ~ *

Tapping his finger against an ornately carved armrest, the Invader listened to yet another of the many boring reports requiring his attention. It was the only indication of restlessness, his demeanor appearing to be fully attentive to the aide delivering a monologue about the number of geese in the new province of Dulce.

Things had gone well through the summer; despite the inescapable destruction of war and siege, the Invader's coffers overflowed with the wealth of his newest acquisition. *Now if those idiots could pull their heads from their arses and bring me the final heir...*

The tempo of his tapping finger sped up with the onset of his irritation. It had been five months since that night — five months that he had waited to view the head of a young princess known as Sabine. In that time, seven members of his personal guard had been put to death for their failure, and two more awaited execution in the dungeons. At this point, he was sure he wasn't receiving further reports because his men valued their skins. *Can't say I blame them.*

As the aide prattled on, graduating from fowl to flora with his accounting of wheat, the Invader's eyes drifted across the audience chamber. Several scribes sat at a table nearby, prepared to pounce on his every word so that history would not be bereft of his wisdom. Courtiers and courtesans from all over his kingdom watched the proceedings, whispering to one another and plotting their games of intrigue. The Royal Guard were positioned at all entrances, the best bowmen of his realm circling the balcony above, ever vigilant for the smallest threat to his person. A few dozen people seeking audience huddled nearby. All in all, the scene was very pretentious and very boring.

"*Enough!*" he ordered. Deafening silence filled the room. Waving at the aide, the Invader said, "To boil it down, We are rich."

Sputtering at the interruption, the aide bowed low. "Aye, Your Royal Majesty."

With a satisfied nod, the Invader waved at the table of scribes. "Good. Give the list to Our scribes so it might be entered into the records."

The murmuring of the spectators resumed as the aide obeyed. Behind the throne, a door opened quietly, an old woman shuffling forward to whisper in the Invader's ear. Again, the chatter of the lords and ladies paused as they watched the witch, only to begin anew as they saw their monarch's eyes narrow in anger.

"Leave Us!" the Invader barked, rising and waving at the gathering. He nodded at his captain, and the Royal Guard stepped forward to urge the people to greater haste. Soon, the only occupants of the huge room were a few of the most loyal members of the Invader's guard, the old woman, and the king himself. At another gesture from the ruler, a chair was placed below the dais for the witch, who settled into it with a sigh.

"Bring them in," the Invader ordered, indicating the door through which the old woman had entered.

Two of his guard hustled over to throw it open, revealing the king's private audience chamber. Three men, travel-worn and wearing the Invader's colors, entered. Stopping before the dais, each man went down on one knee, head bowed.

"Your Royal Highness," their leader said. "We have word of the Dulce heir."

The Invader sat on his throne, eyeing his men with skepticism. "Your information had better be valid, or you'll join your fellow failures," he growled, stroking his beard.

Gulping, the leader nodded. "Aye, my liege. We think it is."

Finger tapping once more, the Invader leaned back. "Rise. Be seated."

As his men did so, the king called for refreshments. After a slave served a platter of meats and cheeses, the Invader watched the trio wolf down their food. Remembering his campaigning youth, he hid a grim smile while sipping his wine. Many a time, he'd returned from the field famished for food, drink, and human companionship. He idly wondered whether these guardsmen would find the third item or end up in the dungeons.

When the men finished eating, the Invader set his wine goblet on the table beside him. "What news have you?"

The leader bowed his head deferentially. "Sire, in the new province of Dulce, there is unrest. It is rumored that an heir to their throne has survived and is gathering the people to revolt."

Eyes narrowing, the Invader scoffed, "There is always unrest when I've taken a neighboring kingdom, and it is always said that an unknown heir is responsible. What makes this a viable threat?"

The soldier reached into his tunic, pulling out a roll of cloth. "This, Your Royal Highness." He stood and unfurled the material, revealing the standard of Prince Liam Dulce Caesar Alfric.

Stunned, the Invader stared at the stylized depiction of a battleaxe, a coiling green dragon running along its handle. In moments, he was down the steps, ripping the battle standard out of his man's hand. "Where did you find this?" he growled.

"We tracked down a small cadre meeting in a village near their old capital. They knew no one else in their Resistance, though this was in their possession."

The Invader crumpled the cloth in his fist, and the soldier flinched. His voice a dangerous rumble, the Invader said, "You didn't bring me the head I asked for."

Doing his best not to tremble, the guard said, "No, my liege. We...I thought this more important to bring to your attention." He straightened, swallowing heavily in fear. "I beg you not to take punishment on my men. It was my order to return. They were obeying their senior officer."

"What's your name?"

Startled, the soldier's facade cracked a little and he answered shakily, "Corporal Edel Grimnirson, sire."

Stepping up to the throne, standard crushed in his grip, the Invader said, "Edel, you made the right decision." As he sat down, he found the obvious relief of the men amusing. "I want a full written account from the three of you. See my scribes. Then you will be off duty for three days. I'll see that you each receive extra compensation in your pay."

Edel, looking from his men to his king, bowed deeply. "Thank you, sire!"

"Dismissed." As the men rose to leave, the Invader leaned forward. "And Edel?" The soldier turned back, his face a reflection of worry and happiness. "When you return to duty, report to the captain of my personal guard...Lieutenant."

When the promotion sank in, a smile crossed Edel's face. "Aye, Your Royal Highness! *Thank* you!"

Quiet reigned in the audience chamber after the patrol left. Face grim, the Invader stared at nothing, eyes restlessly searching as his thoughts spun about like a child's top. His gaze finally settled on the old woman. "Attend Us," he commanded, turning toward the door behind his throne.

This room was smaller — a private audience chamber with a crackling fire and comfortable chairs. Leaving the door open for the witch, the Invader removed his chain of office, laying it on a nearby table before pulling on a thick robe. Immediately, a servant appeared, pouring the king his favorite wine and setting food within easy reach.

The witch hobbled into the room, a guardsman closing the door behind her. Without preamble, she shuffled to a stool near the fire. The servant set another goblet of wine beside her and left the room.

Getting right to the point, the Invader held up the banner still in his fist. "What does this mean, Beltrana? I ran Prince Liam through myself. How can he be a threat to me?"

The old woman reached for the standard, clutching it to her

chest. Her rheumy eyes closed, and she rocked in her chair, muttering.

With vague disgust, the Invader looked away, sipping his wine. Like everyone else, he found witches and their ilk disturbing. He could not deny their powers, however — not since the first one he'd visited so many years ago. After he'd ascended his throne, he'd never been without one as an adviser.

Beltrana fumbled for a pouch at her waist, tossing a handful of stones onto a low table with arcane designs carved into its surface. Her voice, low-pitched and whispery, rubbed not unpleasantly against the Invader's ears. "The one who raises this standard is no threat to you and yours, only a means to an end."

"A means to an end?" he repeated, sitting across from her and leaning forward. "It's impossible. Liam is dead; his entire family was slaughtered. The only one left is his sister."

At the mention of the princess, Beltrana began rocking again. "Your death is nigh; the girl is coming. She will be your downfall."

Angry, the Invader abruptly rose, putting distance between them. "I don't know why I listen to you, old woman," he growled, back turned.

"Because I've never lied to you."

With an exasperated sigh, the king finished his wine, thumping the goblet on the table. He looked over his shoulder. "Is there a chance I'll survive?"

The old woman nodded, showing rotten teeth as she grinned. "There is always that. Always that." Her eyes became sharp as she focused on the man before her. "Do not allow yourself to be fooled, and you will succeed."

Wanting to be alone with his troubled thoughts, the monarch said, "Leave."

* ~ * ~ * ~ * ~ *

Looking over her shoulder, Katerin allowed her gaze to sweep across the five remaining wagons. With a sigh, she returned her attention to the road, pulling her shawl close against the autumn chill. Ros drove the wagon, a light cape draped across her shoulders, her curly blonde hair ruffled by a passing breeze.

With winter coming on, the circus was disbanded for the season. Half the performers were already gone, drifting off toward their homesteads and families with heartfelt farewells and plans to meet come spring. These last wagons were rolling toward the Compound.

"There it is," Ros said, a smile on her face.

Eagerly, Katerin studied the buildings. She heard shouts behind her as the others caught sight of their home.

The road paralleled a stream, a small but wide bridge spanning it and ending before a large one-story dwelling. Smoke belched from the chimney, and Katerin shivered at the promise of warmth. To the left hunkered a barn of nearly the same size, with a fenced area beside it. Chickens scratched the dirt here and there, and a few cows and horses grazed in the pasture beyond.

Ros clucked at her steeds, guiding them across the bridge and into the yard. She circled about to allow the others room to enter before coming to a halt. Grinning at Katerin beside her, she said, "Welcome home, Kat. Let me introduce you to the rest of the family."

By the time Katerin had climbed down from the wagon, most of the others had as well, and there was a loud commotion as people greeted one another. Ilia, who had opted to remain with the princess when they parted company with Gemma and Lucinda, stepped out of the back of Ros' wagon, standing as awkward witness. Wrapping a companionable arm around her handmaiden's waist, Katerin joined her.

Boasting four new faces, the small crowd got exuberant hugs of welcome. Cristof had an older version of himself in a headlock, the pair roughhousing in excitement. An older man listened intently to young Wilm as he prattled on about the season's adventures, Willem and Sati making the occasional comment in translation. Katerin flushed when she noticed the dwarf, Sameer, heatedly kissing a young redhead who knelt before him. It hadn't occurred to her that Sameer's wife would be of normal size. Prudently looking away, she saw Ros walking toward her, an old woman on her arm.

"Here, now, scamp," the woman exclaimed as they neared. "These old ears are far beyond hearing language like that!"

A surprised grin lit Katerin's face at Ros' blush. *I never thought I'd see the day...*

Despite her reddening complexion, Ros responded, "Only when that old tongue starts saying the same things. Where do you think I learned it?"

Scoffing, aged eyes twinkling, the woman slapped Ros' forearm harmlessly. Catching sight of Katerin and Ilia, she said, "You've been picking up strays again, young lady."

Ros burst into a laugh. "Aye, that I have! It's my favorite hobby!" Stopping at the end of her wagon, Ros bowed slightly. "Katerin, Ilia, may I introduce you to Emerita."

The pair curtseyed, Ilia's voice barely above a murmur as she said hello.

Emerita eyed them. "Well, at least these have manners."

Ignoring her, Ros continued smoothly, "Emerita has been with the circus for as long as I can remember. She and her husband, Phizo, are the greatest contortionists known to man."

This got a laugh from the old woman. Leaning forward, she whispered in a conspiratorial fashion, "Young Ros still has not realized we're getting old and decrepit. Why, I can't lift my arm over my head anymore!"

Snorting, the blonde said, "You'll not convince me, Em." Looking over her shoulder, she saw that most of the travel-worn people were drifting toward the main house. "Come, Katerin, Ilia, if I know Em, there's hot stew and freshly baked bread inside."

"Aye, you know me well, scamp," Emerita chuckled. Gathering her skirts, she smiled at the new arrivals. "Welcome home, each of you," she said as she made her way across the yard, leaving the three to follow.

With a slight bow, Ros waved the women forward. "I'll see to the horses before joining you."

"Don't be too long about it," the old woman's voice trailed back. "I'll not hold Cristof away from the stew forever." Those few still outside laughed at the reference to the animal trainer's legendary appetite.

"We'd best get started, then," Ros laughed, moving toward her wagon. She clambered up the side like a monkey, grabbing the reins and guiding the horses to the barn. Behind her, Willem, Cristof, and the two other men did the same.

Katerin stood with her handmaiden, watching the wagons disappear around the side of the house. Ilia shivered, rubbing her arms against the autumn chill even as Katerin tugged her shawl close.

"Here, now, lass," Katerin said, upon seeing that they were the only ones remaining. "Let's get indoors and warm."

"Aye, Kat." As they crossed the yard, Ilia's voice dropped into a murmur. "Do you think that was Cristof's brother?"

Recognizing a bit more than casual interest, Katerin responded in the same low tone. "I believe it is." She hid a smile at the calculating glint in Ilia's eye.

It took a moment for their vision to adjust to the darker interior, and they shivered as warm air, scented with fresh bread, wrapped about them. Most of the returning performers were already settled before the huge fireplace on the left wall. Over Em's protests, Sati helped Sameer's wife dish up healthy portions of stew. Young Wilm, too excited to sit still, ran in circles around the large room. Seated on a small stool, the dwarf held a small squirming bundle in his arms, a tuft of reddish hair peeking out of the cloth, his eyes bright with wonder.

To the right of the crowd was a wooden table that could easily seat twenty or more, half its benches now located before the fire. The back wall was lined with shelves filled with the usual implements and utensils for running a household, extra linens, and even a handful of leather-bound books. Small windows in the two remaining walls let in light.

Emerita bustled forward, pulling the new arrivals toward the group, fussing at them until they were comfortably seated, hot tea and stew within easy reach. Eventually, those who had been out with the horses entered, and another bench was added to the growing crowd. Ros settled on a stool beside Katerin, wolfing down her food as those who had remained behind were brought up to date on the news of the world. Katerin was introduced to Emerita's husband, Phizo, the other half of the aforementioned contortionist team. Additionally, she met Christof's brother, Henry, as well as Joseph, an elderly widower who had spent his time in the circus as a juggler and magician. Sameer's woman, Florin, did buffoonery and danced.

"So," Joseph said, filling his pipe, "what news of the Invader? I've heard at the market that he's taken another kingdom."

As Katerin and Ilia froze, Ros nodded with a grim expression. She leaned forward, setting her empty bowl near the hearth with the rest of the dirty dishes. "Aye. He has. The kingdom of Dulce is no more. Took it near five months ago, from what I gather." Her blonde head turning this way and that, Ros eyed her family. "We were right near the border at the time."

Florin made a small noise, reaching out to rub Sameer's back as she nursed the baby. Frowning, Emerita asked, "Did you have any trouble?"

"Some." Ros shrugged. "He's looking for someone...or was. His guard rousted us one night near Hodsin, but nothing came of it."

"Except the captain becoming completely disgusted with you," Cristof said, chuckling. "And Sameer acting flea-ridden didn't help matters in that regard, either."

The dwarf screwed his craggy face into an ugly expression, scratching roughly at his neck. "I certainly don't understand to what you are referring."

As Sameer continued his itching antics, everyone laughed. Katerin was glad for the distraction, her face quite red at the mention of the Invader's captain storming away. While she had come to terms regarding Ros' Sapphist ways, they still embarrassed her. Ros occasionally made rude comments, but more for entertainment value than anything else. Glancing sidelong at Ros, Katerin caught a flash of dancing eyes, and she felt her blush deepen.

"Well, with our new additions, there'll be some changes in who sleeps where, I gather," Emerita said.

"Aye," Ros nodded, sipping her tea. "Cristof and Henry will have to share again. Kat and Ilia will take Cristof's old room."

Henry turned to his younger brother, punching him on the arm. "You still snore?"

"Never!"

"Aye, he does!" Sameer insisted. "Many's the night I had to sleep under the wagon to get away from the racket!"

Willem, who had been quiet up to that point, nodded. "And I've had to move our wagon to the other side of the encampment!"

"Henry, we'll give you extra pillows to cover your ears," Ros promised with a grin, standing. As the others followed her lead, she said, "Daylight's wasting. Let's get those wagons unpacked and enjoy our first night home."

Katerin was herded outside toward the barn with the rest of the troupe, a mix of emotions stirring her heart.

Part 10

Drumbeat

Panting, heart thumping, crashing through the wilderness. Noises everywhere, the call of wild animals urging her on.

She knew that the Invader and his soldiers were chasing her, tracking her down to kill her. She was royalty, and her life was forfeit. She'd been instructed since she was a toddler that she lived for her people; Her people were gone.

Bursting from behind a bush, she screamed silently at the armored figure before her. Moonlight flashed on the blade above her and she cowered, afraid of the death blow that was coming. Cuddling her doll to her chest, she heard only the scuffle and the jangle of armor, felt the ground tremble as a heavy body hit.

Then a gentle touch fell on her shoulder, and she peered fearfully at her savior. The minstrel smiled, a bloody dove in his hands. "Hush, child. You're safe now."

Struggling to consciousness, Katerin felt hands grasping at her shoulders and tried to push them away. Finally, she awoke to a dark room and Ilia's whispered assurances that all was well. Panting, fighting tears of fear and relief, she stopped resisting Ilia's calming words. Several moments passed, however, before she relaxed into the other woman's embrace. Glad of the dark that hid her discomfort, Katerin pulled away. "Thank you, Ilia. I'll be fine now."

"Are you sure, Kat?"

"Yes," Katerin nodded, wiping an unseen tear from her cheek. "It was just a nightmare. I've had them often since...that night."

Ilia held her, squeezing gently. "As do I sometimes. It must be the strange surroundings that have triggered them."

"It must be." Katerin gently disengaged from Ilia. "Let's go back to sleep," she whispered, lying back down on the large bed. A vague sense of relief filled her as Ilia complied. Curled up on her side, she stared into the darkness, the noises of a strange building about her. Behind her, she could hear Ilia's breathing slow and deepen, until a gentle snore was all she heard. Only then did Katerin relax.

How odd it is, she mused, *that I should miss Ros' presence. Especially since it's not the first night I've slept with Ilia beside me.* Ilia had moved her meager belongings into the circus owner's wagon when Gemma and

Lucinda broke off from the troupe for their home. The women had been sleeping together in the same bed for several days, Ros having shown an unexpected sense of chivalry by bedding down on the floor.

Despite the residual terror of her nightmare, Katerin's eyes closed, and the beginnings of sleep stole over her. Reaching out, she brushed the wall beside the bed, knowing Ros' room was on the other side.

* ~ * ~ * ~ * ~ *

"Thought you'd be asleep, scamp," Emerita said, looking up from her stitching.

Ros, her expression contrite, scratched her unruly curls. "As did I." She fetched up a stool and sat beside the old woman. "You shouldn't be doing that at night, Em. Your eyesight will be ruined."

Emerita chuckled. "Aye, Ros. I'm an old lady, and my eyesight is ruined anyway. Stitching in firelight isn't going to make a difference anymore." With a shrewd gaze, she studied the circus owner's profile. "You've been having nightmares again?"

"Some," Ros admitted with a grimace. Her eyes shifted to the left of the fireplace, to the wall that divided Katerin and Ilia's room from the main area. "I'm not sure what woke me. It might have been Kat."

"Aye," Emerita said with a nod. "I believe I heard something from her room as well."

"Did you? She must have had another bad dream." Ros stared into the fire. "Do you think I should check on her?"

The old woman grinned slightly. "No, I think not. Ilia is with her."

Her hazel eyes blinked and Ros' shoulders slumped — small actions that spoke volumes. "You're right. I'm sure she'll be fine."

"I'm sure she will," Emerita repeated.

The crackling of the fire filled the room. Ros said, "Sati has already spoken to you about them?"

Again, Emerita nodded. "Aye, she has. You cannot expect an old woman not to be curious about her child's new friends."

Ros grinned at the woman beside her before becoming serious again. "I believe the Invader has lost her. Aside from that one time, his guards haven't appeared. I doubt he'd let it go this long if he knew where she was. You know he doesn't allow any heir to live."

"You're convinced she's of the royal family?"

Ros nodded. "The captain was nearly of a mind to take her that night. Only his belief that she shared my bed drove him away. I have heard rumors that the Dulce line is dark of hair and eye. Kat fits it well." Returning her gaze to the fire, she continued, "The clothes she had when we found her, despite being travel-worn, were much too fine. Even Ilia's clothing was nicer than an average woman would wear. And the dagger used to kill one of the men outside the cook wagon was far too ornamental for either of the men to carry."

"And how are you holding up?" The older woman's eyes held concern, the stitching forgotten on her lap.

"I'm fine." Ros saw the raised eyebrow and sat up. "I am!" she insisted. "The nightmares are to be expected. It's hardly a surprise they've returned."

"True enough. You were but a child, and almost skewered before your da and the rest of us. It was a terrifying time. I only worry for you."

Her face relaxed. "I know, Em. And the nightmares no longer fill me with such dread. I'm able to sleep through them most of the time."

"What do you plan to do now?" Emerita asked, allowing the discussion to move on to less upsetting things.

Ros sighed and rubbed her neck. "I'm not certain. I told Kat that she and Ilia could stay as long as they wanted, that I'd not turn them out. It's not like we've gotten incompetence in return. Ilia is doing a fine job with her juggling and buffoonery. And Kat is a wonder with the accounts, has a fine hand at writing, and knows more of healing than the lot of us put together."

"Then they'll remain with us until they wish to leave," the old woman said with a tone of finality.

Ros glanced sidelong at her. "And that's that, eh?"

"Aye. That's that." Emerita smiled, reaching forward to cup the younger woman's cheek. "This circus belongs to you; your da left it to you. Through the years, you've shown all of us nothing but the best of your abilities and judgment. We trust you to take care of your family."

Blushing, Ros whispered, "Thank you, Em. It's good to know."

The tableau lasted just a moment before Emerita leaned back. Her mending went into a basket and she creaked to her feet. "Now, then, it's time for decrepit old women and young scamps to be abed."

"Aye, Em," Ros said with a chuckle, rising as well. She bent and planted a kiss on her friend's wrinkled cheek. "I'll get to bed as soon as I bank the fire."

"Don't be out here 'til the night becomes morning," Emerita scolded as she moved toward the hall that led to the sleeping chambers.

"I won't. I promise." She bid the old woman good night, waiting until she'd gone before sitting on her stool to stare into the flames.

* ~ * ~ * ~ * ~ *

"Gods, this is taking forever!" Liam exclaimed.

Dominic shared a weary glance with the third man at the table. "Yes, my liege," he said, turning to the prince. "But caution is the watchword here. We aren't strong enough in numbers or weapons to achieve our goals."

With a gusty sigh, the teenager rolled his eyes. "There must be *something* we can do," he insisted. "These clandestine meetings are getting us nowhere!"

The third man spoke. "Begging Your Majesty's pardon, but these meetings do have a purpose." At the sour look he received, he chuckled. "Aye, hard for a young man — one bent on the doing rather than the talking — to easily understand, but it's true. These meetings serve to remind your people that you're alive and calling for them to fight for their king and country."

"Torlief has the right of it, sire," Dominic cut in. Clasping his hands and leaning forward on the table, he peered closely at the young man across from him. "Things may be slowly now, but the revolution will begin to snowball through spring and summer. We cannot make a move until everything is in place, or all will be lost." His voice softened. "I was adviser to your father, Liam. He trusted me. I ask that you place your trust in me as well."

Long moments passed before Liam bowed his head. "Yes, Dominic. You have my trust, just as you had that of my father before me. I know you'll only do what's best for the kingdom."

Smiling, Dominic reached out and squeezed the teenager's shoulder. "Thank you, sire. You'll never know how much that means to me."

* ~ * ~ * ~ * ~ *

"There you are, lads! Put some muscle into it!"

With a clash of metal, the two lines met. Each soldier's shield locked with a mate's as they attempted to break through the opposing line's defenses. The arms master shouted encouragement and instruction while the group shifted back and forth in the slush and mud. A score of other soldiers practiced with various weapons around the battlefield, displaying varying levels of skill. Most were unaware of their audience standing on the low wall surrounding the training grounds. Those who noticed fought twice as hard, showing their skills to their liege.

The Invader watched the mock battle, winter sun glinting off the royal seal hanging around his neck. He was wrapped in his cloak to ward off the season's chill. Raising his head, he closed his eyes. *The sun feels good.* Below him, the skirmish continued as he basked.

"Sire?" a voice asked tentatively. "A message for you."

Inhaling deeply, the Invader turned to see a servant holding a roll of parchment. He took it, his cloak falling open to reveal rich trousers and a boiled leather vest, accepting the man's bow with a nod. The king scanned the document, sent from the Dulce province by the adjunct he'd left in charge. "The messenger?"

"In the kitchens, sire, having a meal and awaiting your response."

With a snort, the Invader noted that word of rebellion was strong and growing daily. The group was organized into tiny cells of resisters; any attempt to rout out the leaders was thwarted by the small numbers and lack of pertinent information flowing among them. The Invader was positive who was behind this rebellion: disgruntled lords, still loyal to the Dulce crown, must have discovered the princess. No one would follow a woman into battle, so they'd passed her off as Liam to gain support. He speculated on who the true leader could be.

On the training ground, the battle came to a stop as one line finally broke through the other. The arms master called a halt before any further damage was done, pulling three wounded soldiers out of training and sending them to the surgeons.

Rolling up the parchment, the Invader said, "Have the messenger bed down in the barracks tonight, and see to his mount. I'll have a response by morning."

"Aye, sire."

As the servant left on his errand, the Invader looked at the training ground once more, eyes unseeing. It was time for a return trip to Dulce. *Perhaps for a grand celebration on the first anniversary of its fall.*

A soldier glancing up at his audience paled at the smile he saw on his liege's face.

Part 11

Ros stepped out of the main house and into the yard, where horses were hitched to the supply wagon. Phizo sat atop it, holding the reins and chatting with Sati and Katerin. The two women had made a small nest of blankets against the early winter chill, comfortably awaiting Ros' arrival.

Climbing up the side, Ros settled beside Phizo. "Let's be on our way before Emerita wants something *else*."

Phizo chuckled, snapping the reins. "One of the long lists, eh?" he asked as the steeds started forward.

"Aye," Ros complained, rolling her eyes when the women laughed. "I swear it gets longer each trip! Does she think we'll suffer some bizarre weather and get snowed in for a year?"

"Not at all," Katerin replied. "Given your appetite for her cooking, we've been hard put to keep up with you and Cristof at the dinner table."

Ros shot her a mock scowl for the jibe, earning a gentle touch on the back and a laugh from Katerin.

Phizo guided the horses across the small bridge and toward nearby Kemple. Once every two weeks, members of the troupe took turns going into town for supplies and news of the area. This was Katerin's first trip, and Ros watched as the small woman tried to contain her excitement.

Since they'd settled down for the winter, Ros felt more and more drawn to Katerin. She would look for Katerin's smile in the morning, tease her incessantly to hear the rich laughter, go out of her way to be where Kat was. When Katerin was out of sight, whether it be for a walk or some domestic chore, Ros sorely missed her presence. Interestingly enough, Katerin seemed to be equally enamored, searching Ros out, touching a shoulder or back or knee.

But no doubt that's just wishful thinking on my part. She'd seen Kat act similarly with the rest of the troupe. She simply enjoyed a tactile connection when dealing with others. *I shouldn't allow myself these silly fancies.*

Despite her rambling thoughts, Ros smiled at something Phizo said, responding in kind. Out of the corner of her eye, she saw Katerin watching her intently. Ros glanced back, snaring the dark eyes with a grin, her smile widening at the blush that crawled across the woman's fair skin.

Breaking their gaze, Katerin fiddled with the edge of a blanket in her lap, pretending interest in Sati's chatter.

The Compound wasn't far from the edge of town, and soon they reached the outskirts. Katerin found it odd that the wagon received barely a glance from the townspeople. She was so used to seeing villagers' joy at an approaching circus, that this lack of response was rather disappointing. Looking about, she found that Kemple looked like all the other small towns she'd been in the last few months — yet another unexpected turn in her mind. For some reason, she'd thought it would be...more.

Beside her, Sati pointed out the buildings of interest. "The cobbler lives just down this street; we'll see him after we've been to the weaver's for cloth. There's the inn," the dusky-skinned woman said, pointing to a two-story dwelling with its own well. "The goodwife there makes the best pumpkin pudding in the area. Maybe we'll have time to stop by?" She looked to Ros.

"Aye. We'll have time," Ros answered with a sly grin. She pulled out a scrap of paper. "Em's list isn't *quite* as enormous as I suggested. Besides, she also wants a cask of brandy." She tore the paper in half. "Sati, you and Kat see the weaver and cobbler, while Phizo and I attend to the smithy. We'll meet at the inn after; maybe we'll stop by the baker's for a special treat for tonight's supper."

"That sounds wonderful, Ros," Sati said, smiling. She waved Katerin toward the rungs leading to the ground, folding up the blankets before following.

Ros shifted to give the women room to climb down, but it was impossible for Katerin not to brush against her in the process. Blushing at the strong hand guiding her, she clambered down the steps, not looking at the cause of her distress until she had both feet on the ground. Another wink caused her to redden further, and she glanced up the small lane to cover her blush, rubbing her arm where Ros had touched her.

Ros' smile broadened. *There it is again. What's on her mind when she colors so? It certainly can't be what it looks like.* Her thoughts were interrupted by Sati's squeezing past her to climb down. By the time Ros could focus on Katerin again, the redness had dissipated and cool dark eyes peered at her.

"We'll see you at the inn," Sati said with a wave. She turned, taking Katerin's arm in her own and walking away from the wagon.

Phizo urged the horses forward, the woman beside him watching the pair until they were around a corner. A slight grin flitted over his face at Ros' interest. The developing closeness between Ros and Katerin had been the talk of the Compound for weeks.

When the women were out of sight, Ros turned back. She glanced at the driver and frowned. "What are you smiling at?" she asked, already knowing the cause.

"Nothing," the old man responded with a chuckle, finding the reins suddenly quite interesting.

Her suspicions confirmed, Ros grimaced at the horses. She'd heard about the wagers amongst her friends and had done her fair share of instigating their rumors and stories. It could hardly be her fault that Kat was such fun to tease on the matter. Still, Ros regretted her part in it, wishing she'd never begun the flirting. She'd discovered a serious liking for Kat as well as desire, but the path she'd started them on could only reach a dead end. Kat had decided long ago that Ros was a cad, and Ros had done nothing to change her opinion. It was much safer for everyone concerned anyway.

~~*~*~*

"How long do you think they'll be?" Katerin asked as they found a table. Nearby, a fire crackled on the hearth, dispelling much of the winter chill from her bones.

Sati set their purchases against one wall. "Soon, I should think." She sighed and sank into the chair, pulling a steaming mug toward her. "I believe Em wanted another kitchen knife. And Ros was saying something about having more tent spikes and nails for next season."

Nodding absently, Katerin's fingertips ran along the shoulder bag in her lap. Inside were embroidery threads — crimson, emerald, and a little bit of gold — to finish her sewing project. She'd decided to give Ros an over-tunic for Midwinter's Fest, and had been working on it diligently for three weeks. It would have been a disaster if she hadn't been under Emerita's tutelage. The flickering of firelight caught her eye.

Last year at this time, she had spent her days with her maidens, talking about the various young bachelors at court. Katerin remembered the festival her father had held, shining and aglitter with torches, jewels, and gold. There had been a wonderful ball, and she had danced with every available man from the age of sixteen to sixty. It had been breathless and intoxicating. All was well in the kingdom; the Invader had yet to make his intentions known.

A vision filled her eyes. The same audience hall filled with the dead and dying. She smelled the stink of blood, smoke, and excrement; the sickly sweet odor of gangrene mixed in with the warm green scent of spring. There was a constant low murmur among the wounded and those who cared for them, punctuated by the occasional scream as a surgeon removed a limb or cauterized an injury. Shivering, Katerin looked away from the flames, blindly grabbing for her mug and drinking deeply of the apple-cinnamon tea.

"Are you all right?"

Katerin found warm brown eyes watching her. Flushing, she shrugged. "Yes. I'm fine, Sati. Just a bad memory." Unable to hold her gaze, she glanced away, scanning the inn.

The interior was dark, yet inviting. It wasn't a large establishment — not much larger than the main room of the Compound, but there, the resemblance ended. Several smaller tables were scattered about, three occupied by a few patrons. A counter ran along one wall near the door, and behind it sat a middle-aged man tapping a keg.

Sati leaned forward with a conspiratorial grin. "Is the thread for Ros?"

Katerin immediately cheered up at the mention of her favorite person. "Yes," she answered with a smile, patting the bag in her lap. "Em says I'm doing well with a needle. I'm going to embroider roses along the hem and sleeves."

"She'll love it," Sati praised. "More for the fact that you made it than anything else." She chuckled as Katerin blushed and squirmed. A shadow fell across the table, interrupting them. Looking up, Sati appeared to be surprised. "Lina! You're working here again?"

"Aye, I am. And glad to be back!"

Curious, Katerin studied the new arrival. Lina was tall, almost as tall as Ros, her frame nearly too thin for her height. Her hair was a thick mahogany wave that fell down her back, and she had a face that would have been called "adorable" at court. She wore a simple peasant dress with a soiled apron, upon which she wiped her hands.

"Who's this?" Lina asked, smiling at Katerin.

Sati hastened to make the introductions. "Kat, this is Lina. She works here as a barmaid when she's not off in the countryside tending to sick relatives."

"Pleasure to meet you," Katerin greeted politely.

"We picked up Kat several months ago." Sati's eyes flickered between the two before she said, "She's Ros' personal assistant."

Green eyes narrowed a bit, pinning Katerin, though the smile widened. "Really? Ros' *personal* assistant? How...interesting." Dismissing the subject, Lina turned back to Sati. "Is Ros here today? I do miss her so."

"Aye. She and Phizo are at the smithy and should meet us here soon," Sati said, a bit reluctantly.

"Phizo! How is he? It's been so long since I've heard of any of the troupe," Lina said.

Their chatter turned to gossip as the pair filled each other in on their doings for the past year. Katerin listened avidly, trying to fathom this woman. After several minutes of conversation, she heard voices at the door and turned to see Ros and Phizo entering. Unaccountably, her heart flipped in her chest, and she could feel the heat crawl across her face. *What is it with me today?* she demanded of herself.

She wasn't alone in noticing the new arrivals. Upon seeing Ros approach the bar, Lina excused herself and fairly flew across the room to the blonde's side. "Ros! It's so good to see you!"

Katerin watched Ros' startled but pleased response at Lina's appearance. The two chatted at the bar for a few moments before Phizo left them and came to the table. She wasn't sure, but Katerin thought he seemed a bit disgruntled as he sat, leaning his elbows on the rough wood.

To make conversation, Sati asked, "Were you able to get everything that Em wanted?"

"Aye," the old man said, sipping a mug of ale he'd brought from the bar. "Though we'll have to return for the tent spikes; Amos hadn't any made up. What about you two?"

"Definitely," Sati smiled. "The cobbler has very nice leathers in a variety of colors. I think we should look into having red boots made for Wilm's costume next season. He's worn out his blue ones."

"That would be good."

The discussion continued across from Katerin, though she only paid it half a mind, her attention riveted on the two women at the bar. Her puzzlement grew as Ros sat on a stool rather than join them. Watching Lina constantly touching Ros in some way or another caused a spark of irritation. *Why, she's hanging all over her! How can Ros stand that simpering?* It appeared, however, that the constant attention from the barmaid was quite acceptable to Ros, which caused Katerin's annoyance to grow.

Turning away from the display with a snort, Katerin found two pairs of eyes carefully watching her. She fought to quell the familiar blush with no success, busying herself with brushing an imaginary speck of dust off her sleeve. Phizo and Sati continued their conversation, and she did her best to focus on it, teeth grinding as she tried to place where the anger was coming from.

"So you've gotten a 'personal assistant', eh?" Lina asked, idly running her fingers along Ros' forearm.

Ros chuckled. "Aye. Kat's good with numbers and letters. She helps a great deal with the accounts." Glancing at the woman in question, she wondered about the tense set of Katerin's shoulders, but dismissed it. "She knows some of the healing arts as well. We need someone like that in the troupe."

Lina leaned forward, brushing her breast against Ros' arm. "Is that *all* she helps you with?" she asked, her husky voice hardly carrying beyond them.

Hazel eyes glanced at the table again, a flash of regret in them. Being enamored of the young woman didn't alter the realities of their friendship. *You've got to get over this infatuation, girl.* Reviewing Kat's most recent flirting, Ros snorted to herself. *She obviously isn't aware of what she's doing, else she'd run screaming back to her kingdom in horror.* Ros smiled and returned her full attention to Lina. "Aye. That's all she helps with." With a laugh, she placed her hand over the one resting on her arm.

Lina's answering smile became sultry. "Why don't you stay tonight? It's the slow season, and I'm sure I can leave early."

Deciding an evening's entertainment would help dispel her daydreams, Ros said, "I'd like that."

As Sati had indicated, the pumpkin pudding was wonderful, but Katerin found she had no stomach for it, poking at it with a spoon. The taste was divine, but her undefined anger made her stomach roil. When Ros finally disengaged herself from the barmaid's arm and approached the table, Katerin's spirits rose. *Good! We can go home now.*

Ros sat on the bench beside Katerin with a grin. "How was your shopping trip?"

"Very good, thank you," Katerin responded.

"But she can't tell you what she purchased," Sati added with a conspiratorial smile.

"Really?" A blonde eyebrow rose in interest. "Something for me?"

Blushing, Katerin almost kicked Sati under the table. "Perhaps," she responded tartly, pleased with the warm chuckle that resulted.

"I look forward to seeing whatever it is." Ros handed a couple of coins to Phizo. "Here's to pay for something from the baker. The barkeep will have our keg of brandy ready when you leave. I'll be staying the night here and walking back in the morning."

"What?" Katerin sputtered. She looked at the two across from her, surprised to find resigned acceptance. "Why would you do that?"

The blonde's grin became lecherous. "Well, since you ask…"

"Ros," Sati warned.

Laughing, Ros raised her hands in surrender. "All right! I'll play nice!" Turning back to Katerin, she said, "Lina and I have...much to catch up on. I'll be staying with her tonight." She rose from the table, ignoring the confusion on Katerin's face. "Until tomorrow, then."

Katerin stared blankly at her retreating form, unable or unwilling to understand why Ros would remain in the village rather than return to the Compound. Little doubt was left, however, when Ros wrapped a casual arm about Lina's waist in a full-bodied hug — one that Lina enthusiastically returned before they both left the inn.

As crimson as the thread she had purchased, Katerin wheeled about in her seat, turning her back on their exit. *By the gods! They're lovers!* Visions of Ros holding the barmaid and touching her naked skin came unbidden, and Katerin closed her eyes at the onslaught, swaying slightly in her seat.

A hand rested lightly on her clenched fist. "Kat? Are you all right?"

Katerin opened her eyes to see Sati's compassionate face. She tried to respond, unable to do more than stammer through the shock and burgeoning anger.

Phizo, looking decidedly uncomfortable, rose from his seat. "I'll go load up the keg," he said as he left them.

"Kat?"

Anger soon won the battle for dominance. Black eyes flashing, Katerin pulled away from Sati's touch, putting her fists in her lap. "You *knew* they were lovers," she hissed.

Taken aback at the woman's vehemence, Sati sat up straighter. "Aye. I knew," she answered calmly. "Though it doesn't happen often. Lina serves only to satisfy certain...needs Ros has."

"Needs?" Katerin sputtered. "We *all* have needs! That doesn't mean we should whore ourselves about!" Even as the vicious words spilled from her mouth, she wanted to call them back. Her irrational fury warred with shame as she watched her friend's eyes grow cold. "I'm sorry, Sati. I—"

"No." The woman held up her hand. "I'll not discuss it here." Rising, she picked up her purchases. "Come along or stay, Kat. It's your choice. We won't wait long for you."

Katerin stared down, watching the splash of a tear hit the tabletop. She felt hollow and lost, worse than she had in those dark days of running before she found the circus. The Compound had become home; the troupe, family. Slowly, Katerin rose and shouldered her bag. She wiped away the tears on her face before leaving the inn.

* ~ * ~ * ~ * ~ *

Silence enveloped the ride home. Sati took Ros' place by Phizo, leaving the princess to sit alone in the puddle of blankets. Katerin's heart was a knot of confusion. Anger, envy, and deep sorrow filled her, forcing her to concentrate foremost on not crying. Instinctively, she refused to think about Lina, knowing that to do so would be her undoing. Only her royal training kept the tears at bay.

Soon, it was over. Katerin sped down the side of the wagon and into the main building. Emerita barely had time to acknowledge her arrival before she stormed into her room. Throwing herself onto the bed she shared with Ilia, she burst into tears. A part of her childishly awaited someone — anyone — to interrupt her pitiful wallowing with words of sympathy. No one came.

In the absence of a distraction, her sobbing intensified. *How could she do this to me? Running off to sleep with a barmaid...who does she think she is?* Fury overcame Katerin, and she beat on her pillow as she cried. Exhaustion eventually overcame her, tears fading to leave swollen eyes and a runny nose in their wake. The numbness was a relief, though she couldn't drift off to sleep. Every time her eyes closed, a vision of Ros pressed against Lina's naked form would appear.

The day passed into evening. Noises from the wall adjoining the main room attested to continued life. Supper was prepared and eaten, the troupe gathering about the fireplace afterward to entertain one another with stories and songs. Stewing in her melancholy, Katerin listened to the familiar sounds, feeling hollow and alone.

The knock, when it occurred, caused Katerin to jump. Hastily sitting up, she rubbed her face. "Come in," she said in a rough voice.

Emerita poked her head into the sleeping chamber. "Would you mind a visitor?"

A combination of relief and irritation moved through her. "Yes, I mind," Katerin said, her royal blood shining through as she lifted her nose into the air. "I wish to be alone."

Raising an eyebrow, the old woman stepped back. "Fine. I'll leave you to your self-pity."

"Wait!" Katerin leaped to her feet, heart pounding at the threat. Wilting under the stern but kindly gaze, she dropped her eyes. "I'm sorry, Em. I don't know what's come over me this afternoon. Please stay."

Nodding, Emerita entered, closing the door behind her. "Sati told me that you were out of sorts about Ros," she said as she sat on the bed, the young woman joining her.

A watery snort erupted from Katerin, and she looked away, tears making a rapid return. "'Out of sorts', that's an interesting phrase."

Eyeing the young woman's profile, Emerita said, "She says you're acting the jilted lover."

"I most certainly am *not!*"

"Aye, I agree. Which begs the question — why are you acting like one?"

Katerin began huffing, anger making a glorious comeback. Emerita let her sputter, watching with mild interest. Unable to come up with a coherent reply, Katerin felt her fury dissipate, leaving her feeling emotionally battered.

Silence stood between them for long moments. With a gentle sigh, Emerita reached for the young woman's hand. Cradling it, she said, "You're angry at Ros for staying with Lina this night. You're jealous."

Katerin attempted to pull away, but the old woman's grip was surprisingly strong. "You can lie about it to yourself as much as you'd like, but I'll not allow my family to be disrupted as a result." Emerita released the now balled-up fist. "You must come to terms with your emotions, girl."

Dark hair obscured Katerin's face as she hung her head.

"Anyone with eyes can see that you love her." Emerita allowed a slow grin to cross her lips as the woman peered up at her. "Aye, and she loves you too."

Tears spilled down Katerin's face. "Then why is she there and not *here*, Em?" she asked, hating the plaintive waver in her voice.

"You've never given her cause." The old woman's eyes searched the room even as her mind sought to convey the words. "Your opinion of Sapphists is no secret, Kat. Whether you harbor these thoughts because of experience or upbringing, I don't know. Ros is a Sapphist, like it or no."

Katerin blushed at the old woman's candor. It took quite a bit of strength to not squirm. "Where I come from...it's...frowned upon," she finally allowed. *Especially for the heir to the throne.*

"Aye. It is in many places," Emerita said, nodding. Her voice became unyielding as she said, "But not here."

Chastised, Katerin nodded in mute agreement, fresh tears falling into her lap.

Emerita eased her stern features, unwilling to let the young woman suffer alone. Gathering her into her arms, she rocked her gently, pleased that Katerin relaxed into the embrace.

The tears came back with a vengeance. Heart-wrenching sobs shook Katerin's small form as she mourned her situation. Emerita never wavered, holding her close. Even after the weeping finally let up, she remained in place, her head in a soft lap, aged fingers running through her hair. She still felt hollow, but the gentle caress eased the ache in Katerin's chest.

"It's high time you made a decision, Kat. You can accept Ros' love and return it freely," the old woman murmured, "or you can release her in your heart, no harm done."

Katerin sniffled, forcing herself to sit up, pulling away from the comforting touch. "I've been too long denying it, Em," she said, wiping her face. "Ros wouldn't have me now anyway. She's Lina to bed, in any case."

"You're wrong, Kat. If you crooked your finger, Ros would come running." At the incredulous glance, Emerita chuckled. "Aye! We know it, even if neither of you does. The question's not whether you two love each other, it's whether the pair of you will fight for the love you feel."

Katerin was caught off guard by the statement, and her troubled expression faded into thought. Not until Emerita reached the door did the young woman return to the present.

"Sati and Florin have put aside dinner for you. Ilia said she'd be happy to bring it if you wish."

Raising her chin, Katerin rose. *I must get on with things.* "That won't be necessary, Em. I'll come to the hall to eat. Thank you."

The old woman smiled, reaching out to take Katerin's hand. "Good. We miss your presence this night." Emerita led the young woman out of the solitary room.

Part 12

"...And on the twenty-third day of the fourth month, We, His Royal Majesty Germaine Carlos William Cassaidie, have ordered a grand celebration in the Dulce province to commemorate the first anniversary of its...inclusion in Our kingdom!"

The crowd murmured. The court herald swallowed nervously but went on. "The finest entertainment has been invited: dancers, musicians, racers, circuses, and acting troupes. Firemount Field will be converted to tournament grounds, and all warriors near and far are invited to test their mettle against one another. We will be in attendance as judge.

"The celebration will last a fortnight, and We ask all of Our subjects to attend. Signed by Our hand, the eighth day of the eleventh month."

As the herald continued to other announcements, Dominic stopped listening, his mind awhirl. *Fourth month, eh? That might be the perfect time.*

Planning the rebellion had been a logistical nightmare. Recruiting the disaffected public and loyal followers to Liam's banner hadn't been as difficult as pinning down a time and date to act. The Invader had already taken the castle once; taking it again wouldn't be that hard, especially with his soldiers in residence.

But killing the Invader...now, that would be far better. The royal brat would triple his diplomatic power base by slaying the usurper. Thoughts heavy on his mind, the aide stroked his mustache as he left the square.

* ~ * ~ * ~ * ~ *

Undoubtedly, the dawning hour is the most beautiful, Ros thought. The morning quiet was broken only by the crunch of her footsteps on the frozen road. Everything was still, most townsfolk still abed as local farmers tended to their early chores.

Inhaling deeply of the chill air, Ros wrinkled her nose, perversely enjoying the numbness of her face. She looked up into the sky, noting the low clouds. *It will snow soon. I'd best check the tiger's enclosure with*

Cristof — make sure she'll be warm enough.

Her thoughts wandered to the previous evening's activities, and Ros smiled, unconsciously licking her lips. As usual, her liaison with Lina left her feeling playful and lazy, relaxed on levels she usually couldn't attain on her own. It had been embarrassing, calling out Kat's name at one point. Fortunately, Lina understood far more about the situation than Ros gave her credit for. They spoke at great length before the barmaid pounced on Ros, insisting that *her* name would be the next one called in passion. *And call it I did*, she thought with a smirk.

As she came over a small rise, the Compound came into sight. Surprisingly, smoke already trickled from the chimney. *Em must be baking today*, she thought, though it seemed that the matriarch of the troupe had finished that little chore a day or so earlier. With a shrug, she continued walking.

As they inevitably did, her thoughts turned to Katerin. Ros pulled her cape tighter around her throat. She truly wished things were different between them. Given Katerin's background, Ros was certain her flirtations were merely larks as Katerin learned womanly ways. Katerin was safe in teasing Ros, knowing nothing would ever come of it. While it was heartening to know that the young woman trusted her so, it didn't serve to make things easier for Ros. *Had Kat remained a princess in her kingdom, she'd never have acted in such a manner.*

Which brought up another line of thought. The Invader was known the world over for his dogged stubbornness. Unless his men had lied and another young woman had been killed in Katerin's place, he was still looking for her. Unfortunately, the circus' route took them precariously through the old Dulce kingdom. *To change our normal circuit for no apparent reason would create suspicion. What then, eh?*

Ros worried over the topic — a familiar habit for the past few months — as her steps brought her closer to home.

~~*~*~*

As the door opened, Katerin looked up from her sewing to see the lanky circus owner enter. Heart shivering, she tried to maintain an air of calm as she set her project in the basket at her feet.

Ros, deep in thought, didn't initially notice Katerin's presence. She took off her cape and hung it on a hook behind the door. Turning, she spied the object of her musings, a pleased smile crossing her face. "Good morning, Kat. I didn't expect to see you up so early."

"Good morning," Katerin said, returning the smile. "I had some difficulty sleeping, so I thought I'd do some work on my stitching."

The ghost of a frown flickered in Ros' eyes. "Nightmares?" she asked, settling down on a stool.

Katerin blushed, looking away. "Sometimes," she murmured. Raising her chin in subtle defiance, she captured the woman's eyes. "But not last night."

Ros blinked. "Oh," she said, at a loss. *How does she pull the rug out from under me so easily?*

With a small laugh, Katerin leaned forward and patted Ros' hand. Swallowing her envy, she sat back in her chair, a small grin on her face. "How was your visit with Lina?"

"It was...relaxing. We haven't seen each other in well over a year. She's been—"

"Taking care of her sick grandfather in the country," Katerin finished, not wanting to continue that line of discussion, despite the fact she'd begun it. "She told me. At the inn yesterday." *You are acting like such a ninny*, she scolded herself.

Watching Katerin appear to be intensely interested in a speck of lint on her lap, Ros wondered, *Is that jealousy I see?* After a slight hesitation, Ros rejected her thought. *Of course not. What am I thinking?*

Katerin sighed. "I apologize," she said, looking ruefully at the circus owner. "I...I didn't get much sleep last night, as I said. I do not wish to be rude."

"I understand," Ros answered, not comprehending in the least.

"No, you don't," Katerin said, smiling despite herself. *Get on with it, woman! You're the Princess Royal, for gods' sakes! Show some backbone.* Inhaling deeply, she reached for Ros' hands, taking them in hers. "As I was told last evening, I've been a bit out of sorts since yesterday. When you stayed in the village, I—" Katerin squeezed Ros' hands, forging on. "I was jealous. There! I *said* it!"

Frowning, Ros attempted to make some sense of the words. She was half-amused by the proud smile that beamed her way, belying Katerin's statement. *Jealous? Of what? Who?* "Lina?" she finally asked. *Why would she be jealous? Unless...*

"Yes."

Ros chuckled at the suddenly cheerful woman across from her. "I'm not sure why you'd feel that way, Kat, but no worries," she said. "Spending time with Lina doesn't detract from our time together."

Crestfallen, Katerin released the blonde's hands, shoulders slumping. "You do *not* understand what I meant at all."

She can't be saying what I think she's saying. Pulling back, her own expression serious, Ros asked softly, "Are you aware that Lina and I did more than talk through the night?"

"Yes," Katerin said with a grimace. "I am."

Rubbing her face, Ros considered her next words carefully. "And this caused you anxiety because...?" When she received no answer, she looked at Katerin. "You've known from the beginning what I was. My apologies if the truth of the matter should suddenly hurt your feelings in some way, but I'll not behave like a virgin to assuage your sensitivities, Katerin."

With a groan, Katerin hastily rose to her feet. "I'm sorry. I shouldn't have said anything." Before she could be intercepted, she rushed from the room.

Hearing a door closing gently, Ros sighed and dropped her head. *Made a mess of that, I'm sure.* The good feelings she'd floated on after the evening with Lina had long since disappeared; a vague headache began to assail her.

~~*~*~*

Quite at a loss, Ilia watched from her seat on the bed as Katerin paced the room.

"Honestly, I don't have the slightest clue!" Katerin said, lips pursed in agitation. "How can I get past this?"

Ilia's eyes widened when she realized the question wasn't rhetorical. Her former liege and current roommate seriously considered her, expecting an answer. "I certainly wouldn't know, Kat!" she insisted, standing. Her pale features reddened. "I'm of the same mind about Henry. The silly man doesn't even know I exist."

Katerin tsked at herself. "I know! Run and get Em. She's known them both for a time. Perhaps she'll have some ideas."

Ilia decided the idea was a fine one. "I'll be right back."

In her absence, Katerin returned to pacing. Her conversation with Ros had been a complete failure; she had no idea of how to proceed. Now that she'd changed her mind about Ros, getting that thick blonde skull turned to the idea promised to be a difficult task.

Katerin's training in court included etiquette and grace, her future one of regal childbearing for whatever husband her father chose for her. She'd never learned how to entice a man to her, let alone a woman. There was no cause. Any man would be a fool not to marry a princess and expand his lands and titles. Yet here she paced, in the exact predicament she'd never trained for. Katerin had to chuckle. She'd spent a good deal of time these last few months dealing with predicaments for which she'd never been trained. In that respect, this would be nothing new.

The door opened, and Ilia ushered Em, Sati, and Florin into the room. Katerin's eyebrows rose, her skin flushing. "I didn't expect everyone," she said as the door closed firmly behind Ilia.

"Well, you didn't get everyone," Em said, settling on the bed with Florin. Sati leaned against the door, and Ilia settled in the only chair. "Unless you'd like me to call the menfolk and Ros in here?"

"No!" Katerin said, a rueful grin on her face as she saw the older woman's impish smile. "That won't be necessary, I think."

"So Ilia said you've a problem?" Sati asked.

Uncertain how to proceed, Katerin nodded vaguely and looked away from the gathered women.

"You've a mind to crook your finger at Ros?" Em asked, referring to their discussion the previous night.

Florin gasped, clapping her hands over her mouth in delighted surprise.

At the door, Sati murmured, "It's about time."

Katerin, thoroughly embarrassed, sighed. "Yes." She took a deep breath and squared her shoulders. "It's past time for me to 'crook my finger'. If what you say is true..."

"Oh, it is, I assure you," the older woman said, smiling.

"What's true?" Ilia asked.

"Our Ros is smitten by this young woman," Sati said, arms crossed over her chest, her eyes dancing. "Those of us on the road knew it months ago."

"That long?" Katerin asked, startled.

"Aye," Sati said. "You thought the men were wagering on the pair of you without some hint to urge them on?"

Katerin dropped her gaze. "I wasn't certain," she finally said, her voice almost a mumble.

Em scooted to one side, making room on the bed. "Come, sit, Kat. Now you know the truth of it, what would you have us do?"

Katerin sat between the old woman and Florin. Her initial anxiety faded in their presence; a sense of belonging washing over her, bolstering her courage. "It's not so much what you can do, but what I can do," she said. "I...I'm at an impasse. I tried to speak to Ros this morning when she returned, but...I didn't speak correctly. She didn't understand my meaning." Dejected, she let her shoulders slump. "I don't know how to let her know things have changed with me."

"Telling her you were wrong isn't possible?"

Something in Katerin's chest tightened. "No," she said to Florin. "It's not."

"Kat is as stubborn as Ros when it comes to being wrong," Sati informed the slight redhead. "I've never heard either of them admit it."

Despite the serious topic, Ilia chuckled. "And my! The sparks that would fly over such a thing!"

"Aye. Watching these two butt heads has been quite entertaining this season."

Em draped her arm across Katerin's shoulder. "Enough, you two."

Ilia looked chagrined, though Sati's smile was unrepentant.

"I think I understand the problem," Em continued. "She's made her decision about you already. Unless you force the issue, Ros will remain honorable to her intentions."

"Yes! That's it exactly!" Katerin said. "When I spoke with her this morning, it seemed as though she didn't want to consider that things had changed, that *I* had changed. I could almost see her comprehension before she took another tack entirely."

"But how do you force a stubborn mule like Ros?" Florin asked. "I've only known her two years. She doesn't strike me as the type of woman to change her mind once it's set."

"She isn't," Em said. At Katerin's slump, the old woman smiled and added, "For the most part. Kat here needs to show the scamp how much she's loved, that's all."

Florin's eyes lit up and she smiled. "So Ros needs *romancing*?"

"Aye, I believe so."

From the door, Sati laughed and eyed Katerin intently. "If you wish to romance her, you must hit her over the head with it. She's intelligent and compassionate, but not too bright about what's sitting in front of her."

Em laughed. "Such could be said for most men as well."

"Even Henry?" Ilia asked. The room quieted and she flushed deeply, dropping her gaze as the women stared at her.

"Well, now," Sati said, "seems love is in the very air we breathe, doesn't it?"

"It most certainly does." Florin smiled at Ilia kindly.

"I'd say even Henry will be susceptible to the proper feminine charms," Em said, reaching out to squeeze Ilia's knee.

Katerin frowned. "So how does one go about romancing another? It's not something I've been taught."

"You've never flirted with a man just to see what would happen?"

"No, I've not. My family was...very strict," Katerin said, looking away from Florin's skepticism. She didn't see the quick glance between Sati and Em.

Ilia pursed her lips. "I've flirted before, but it seems that doesn't work with Henry. He doesn't respond in the manner of other men."

"I believe Henry thinks of himself as being duller than Cristof.

Therefore, no woman would really want much to do with him."

"That's preposterous!" Ilia's blue eyes flashed dangerously. "He's a very interesting man!" Her ire faded at the knowing looks around her, and she colored again.

Florin took Katerin's hand. "I know what you need do with Ros, Kat. Show her you love her — in *all* the ways women can love."

"Aye. I think she'd fall for that one, no doubt," Sati said.

Katerin's eyes narrowed as she puzzled over the statement. "I do not understand. You mean *bed* her?"

"Well, ultimately."

"Florin!" Em raised an eyebrow at the now-giggling woman.

Katerin chuckled, amazed she could laugh about such a thing with her face as heated as it was.

Sati said, "What Florin means is to treat Ros as if you were already lovers."

"Aye, that's what I meant." Florin fought to control her laughter.

Shivering, Katerin asked, "How can I do that if we're not?"

"It's not so much the intimacy," Em said. "It's the little things that couples do for one another every day."

Ilia's eyes lit up. "Like when you pour water for Willem at breakfast," she said to Sati. "You touch him in a manner to remind him how close you are."

Sati nodded. "That's it exactly." She turned her attention back to Katerin. "If you were to take over the meal serving as far as Ros is concerned, you'd do the same — act as if you were already lovers."

Unconvinced, Katerin frowned. "I don't see how that would make a difference."

"It's a subtle thing," Florin said. "Though Ros has already made a decision about you, your actions will cause her to rethink it on such a deep level, she'll never know when she changed her mind."

"And she *will* change her mind, Kat," Em said, her voice reassuring. "I told you last night, she loves you dearly."

"Aye, she does," Sati said.

"Will this work on Henry as well?" Ilia asked.

"I guarantee it will work on Henry," Florin said, smiling at Ilia. "He's a lonely man who's pining away for a woman, though he doesn't know it."

"And *you* are a matchmaker gone mad," Em said, laughing. "Florin can never leave well enough alone when it comes to romance." She gave Ilia a warm smile. "She's also never wrong when it comes to her skills."

For the remainder of the morning and afternoon, the women clustered in the small room to discuss plans of action. Every manner of situation brought up was met with suggestions for the two women to use in their respective quests. As the last of the women left, Katerin leaned against the door and sighed. The prize was within sight, and she finally held hope in her heart that she would be the victor.

～～*～*～*

"You'd be best served, Highness, by tossing that traitorous bastard out."

Liam sighed as he formulated a response to the farmer before him. "I'll not rid the rebellion of a loyal ally. Dom has done more for us than any other man since the Invader stole our kingdom."

"Maybe so, maybe no," the farmer said, spitting to one side in disgust. "Yet I've heard tales. Heard your loyal aide had a visit with the Invader the day after you were run through. My cousin Radis saw him in the royal wing."

"Your cousin must be mistaken, Felin," the teenager insisted. "Dom left the castle the night before. He told me so." *Didn't he?*

"Aye. He told you so. And gods above, what that snake speaks is golden truth" was the sarcastic response.

Liam bristled but was waved down. "No, young pup. You believe what you want. And maybe when this is over, you'll remember my words and either heed them or send me to the gallows." Again, Felin waved the younger man into silence. "Be that as it may, I'll still fight. But not for you, lad. I fight for the memory of your father, and hope that someday you'll pull the wool from your eyes." With a tug at his forelock, more an automatic gesture than anything else, Felin stomped out of the room.

Slumping into a chair in frustration, Liam sighed again. *Bleeding Sif! As if we've not enough problems!*

Unfortunately, this was not the first whiff of unrest regarding Dominic's proximity to the crown. There had been too many hints and innuendoes to ignore. *But if he is in league with the Invader, why is he here? It would have been far easier to kill me as I lay on my sickbed. Why the plotting to get my crown?*

Unless Dominic plans on taking the crown from me once I've received it.

Although that thought was sobering, it still didn't feel right. Liam vowed to keep a closer eye on his chief aide.

Part 13

Ros sat at the table. Around her, the members of her extended family ate breakfast boisterously, an excited atmosphere filling the air. Mingling with the smell of Sati's famous cherry hotcakes was the aroma of pine boughs that had been brought in to decorate the Compound for Midwinter's Fest. With a smug grin, she watched the people she loved, happy that another winter with her friends and family held such joy.

Before having a third helping of food, Willem coaxed his young son into finishing his mug of milk. The old man, Josef, tickled Florin beside him while her husband, Sameer, looked on with a grin. Their baby perched on Ilia's hip, eyes wide, as the willowy blonde set a generous plate before Henry. The animal trainer, Cristof, chatted amiably with Phizo about the coming season. Sati worked at the fire while Emerita and Kat kept her company, eating their breakfast there and delivering food to the great table.

As Ros' eyes fell on Katerin, she looked up. The woman's face lit with a soft smile before she turned back to the conversation in which she was engaged. Unaccountably blushing, Ros became intent on her food. To say that the past few weeks had been perplexing would be an understatement. Since that cryptic conversation after Ros' return from Lina's, Kat had refused to discuss it. Instead, she'd spent the rest of that day sequestered in her room, allowing only the other women entrance.

Ros squirmed at the memory of the looks she'd received from Katerin's visitors. They had run the gamut from angry dissatisfaction to mysterious smiles, and it was beyond her which was worse. The men only chuckled at her complaints, patted her on the shoulder and offered vague platitudes that passed for wisdom. After a week of trying to persuade Katerin to talk, Ros had finally surrendered.

She's as stubborn as I am, she thought, taking a bite of breakfast.

Across the table, Ilia leaned in close to Henry, hand on his shoulder for balance, as she poured him another mug of cider. Henry flushed at the contact, but smiled up at Ilia in thanks.

Hiding her own smile, Ros took a long draught of her own cider. *He's falling hard! I wonder — will Ilia remain behind this season? Or will*

Henry join us? A hand on her shoulder distracted her, and she looked to see Kat holding a kettle, smiling down at her.

"Would you like more cider?"

Frozen for just an instant under the warm regard, Ros mentally shook herself. Her training came to the fore and she grinned back, holding out her mug. "Aye, I would. Thank you."

Katerin's smile widened, and she leaned in to pour, breast brushing against Ros' shoulder. "How's breakfast?"

Ros flushed at the contact but maintained her composure. "My best to the chef and her assistants. You've outdone yourselves this morning."

"I'll convey the message," Katerin said with a grin before moving to offer cider to the others.

She watched Katerin make a circuit of the table, unaware that Henry eyed Ilia in the same manner.

* ~ * ~ * ~ * ~ *

Katerin laughed, clapping her hands as Cristof and Sameer bested Henry. The animal trainer had pelted his brother with snowballs, driving him backward to trip over the dwarf's huddled form. Before Henry could do more than flail on the ground, his opponents were on him, tickling him and filling his clothes with snow until he yielded.

Beside Katerin, Ilia held a hand to her lips; whether it was to stifle a grin or a gasp of concern was uncertain.

Florin wrapped a companionable arm across Ilia's shoulder. "You know he deserved it," she said, laughing. "Throwing his brother into the snowbank was uncalled for."

Ilia leaned into the hug, and her eyes danced as she chuckled. "I know. Henry can be such a scamp!" she said with obvious affection.

Behind the pair, Katerin exchanged a knowing look with Sati. A yell brought their attention back to the yard.

Ros and Willem, with the eager assistance of the Compound's only child, voiced battle cries as they attacked the three others in the yard. Setting their differences aside, Sameer and the brothers left off their fight to defend themselves.

Snowballs flew fast and furiously among the opponents while the women watched from the front step, rooting for their favorites. The noise was so great that the older members of the family joined the audience, Phizo with the babe in his arms.

Young Wilm apparently decided to have pity on the enemy and began lobbing snowballs at his teammates from behind. With an incredulous growl, Ros turned to grab the giggling boy, who took off running for all he was worth.

Katerin laughed so hard at their antics that tears came to her eyes. This Midwinter's Fest was so different from those of her upbringing — staid, formal occasions that were primarily for politicking among the nobles. With the excitement and activity, she'd hardly had an opportunity to be homesick.

A wayward snowball smacked her shoulder, icy flakes exploding to spray the audience as well as settle into her bodice. The women cried out at the attack; Phizo and Josef successfully shielded the baby.

Emerita was the furthest back. She wiped her face with a mock scowl. "I'd best start supper." The two old men agreed with her, shuffling inside and firmly closing the door.

The snow warriors watched Katerin with expressions that ranged from chagrin to amusement.

Looking up, mouth agape in shock at the attack, Katerin fastened her eyes upon Ros. The circus owner made every attempt to appear contrite, despite the fact that she was shaking with contained laughter. Unable to hold her composure under Kat's startled gaze, Ros burst into guffaws, followed by those of her cohorts.

Katerin's eyes narrowed as she looked to the other "victims". "I say we get them back," she suggested. Seeing unanimous agreement, Katerin pointed at Ros. "You're next!"

With that, Katerin and the women rushed their targets, abandoning shawls and cloaks while scooping copious amounts of snow from the ground. Wilm was the only one to respond immediately, taking advantage of the situation to score another hit on Ros.

The astonished expression on Ros' face was beyond price as Katerin bore down on her intended victim. Not content to throw her missiles, she marched forward with every intention of rubbing Ros' face in snow. Behind her, there were whoops and hollers as the women joined the fray.

Ros' uncertainty was nearly her undoing as she gaped at the approaching woman. *She can't be serious.* At the last possible moment, she realized the danger and dashed away, Kat chasing her. "I apologize!" she called over her shoulder. "I was aiming for Sameer! He was running for the door!"

Katerin didn't respond. Caught up in the chase, she followed her opponent, a fierce grin on her face.

Cristof, his brother, and the dwarf remained together, ducking down the side of the main building for protection against Florin and Ilia. Sati had her husband on the ground, stuffing snow into his tunic as Wilm jumped around them, laughing.

Leading Katerin on a merry chase, Ros continued to protest her innocence as her opponent disregarded every word. Ros slowly realized that nothing would change her fate. *If I'm to be packed in snow, best have fun in the process.*

It was Katerin's turn for startlement when Ros turned mid-chase and began advancing, an evil glint in her eye. Tables turned on her, Katerin hared away with a giggle, and the chase resumed. Their path took them around the main building, where they danced back and forth at the woodpile, Ros voicing a series of threats and Katerin impishly egging her on. Katerin broke away, making a dash for the barn and relative safety. Scrambling, Ros was only a step behind, reaching out with long arms and grabbing her prey around the waist.

Katerin stumbled, yelping as she fell forward. In an effort to protect the smaller woman from injury, Ros pulled her close and rolled, falling onto the snow with Katerin on top.

Laughing, Katerin twisted, attempting to get the upper hand, but the grip on her waist tightened.

"Oh, no, you don't," Ros growled, pinning the woman. "We'll see who's next now!" One arm keeping Kat in place, she dug her fingers into the woman's ribs, delighted to find how ticklish she was.

It wasn't long before Katerin begged for mercy against the onslaught, yielding to the superior force. *This time.* She lay in happy exhaustion on her human mattress, chest aching as she caught her breath.

Despite the snow melting against her back, Ros held Katerin close, inhaling deeply of the scent from the black hair against her cheek. *It would be so easy,* she mused, eyeing a delicate ear just within reach. Stiffening at the thought, Ros gasped. *Stop that! Stop this!* She loosened her grip, urging Katerin to rise.

Katerin's eyes, which had been blissfully closed in the loving sensation of being held, shot open. The voices of her friends whispered in her ears.

Emerita: *"She's made her decision about you already. Unless you force the issue, Ros will remain honorable to her intentions."*

Sati: *"If you wish to romance her, you must hit her over the head with it. She's intelligent and compassionate, but not too bright about what's sitting in front of her."*

Florin: *"Show her you love her — in all the ways women can love."*

Rather than allow Ros to squirm out from under her, Katerin turned until she straddled slim hips.

This is not an improvement, Ros thought, hands automatically resting on Katerin's waist. "Still going to get me?" Ros asked.

Swallowing her sudden anxiety, Katerin leaned close. "Yes," she breathed as their lips met for the first time.

~~*~*~*

Liam stared into the distance, unseeing.

The difference between this Midwinter and last was a gulf beyond grasping, a year of darkness weighing upon his shoulders. He could hear the ghostly echoes of music and conversation, see his family happy and whole as they celebrated the coming spring with joy in their hearts.

A dark scene flashed across the flames: blood gushing from his mother's throat, her mouth open in a silent scream; the Invader looking down at them, sword in hand, a grim expression on his face. Liam felt a vague twinge in his chest and idly rubbed it.

"Would you like more wine, sire?"

Blinking, he returned to the present. "Yes, Dom. Thank you."

Dominic poured from a flagon of mulled wine warming at the fire, filling a mug for himself before sitting in an armchair. *No doubt the brat's homesick for the holidays.* "Next Midwinter will be remarkably different," he mused, pretending to be deep in thought.

"Yes, it will," Liam murmured. "I shall be king, and my family will be avenged."

"Yes." A log settled in the fireplace, crunching.

Dominic cast around in his mind for a suitable course of action. Push the lad to tears, or cheer him? The former could definitely serve his purpose, weakening the young man further. On the other hand, Liam's bloodline was proud and strong. Perhaps the latter would be more appropriate.

"Your father would be very proud of you," the aide said. At Liam's surprised and wistful gaze, he smiled and nodded. "Yes, he would. You've come quite a way down the path of adulthood, surmounting obstacles that would make a brave man quiver." Dominic leaned forward, his voice lowering, drawing the teenager closer. "Your blood is telling."

Liam's eyes stung. "Thank you, Dom," he said, voice husky. "That's good to know."

Content he'd chosen his words well, the aide sipped his wine.

Frowning, Liam tried to recall a time when his father had met with Dominic. Granted, he was but a lad and not privy to the comings and goings of the court, but it seemed to him the aide had sat far away from the king during the last Midwinter's Fest — at the tables reserved for the lower vassals, if he recalled correctly.

If he held as much sway as he suggests, wouldn't Dominic have sat at the high table with the rest of us?

* ~ * ~ * ~ * ~ *

Ros stared at the ceiling, watching the flickering shadows cast by the candle flame. She lay on her bed, tired but unable to sleep. Her mind racing, Ros let her thoughts take her where they willed.

The evening had brought more laughter and joy to the Compound's inhabitants. An early supper of immense proportions was set, and the family proceeded to feast well into the night. Using the last wizened apples in the larder, Florin presented them a sticky sweet dessert to top it off.

Inhaling, Ros felt the not-quite-comfortable sensation of fullness. Despite this, the temptation to sneak out to the common room for a nibble was nearly overpowering. *I could check the Summer Finding log*, she thought.

Not motivated enough to move just yet, she rolled over instead, eyes lighting on the small table that she used as a desk. On it was a small mound of items — gifts from her family. Among the lot of them, Ros had a new set of clothes for the center ring. In addition, she had some new parchment, a new quill, and the last jug of Joseph's homemade ale.

The best gift by far, however, was an over-tunic that Katerin had given her. Ros smiled, remembering the light blush powdering the small woman's face as she held out the package. Fading, the vision was replaced by another: Katerin happy and flushed with exertion, leaning close.

Unconsciously, Ros fingered her lips in an attempt to recapture the moment. Katerin's mouth had been warm and still tasted of Sati's hotcakes. Her touch had been both tentative and purposeful, tongue flickering in to tease before withdrawing. It had so startled Ros that she'd been flummoxed afterwards, barely able to pull her lanky frame out of the snowdrift as Katerin giggled and ran away.

For the remainder of the day, Ros had attempted to get Katerin alone, coming up with all manner of schemes to attain her goal. However, the other women interrupted, interfered, and just plain insisted that their concerns were more important. Ros was positive she was being toyed with, and it was frustrating in the extreme even as it was humorous.

Who knew how well Kat could fit into our family? Ros sighed and returned to her daydreams.

A gentle tap on her door drew her back. Ros glanced at the candle, surprised to see how low it had burned. Another tap galvanized her, and she rose, donning a robe before crossing the room. She wasn't surprised to find Katerin standing uncertainly in the hall, and they stared at each other a few moments.

A faint grin flickered on Katerin's lips. "May I come in?" she asked in a quiet voice.

"Certainly!" Ros stood back, allowing the small woman entry. She paused in thought before pulling her robe tighter and shutting the door.

"I hope I didn't wake you," Katerin said, turning to face the blonde.

Ros shook her head, waving at the only chair. "You didn't. I was still up." She sat on her bed.

Katerin nodded, sitting where indicated. They glanced about, unsure what to say. Finally, Katerin said, "I fear I've been put out of my room for the night."

Frowning, Ros leaned forward. "Did you and Ilia have a disagreement?"

Katerin colored, dropping her gaze to her fidgeting hands. "No, that's not what happened." She chewed her upper lip. "Henry came by for a...a visit."

"A visit?" As understanding washed over her, Ros immediately glanced at the wall that the two rooms shared, eyebrows reaching her hairline.

"Yes," Katerin answered the unspoken question.

"I see," Ros murmured, searching for a possible solution. Gingerly, she stood, gesturing to her bed. "By all means, Kat, sleep here. I'll...uh...check on the fire and bed down in the common room."

Katerin stood as well, stepping forward to intercept her. "That's not necessary, Ros," she said. "This bed is certainly larger than the one in your wagon. There's room for both of us."

Ros gazed at her, an almost-wistful expression on her face. "I don't think that would be a good idea, Katerin."

Bolstering her courage, Katerin moved closer, stopping a hair's breadth away. She licked her lips and said in a low voice, "I believe it's a *very* good idea."

A tingle passed through Ros' nerves, and she swallowed. "Kat," she said, taking a step backward, "perhaps you had too much brandy this evening. Go to bed and we'll talk come morning."

Sighing, a petulant flash in her eyes, Katerin closed the distance between them. "Allow me to speak plainly, Ros," she said.

Before Ros could answer, she was soundly kissed. No tentative teasing this — the lips on hers were firm; hands in her hair held her close. Against her better judgment, Ros responded, tasting what she'd dreamed of for months.

    The kiss broke off, and they leaned into each other, breathless. "Ravish me, Ros," Katerin whispered.

    "I thought you'd never ask."

Part 14

Katerin stood, hands on hips, frowning at the clothing on the bed. How it would all fit in the wagon was beyond her. Ros insisted that she'd been able to store more in their traveling abode than this, however, so Katerin dutifully returned to folding and sorting, muttering imprecations in the process. *Difficult to imagine that less than a year ago, I hardly owned enough to fill a satchel. Now I have too much!*

She shook out one of Ros' shirts, pausing to bring it to her face and inhale. That wasn't the only thing that had changed these past three months. The aroma of her lover brought tingles of memory across her mind and skin, recollections of long winter nights keeping one another warm and pleasured in this very bed.

Katerin's only regret was her secret. She had learned so much about Ros as they cuddled through the season, discovered her hopes and dreams, her childhood fears and wishes. Yet she couldn't reciprocate those things, not without revealing her true background.

"How goes the battle?"

She set aside her melancholy, turning to step into the welcome embrace. "Not well, I deem. I'm prepared to surrender." She snuggled closer, smiling at the raspy chuckle.

"You're doing fine," Ros assured her. "The wagon is clean and aired. Henry and Phizo are touching up the paint, and Em has the bedding out in the sun." She gave Katerin a squeeze before releasing her, sitting in the room's only chair.

Not willing to let her get too far away, Katerin followed, standing between long legs and running her hand through curly blonde hair. "How long before we leave, then?"

Ros smiled lazily, caressing Katerin's side. "Not long. We're only awaiting two wagons; Daiki and Habibah should show up any day now. I expect Gemma and Lucinda by the end of the week." She leaned forward, pillowing her head on Katerin's belly.

Closing her eyes, Katerin held Ros close. "It should prove to be an interesting season."

"Aye, it should," came the muffled answer.

Katerin smiled and looked at the tousled head. "But it will never get started if I don't finish the sorting."

After a grunt of agreement, Ros pulled away with a rueful grin. "There *is* that." She released her lover, watching her move back to their bed. "I'm debating the need to bring a third stock wagon. What with Sameer's family and Henry coming along, it would behoove us to have the extra stores."

"It would," Katerin agreed, pushing through a pile of shifts.

Her eyes drifting along the items to be packed, Ros blinked and pursed her lips. She rose and went to an open chest along the wall, rummaging within it until she retrieved what she was looking for. Ros surreptitiously glanced over her shoulder at Katerin. Sighing, shoulders straightening, she said, "Don't forget this."

At first, Katerin thought it was Isabella, the doll she'd carted halfway across the countryside in her wild flight from the Invader. It occurred to her, however, that this doll's flaxen hair was of a darker shade, the clothing yellowed and unfamiliar. Blinking, she looked into Ros' eyes. "*You* own a doll?"

Ros sighed again, looking away. "Aye, and she goes wherever I go. Her name's Grace, and she's my luck."

Trying very hard to suppress her amusement, Katerin couldn't help but allow a small smile as she stepped forward. Rather than take the doll, she wrapped her arms about Ros' waist and hugged her. "You're adorable when you blush," she said.

Regardless of her tint, Ros chuckled. "Why, thank you, madam. I shall endeavor to do it for you more often."

"See that you do." Katerin yelped and pulled away, rubbing her rear as she waggled a finger at Ros. "Best watch yourself, love," she warned with a grin. "I know where you sleep."

Attempting to look contrite, Ros failed miserably. "Aye, you do. I'll be on my best behavior, madam."

Katerin's grin widened, and she moved back into an embrace. "Good. I'll reward your best behavior," she murmured, tilting her face for a kiss. Her offer accepted, Katerin closed her eyes and sank into her lover's arms.

A door slammed, and pounding feet neared. They barely had time to break off their kiss when young Wilm slid to a halt in the open doorway. "Daiki and Habibah are here!" he yelled before dashing off to share the news with anyone else indoors, leaving an excited wake behind him.

"I believe that's our cue to go welcome them," Ros said, smiling.

"I believe you're right" was the response.

Stopping only long enough to set the doll with the rest of the items to be packed, the pair left their room.

* ~ * ~ * ~ * ~ *

Ros read the parchment, her lips pressed together and her brow furrowed. Daiki sat nearby on a stump, waiting as he petted a puppy. They were alone at the woodpile, the rest of the family going about their chores in and around the Compound.

"When did this come out?" she asked, clenching the public notice.

"About Midwinter." Daiki set the squirming pup down. "Last fall, there was a proclamation regarding the celebration. I suppose this is their 'invitation'."

Nodding, Ros said, "I'd heard about the celebration. I was hoping to avoid it." Crumpling the parchment, she added, "I hadn't expected a personal request."

Daiki shrugged. "Apparently, every traveling troupe of actors, circuses, or minstrels that goes through the area has received one. The Invader means this to be a grand party — a reminder of who holds the reins in the Dulce Province." He watched her carefully. "What are we going to do?"

Ros inhaled deeply, straightening. "We gather everyone and discuss it."

"In the hall or out here?" the man asked, scooping up the puppy and rising.

"Out here, I should think. More room and light."

With a nod, Daiki headed for the main building. "I'll see to it."

After a vague wave of acknowledgment, Ros turned away, staring into space. She opened the parchment once more, scanning the contents.

> *The presence of the Adamsson Circus is required at the Grand Celebration of His Royal Majesty Germaine Carlos William Cassaidie, to be held on the twenty-third day of the fourth month. A section of Firemount Field has been reserved for your troupe's tent and wagons. You are scheduled to perform before the king on the afternoon of the twenty-sixth day.*

Again, Ros crumpled the parchment in one hand and stared at the horizon. *Bleeding Sif, not even given a choice. We're already scheduled to perform for the bastard. How much does he know?*

Soon, the troupe gathered by the woodpile. Two benches were brought out, as well as several stools, the remainder of the family standing or using pieces of firewood as seating. Ros gave Katerin a significant look, receiving a puzzled frown before she began. Holding the parchment out to Abdullah, who was closest, she said, "I've received an order to attend the Invader's celebration in the Dulce Province."

Katerin blanched and wobbled before sitting down. Ilia also paled, leaving Henry's side to hold her mistress.

"Who is he to order us?" Martim asked. He sniffed and flexed well-defined muscles. "He doesn't command us. We're not even in the same kingdom."

There was a rumble of agreement, though Ros noted the older and wiser members kept their tongues. "Aye, 'tis true. But a fair half of our route is now within the Invader's borders. If we refuse, he can decide not to allow us entry." She sought eye contact with her family. "We know how hard it is to open a new route. The question is, will it be worth it to ignore this?"

"No," said a soft voice.

Everyone turned to a still-pale Katerin.

"The Invader's taken four kingdoms in his reign. If he takes more, your routes will become increasingly smaller. You can't afford to re-route every time he conquers another kingdom."

Martim shrugged. He passed the parchment on without reading it. "So? We go. We'll probably make a good penny in the process. What's the difficulty?" Ducking, he barely avoided a cuff from Usiku, who was standing behind him.

"In case you've forgotten, what with that empty space between your ears," the black man said, nose wrinkled, "it was the Invader's man who was killed in our camp last season."

Before Martim could respond, Ros cut in, drawing their attention back to the issue, "Aye. Are we receiving this 'invitation' because of that, or not?" Silence met her question. "Daiki says he's heard of other troupes and minstrels receiving this order. Is it a ruse to draw us in? Or is it what it seems to be: the Invader celebrating his new province?"

"There's rumor that a Dulce heir is stirring up rebellion in the province," Habibah said in a quiet voice. Despite her lack of projection, all heads turned her way.

"That's impossible!" Katerin, who had risen, froze under the collective stare of the troupe. She wilted somewhat, mouth open to explain her outburst, but nothing came. Ilia stood close with hand on her shoulder, providing a measure of support. Katerin's gaze flickered over the gathering, finally finding Ros'. Love and understanding seemed to flow between them, and Katerin stood taller, gaining strength from the look. "I have it on very good authority that none of the heirs to the Dulce throne survived. Save one."

Willem said, "We know, Kat. The guards rousted us a few nights after you joined us. Remember?" He smiled warmly. "It's no secret they were looking for a woman."

Flabbergasted, Katerin became speechless once more.

Habibah tilted her head. "But the rumors from Dulce are that a crown *prince* survived."

Katerin's eyes narrowed as she frowned in thought. *That cannot be. My brothers are dead.* She recalled Hector's statement when they'd met that fateful night. "*Nay, Your Highness. I saw the Invader run them through.*" Her musings were interrupted by Ros' voice.

"So there are rumors of unrest, and he plans a celebration. For what? To thumb his nose at any rebellion? To let them see how unconcerned he is? Damn if that man isn't an arrogant bastard."

"Are we going, then?" Sameer asked. Beside him, Florin suckled their baby.

Ros sighed and nodded. "Aye. We're going. We've really been given no choice." Looking at her family, she said, "Anyone who doesn't wish to follow can split off before we enter the city," she looked at Katerin, "lay low and camp until the celebration is complete." There was a general murmur as the people discussed their options.

For the first time, Emerita spoke up. "Phizo, love, get our wagon from the barn. We're going along."

"Em," Ros said, stepping forward, "it'll be all right. You don't need to come."

The old woman smiled, patting Ros' cheek gently. "My family needs me. We're old and decrepit, but Phizo's good with the horses and I can cook." She smirked at Ros before going to Katerin and taking the woman's arm in hers. "The fewer worries, the better."

"Em..." Katerin murmured.

"Hush, Kat. The decision's made."

Ros sighed again, a mixture of irritation and pleasure on her face. "Don't bother, Katerin. Once she's made up her mind, that's the end of it." She ignored the chuckle from the old woman, turning to the rest of the troupe. "We go. Those who want to stay away can camp outside the city. In the meantime, we've much work to do in preparation. We've a hard road ahead if we're to be there in time. I want us ready to leave a day or so after Gemma and Lucinda arrive."

Obviously dismissed, the group separated, returning to their chores. Ilia stayed behind until Katerin urged her away. Em, after another squeeze, let go of the brunette's arm and went to her husband, the pair drifting toward the barn.

Katerin stepped into her lover's welcome embrace. "We must talk," she said.

"Aye."

* ~ * ~ * ~ * ~ *

Katerin stood in the center of their room, arms wrapped about her. She heard Ros closing the door behind her and shivered, a weight building in her chest. *You knew it would happen sooner or later!* she scolded herself. *Get on with it!* Warm hands on her shoulders pulled her from her self-castigation. Katerin turned, releasing the death grip on her arms to cling to her lover. Tears stung the back of her eyes and she closed them, wishing the emotions away.

"It's all right, Kat," Ros murmured. "You're safe."

Sniffing, Katerin nodded. "I know," came the muffled response. She swallowed past a tight throat and pulled back slightly. Looking into concerned eyes, Katerin said, "But I fear you'll not have me when I say what I must."

Ros hugged her again. "Nothing you can say will change my opinion of you, Kat," she assured her.

"Be that as it may," Katerin said, unconvinced, dropping eye contact. With reluctance, she pulled out of the comforting embrace, returning to her original stance. Refusing to look at her lover, she said, "I'm sure you have some suspicions of where I came from — why the Invader's man was killed in your camp." She shuddered, remembering the sounds of skirmish and the voice proclaiming Hector dead. "My name is Sabine. I am the daughter of King Frederick of Dulce, the sole surviving heir to the throne, and the Invader is looking for *me*."

Inhaling, fighting back tears, Katerin whirled about, straightening her shoulders and standing tall. "Ilia is one of my handmaidens. The second man you found dead was Hector, former royal guard and my man-at-arms." Part of Katerin wanted to gibber in relief at the confession, but she wouldn't allow it, resorting to her royal training. She studied her lover, expecting anger, dismay, or confusion. To her surprise, Ros' face held a bemused grin. "You *knew*?" she blurted.

Ros nodded slightly. "I *suspected*," she corrected gently. "I figured you to be a royal; I just didn't know which one." Her demeanor became solemn. "Which makes this *invitation* much more ominous."

Deflated, drained, Katerin sat on the bed with a flounce, not heeding the clothing there. "Yes, I know." She chewed her lower lip. "I know that my brothers didn't survive. Hector told me he'd seen my whole family run through, my mother included."

The blonde sat beside Katerin, gathering her into a hug. "I'm sorry," she said. "To lose your family in such a violent and sudden way isn't easy."

Ros' words opened a floodgate. Katerin, unable to hold back any longer, burst into tears, burrowing into her lover's arms. Ros held her close, rocking gently as a year's worth of pain and worry released. When the crying died down, Katerin realized she was curled up and cradled in Ros' arms. She snuffled a bit, wiping her face on her sleeve. "Thank you," she whispered.

Hugging her, Ros whispered back, "Of course. I love you, Kat. That hasn't changed."

This comment almost set off more tears, but Katerin fought them, pulling out of the embrace. "I love you, too, Ros."

Ros leaned in with a smile and kissed her on the forehead. "I know." After a careful study, deciding that Katerin was emotionally composed, Ros said, "So, with that off your chest, we need to plan a course of action."

"Yes, we do," Katerin agreed, nodding. Her eyes, still red and watery, peered at Ros. "I do not wish to put you or the troupe in danger, but I do not think I can stay here the entire season without you." She stared at her hands.

Ros rubbed Katerin's back. "I don't want you to remain here either." At the tentative look Katerin gave her, she smiled. "I'd miss you far too much for my own good. The season would be...empty."

A ghost of a smile crossed Katerin's lips.

"So the question is how we go about our profession without putting you in danger."

"Do you think this is a ruse to draw us in — me in?" Katerin asked, turning to her lover.

"I don't believe so. It's too elaborate a plot. The Invader is an arrogant man, aye, but he's a conqueror, not the type to play court games." Ros gave her a sardonic smile. "Subtlety is not his suit."

"Yes, there is that," Katerin said.

"I think that the rumor of a Dulce rebellion is what's at the heart of this. He's either had another young woman killed, thinking it was you, or he's decided that a show of force is necessary to forestall any revolution." Ros took Katerin's hand, rubbing it idly as she thought. "He might be confused about your gender, thinking a prince *did* escape his blade. He may be looking for a young man."

The thought of another woman taking her place in death caused Katerin to shudder. "Who is stirring rebellion in Dulce?" she wondered aloud. "None of my family survived. Do you think a lord of father's court is attempting a ruse of his own?"

Ros shrugged. "I cannot say. It could be any number of people."

She paused. "You're heir to a throne, Kat. Do you wish to retake it?"

"*No!*" Katerin exclaimed, body stiffening. Realizing she had perhaps spoken too adamantly, she blushed and relaxed. "No. I have no training for it. I have no army. My only worth to the throne would be to my future husband and the children I would have." Her gaze was imploring. "I cannot lose you!" she insisted.

Nodding, Ros squeezed her lover's hand. "You won't, Kat. I had to ask. I had to know."

Reddening, Katerin nodded.

"I'm very ill at ease with the idea of leaving any of the troupe outside the city during the festivities," Ros said. "If it is this 'prince' he's searching for, he may have patrols sweeping the area, more vigilant than ever due to the special nature of this celebration. I believe everyone will be safer staying at Firemount Field in our encampment." She inhaled deeply, looking at Katerin. "You, however, will remain in the wagon during our forced audience, along with anyone else who wants to be absent. Ilia comes to mind."

Katerin nodded. "Yes, that would be for the best."

Rising, Ros helped her lover to her feet, pulling her into an embrace. "So, we're decided, then? You come along and stay in camp, and then we'll leave, returning to our normal route?"

Hearing the heartbeat in Ros' chest, Katerin murmured. "We're decided."

~~*~*~*

The procession stopped despite being within an hour's travel of their final destination. Camp was set as usual — the Invader's tents and environs at the center of a large circle. As befitted their rank and station, the lords of his court spiraled outward, the area liberally sprinkled with fire pits, pickets, servant quarters, and the tents of his Royal Guard. Rimming camp were the regular guards, setting a perimeter and keeping their liege safe.

Looking over his encampment, the Invader smiled, imagining the curses of his subjects as they were forced to endure yet another night in the "wilds". *It'll be good for them*, he thought, a derisive smile twisting his lips. *Make them appreciate their homes and money, and the leadership that keeps them fat and spoiled.*

He, on the other hand, was in his element. Many a night he'd spent in similar camps, surrounded by his generals, working on a plan of attack against his enemy. Inhaling deeply, the Invader remembered campaigns past. It had been from that very spot the previous year that he'd made his final attack on the Dulce capital. He relived the memory, seeing pompous lords replaced by confident generals, hearing the scrape of weapons being sharpened and the gentle murmur of men preparing for war.

"Your Royal Highness?"

Turning, the Invader found the captain of his Royal Guard waiting respectfully. "Yes, Semelo?"

Having spent many years in the Invader's employ, two of them as captain, Semelo appeared to lack the typical nervousness in his ruler's presence. "The lords are requesting an audience with you, sire," he said, stepping forward. "I believe they're interested in knowing when we'll be leaving for the city."

"Led by Duke Agnar, no doubt." At the captain's nod, the Invader smiled. "Have the herald make an announcement. We'll be here until sunrise. I want the guard looking their best: weapons sharp, armor polished." Looking to the distant city, he said, "Tomorrow's procession will be spectacular."

"Aye, sire," Semelo nodded, bowing and backing away.

Alone once more, the Invader murmured, "We'll see if I can flush you out, Princess. You and your...benefactor."

* ~ * ~ * ~ * ~ *

With a sneer of distaste, Dominic watched from behind a curtain as the Invader arrived. Having ensconced himself at an inn two nights prior, he wanted to be on the Invader's route into the city. The owner of the establishment was a member of the rebellion and more than willing to give up the price of a room for a good cause. Eyes lighting on the hated figure, Dominic's face twisted further. *Bastard!*

In a display of confidence, the Invader rode at the head of his procession without visible armor. He was clad in light-beige breeches and tunic, his deep-red cloak thrown back off his shoulders. The only jewelry on his person was that of his office: a signet ring, a thick chain about his neck, and a gold circlet on his head. He waved at the cheering crowd, his smile belied by the well-worn sword belt at his waist.

It wasn't lost on Dominic that the city guard glared at the masses, their threat evident. *Yes, applaud the bastard who killed your friends and family, or join them in death.* Regardless of the hypocrisy, the former aide felt grudging respect for the Invader's tactics. *If it weren't for Liam, these fools wouldn't need the prodding. They'd blithely go about their lives in subservience to a usurper.*

When the Invader was past, Dominic let the curtain return to its place; he was not interested in the courtiers and servants. He had the crowd peppered with contacts; they would report to him on the strength and numbers of the Invader's men before they even arrived at the castle.

"I should go."

Dominic turned to his guest, almost surprised to find him there. "Yes. Get there before him. Don't cause suspicion, and report to me this time tomorrow." He smiled. "The Invader will be on his guard, so be careful in the palace."

Rising, the man straightened the royal livery he wore. "Aye, I will." He paused in thought. "I may not be able to get away tomorrow."

"I understand. If I don't see you in three days, we go underground." Nothing further was said between them as the spy left the room.

Dominic went to a table, ignoring the tray of food. He poured another glass of wine and sipped thoughtfully. *I'm very glad the royal bratling agreed to remain in our rooms. Just what we need is for him to be found wandering the streets during this festival.* Considering Prince Liam had already done such a thing, the aide frowned. *Best I go check on him.*

Grabbing his cloak, Dominic left the room, locking the door behind him.

Part 15

The weather was unseasonably warm. Katerin wiped sweat off her neck with a kerchief, the wagon rocking gently around her. In the interest of safety, she and Ilia remained inside their respective abodes while the troupe traveled through the city. She perched on the bed, comforted by knowing that Ros was directly above her, driving the team.

Their entry into the city had been easier than one would have expected with a rebellion in full bloom. In anticipation, Katerin dressed in rags that stank of soot from the fire pits. Her short hair was disheveled, and dark streaks smudged her skin. The gate guards insisted on seeing the contents of the wagons, and the princess affected her simpleton routine. Whether it worked due to her improved acting or to the fact the guards were mortally busy with the large influx of crowds into the city was debatable. In either case, they were waved through without incident.

Beyond the walls, Katerin could hear the familiar noises of a large city. That it was *her* city only made the lump in her throat more solid, and she was uncertain whether she should mourn or scream. Over the months, she had entertained herself with dreams: her family intact, the Invader never having been there, and life continuing as it had before. Since she'd become involved with Ros, however, those fancies had faded. If things hadn't gone as they had, she'd never have met the circus owner, never have understood the love of two women, the love of Ros.

But gods, the price! she thought. Using the kerchief, she dabbed her eyes. A headache niggled at the back of her neck and Katerin sat up, rolling her shoulders to loosen the muscles. "Enough of that," she murmured. "Self-pity will get you nowhere." Moving to the edge of the bed, she leaned closer to the shutters, cracking one open to see outside.

The streets weren't as crowded now that they'd passed through the gate. There were far more people than Katerin had seen in one place in some time, however. Ros had wisely avoided the market, knowing they'd be considerably slowed there. Not having spent much time in the city proper, Katerin wasn't sure where they were in relation to the castle and Firemount Field. The two were side by side; the field having been used frequently for outdoor parties and tournaments during her father's reign.

Katerin closed the shutter as the wagon drew alongside the field, where guards were prominently stationed on the perimeter. After a few moments, the wagon lumbered to a stop, and she heard Ros climbing down the side. Her lover had an amiable chat with the guards, showing them her invitation and receiving directions to the troupe's designated area. Katerin heaved a sigh when no further search was made. Ros returned to the driver's seat, and Katerin felt the lurch of movement.

Noises outside indicated a different population. Katerin could hear music — pipes, drums, lutes — and the grunts and shouts unique to those practicing the entertainer's profession. Soon, the wagon stopped, and Ros dismounted once more. Her voice rose as she ordered the rest of the troupe to their places.

Several moments later, the wagon door opened. "I think it's safe for you to come out," Ros said. "We're centrally located in the field, and the guard is remaining on the outskirts."

With a flutter of nerves, Katerin nodded. Hearing the troupe's familiar sounds as they set up camp eased her anxiety. She came forward, taking Ros' hand and stepping out of the wagon. The racket became much louder. As Katerin slowly turned, she could see another circus troupe in a practice session, three minstrels, singing to the accompaniment of four musicians, and a menagerie of exotic-looking animals. "So many!" she blurted, eyes wide.

Ros chuckled, draping her arm across the smaller woman's shoulders. "Aye, and more where these came from. I daresay the Invader hired acts from as far away as the Contrin Seas."

Katerin stared in amazement. *Even Father never went to such expense.*

"I'm required to check in at the registrar's," Ros said. She squeezed her lover. "Will you be all right?"

Tinting at the evident concern, Katerin smiled. "I'll be fine, Ros. Do what needs doing." She looked about at her friends. "I've plenty of people to keep an eye on me."

Reluctant, Ros lingered. "Well, then," she finally said, "best get on with it. I'll be back as soon as may be."

Katerin smiled, gently slipping away. "I'll see how Em and Phizo are doing," she said. "They could probably use some assistance."

"Aye." Ros watched her lover walk away. *Have I made the right decision, bringing her here?* "Worried" didn't even begin to describe her state of mind. She truly felt, however, that there was no other option. *Not to follow the Invader's directive would cripple the troupe's route. And to leave her behind would cripple me.*

Sighing, Ros shook herself out of her reverie. "Let's get cracking. Two days, and we'll be gone." She left the troupe, heading for the registrar's.

* ~ * ~ * ~ * ~ *

From the window, the Invader regarded Firemount Field with satisfaction. It was a jumble of activity, with more entertainers arriving every hour. The tourney grounds proper had been prepared with new fencing and paint, and the stands had been repaired in preparation for an audience. To one side were the tents of those who wanted to win a hefty purse at the upcoming tournament.

He saw a tall blonde woman in men's clothing approach the registrar. *A woman running an entertainment troupe?* Noting the sword and her obvious comfort with it, he thought, *Probably a Sapphist to boot. Pity. She's beautiful.*

A scratch at the door interrupted his thoughts and he turned away, picking up his forgotten glass of wine. "Come in."

Semelo opened the door and bowed before entering. "Your Majesty," he said, "I believe we've found a spy from the rebellion."

Instantly alert, the Invader set his glass on a nearby table, waving the man into the room. "Who and how?"

Closing the door behind him, the captain stepped closer. "His name is Travis. He was hired last summer in the kitchens. We caught him purely by accident." Semelo grimaced. "One of the ovens overheated and started a fire. The smoke wasn't acting properly; it hovered near one wall rather than going for the windows and doors. When the fire was out, I investigated and found a passageway. He was inside, unconscious."

The Invader scowled. "Where does this passage lead?"

"Well, sire, we had reports that your drawing room was on fire, but no flames were found. I can assume that is where it ends." Semelo nodded. "I've already sent a squad into the kitchen passageway. I've detailed another to your drawing room. If there's anyone between, we'll flush him out."

"Where is the spy?"

"The dungeons, Your Majesty, awaiting an...audience with you."

The Invader grinned. "You know me well, Semelo." He gestured toward the door, stopping to pick up a pair of gloves before following. "Let's go see our little friend, shall we?"

* ~ * ~ * ~ * ~ *

As expected, the guards surrounding the field were to keep the entertainers in rather than the populace out. Though everyone enjoyed them, most troupes were considered to be potentially dangerous — traveling warrens of immoral people who would think nothing of stealing the food from a workingman's table. Only scoundrels and rogues could thrive in the unstable lifestyle.

With little effort, Dominic was able to gain entrance. *Where else can I loiter about near the castle without question?* He wore peasant clothes, dusty and brown, appearing like many of the visitors who found the lure of entertainers stronger than common sense. Drifting along, he watched the castle, ignoring jugglers, contortionists, and musicians.

The soldiers on the wall had been doubled since the Invader's arrival, which was to be expected. Dominic was certain the usurper was here because of the rebellion. It was impossible to hide a revolution of such magnitude. A few cells had been discovered over the year, and there was no doubt that rumors fairly flew to the Invader's ears. Fortunately, none of the rumors were vital.

Two boys raced past the aide, breathless as they explored the grounds, and he absently checked his belt pouch. Finding it unmolested, Dominic continued wandering.

Reports coming in indicated that the Invader had brought more courtiers than army. All counts totaled roughly twelve hundred soldiers in and around the city, not including the Royal Guard. With proper planning, the Invader would be dead and Liam king before the end of this "celebration". All he needed now was Travis' report from inside.

Time was of the essence. Liam was becoming an increasing problem, insisting the rebellion push through before everything was in place. So far, the older and wiser leaders had headed the young hotblood off, but it was anyone's guess how long their control would last. *If the royal bratling has a mind to start early, we don't have the means to stop him.*

Dominic realized he was woolgathering, staring at a circus troupe as they rehearsed. There was no more information to be had there, and he turned to leave. The sound of footsteps behind him didn't register until he intercepted a running person, the pair crashing into each other.

Almost falling, Dominic grabbed the runner's thin shoulders to keep his balance. "Watch where you're going, fool," he growled.

"My apologies, sir," a woman's voice answered. "Are you all right?"

"No thanks to *you*," the aide said, finally looking at the woman. Then his eyes widened and he clutched her in his grasp, giving her a shake. "Your Highness?" he hissed.

Heart in her throat, Katerin stepped back. "You mistake me for someone else, sir." *He looks familiar. A courtier of father's?* She desperately cast about with her eyes, but none of her friends was near.

Remembering where he was, Dominic quickly looked around before bodily dragging the princess to the side of a wagon. "Are you mad?" he demanded in a whisper. "What on earth are you *doing* here?"

"You're hurting me," Katerin said. His hands dropped as though they'd been burned. *I think his name's Dominic, isn't it?* "I don't know who you think I am, but you're mistaken." *Of all the people to find me, it has to be a minor courtier turned peasant.*

Leaning forward with menace, Dominic said, "You may be able to fool these...people, Princess, but I know who you are."

Katerin realized he wasn't going to accept her innocence. *Deal with things now; Ros will know what to do after.* "My title isn't necessary, sir. I'm known as Katerin now."

Triumphant, it was all Dominic could do not to crow aloud. He stepped back, looking her over. Katerin wore rags that were filthier than his, dirt smudging her skin and her hair mussed. *She's still the image of her mother*, he thought, repressing a sneer. "I'm so glad to see you survived!" he said. "We'd heard you escaped the Invader's wrath that night."

We? Dear gods, could he be involved in this rebellion? "Yes. It wasn't easy. I hid during the day and traveled at night until I was out of the kingdom."

"Alone?" *Not bloody likely.*

Katerin nodded. "Yes. A few weeks later, I found the troupe, and I've been with them ever since." *If he is with the rebellion...* "I've heard rumor that one of my brothers survived as well."

Dominic's smile faded. "No, Your Highness. As far as I know, no one but you lived through that night."

"Don't call me that," Katerin said absently, feeling a bit of her heart wither with the death of hope. "Princess Sabine didn't live through that night...Dominic, isn't it?"

"Yes," he answered, resorting to a nod rather than a bow. "Are you sure, Lady? The throne..." Her dark eyes became intent and Dominic was snared by them. *Just like her mother's.*

"Are you still loyal to my father?" Katerin demanded.

Appearing to be properly horrified by the question, Dominic said, "*Absolutely*, Your...I mean, Katerin."

"Then *everyone* in the Dulce royal bloodline is dead. Is that understood, Dominic?"

The aide studied Katerin for long moments. "Yes. Everyone." *So.*

Not interested in regaining the throne, eh? Although that could be a blessing, why?

"Kat!"

Dominic turned to see a tall blonde approach, eyeing him suspiciously.

"Are you all right?" the newcomer asked Katerin, her gaze never leaving the man.

Blushing, Katerin nodded, stepping into a hug. "Yes, I'm fine," she said, ignoring Dominic's raised brow.

"Can I help you?" Ros asked him, her tone anything but helpful.

"No, thank you. The lady and I ran into each other. I just stopped to be certain she was unharmed." *That's it, then? Found yourself a woman lover?*

Ros glanced at Katerin. "She appears to be fine, thank you. However, we have rehearsal," she hinted.

Taking his cue, Dominic nodded. "My apologies for the interruption." To Katerin, he said, "Be careful, young lady. You never know who you'll run into."

"I understand," Katerin said.

With a bow, Dominic scurried away, mind spinning.

Watching, Ros asked, "Who is he?"

"I'm not sure," Katerin said. "Either a minor court official or a lord."

"He recognized you," Ros stated with certainty. She turned to her lover. "Didn't he?"

Swallowing, Katerin dropped her gaze and nodded. "Yes, he did." Ros' body stiffened as she continued. "I think things will be fine. Our presentation is tomorrow afternoon. I doubt Dominic will have time to do anything before then, even if he's of a mind to."

Ros said, "Aye, there's the rub. Will he have a mind to?" Her eyes searched the immediate area, alert for guards appearing out of nowhere to collect Katerin for the Invader's axe. "We have to get you out of here. I'll have Martim and Tommaso go with you."

"No."

Narrowing her eyes, Ros glared at her. "We *must* get you away," she said, apparently hoping that repetition would lead to agreement. "If he recognized you, any number of others could."

"I don't think so. The only reason he did was because we ran into one another." Raising her hands and stepping away, Katerin continued, "Where will I go, outside the gates? You recall the patrols along the roads as well as I. Getting into the city was easy. Getting out — ahead of schedule, I might add — will not. We've got guards here at the field, guards at the city gates and guards on patrol looking for an elusive prince who doesn't exist. It would be less safe than where I am now."

"Kat..."

Katerin, her royal dander up, shook her head. "No, Ros. Growling at me won't change a thing. Dominic isn't in the employ of the Invader. If he were, do you think he'd dress like a peasant? He's got something to do with the rebellion; I'm sure of it. If he were to turn me in, it would decimate any faction trying to displace the Invader." Sighing, Katerin said, "If he were to turn me in, do you think we'd get through the field? If anything, Dominic will be scheming how to get me into the rebellion. He has only a trumped-up figurehead. It would be idiocy to give me over when he could use me to his advantage. I'm safe for the moment. Though we leave as soon as the show is over."

Uncertain, but recognizing the truth of Katerin's words, Ros chewed her lower lip. "We'll post a guard for the rest of our stay," she finally said. "I want everyone packed and ready to leave the minute we're through this morass."

Relieved that her friends would be safe, Katerin smiled. "I'm sure it will be fine, Ros." She slipped into a comforting hug.

"I hope you're right," Ros whispered.

* ~ * ~ * ~ * ~ *

Kemplak's hells! Why couldn't I have found her last year? Dominic grumbled as he returned his pass to the guard. Sliding easily into pedestrian traffic, he worried about the new development.

The segregation of the entertainers was a boon. *At least she won't be ambling along the streets to be discovered.* Fortunate as well was her disguise. Despite his knowledge that Princess Sabine had survived, Dominic wouldn't have known her to look at her.

If the girl is fool enough to come here, though, he turned off the main thoroughfare, *what other absurdity will she be party to? How can I use this?*

Telling Liam his sister lived was out of the question. The young man was distracted enough; this news would only draw his attention away from the goal. They were too close to the throne to risk it.

Dominic had already lied to Sabine about the prince. *Gods help us if she finds out! Her lack of common sense could uncover us all.* Putting the final straw on things, Travis was late checking in by a full day. Others in Dominic's network of spies had heard nothing about him. *Either he's been compromised, or he's unable to leave.*

Too many variables made for little control, and Dominic detested the situation. If Travis didn't report by the end of the day,

Dominic would be forced to act. Everything was in place; the rebellion only awaited his word. Should the Invader have gotten the information, Dominic could see little recourse other than an early attack. A later attack would guarantee a loss. *And I very much doubt I could talk the royal bratling into delaying.*

Worst case, Travis had been discovered and the Invader had received information on the rebels' attack. The best option was to advance their timetable and possibly distract the ruler.

As Dominic neared the hovel he shared with Liam, he stopped in his tracks. Oblivious to the jostle and curses of those pushing past, a smile crossed his face. *What better distraction than a hunted princess?*

* ~ * ~ * ~ * ~ *

The Invader wiped his hands on a towel, leaving streaks of crimson gore. "Clean that up," he instructed, nodding at the body crumpled behind him. As guards hastened to obey, he said, "Remove the head and hang it from the main gates."

"Aye, sire," the jailer said, bowing.

Turning, the Invader raised his hand. "No." He stood in thought as everyone paused. "Destroy it instead. When this is over, I'll have other heads to decorate the castle walls."

"Aye, sire."

Looking down, the Invader noted his tunic was a mess. *I'll have a bath drawn when I return to my quarters.* As he left the dungeons, he said, "Semelo," not bothering to see whether or not his captain followed. Climbing the narrow steps, he was amused by the visible recoil of the guard at the door.

Out in the courtyard, the Invader inhaled deeply, chasing away the scent of blood and death that clung to him. Although the odor was reminiscent of a battlefield, it wasn't the same when it was derived from a helpless opponent. Grimacing, he removed his tunic, tossing the offending material to the ground.

Behind him, Semelo spoke softly to the guards. Clothing rustled, and he approached his liege. "Sire, wear this."

"Thank you, Captain," the Invader said, taking the offered tunic. "See that the guardsman is properly rewarded."

"Aye, Your Majesty. I'll see to his compensation."

The tunic was tight in the shoulders, but fit well enough. The coppery smell of blood still tickled the Invader's nostrils, and he started walking across the courtyard, his captain trailing behind.

Dominic's name coming from ravaged lips was hardly a surprise. *If anyone would be behind this misbegotten attempt, it would be he*, the

Invader thought. *With no prince, however...does he think he can be king? Unless he's discovered Sabine.*

To start things off, Dominic planned to instigate a riot coinciding with the day after the fall of the kingdom, only four days away. *The day I ousted him.* He hoped that the guard would be more lax, having seen the official anniversary come and go without incident. *Should he discover I've found him out, he'll move the time forward and change some of the particulars.*

The spy wasn't privy to any more information than the time and date, and he didn't call out many names. He mentioned Dominic, the long-dead Liam, and three others. Finding them in the crowded streets of revelers would be impossible, though the spy had mentioned an inn that Dominic frequented.

Pausing at a door that led into the castle, he said, "Send a squad to the Dancing Bird, and roust the owner. I want him publicly flogged for treason before his arrest. Bring in his family as well. Make it loud and very noticeable. I want their leaders to know that I'm aware of them."

Semelo bowed. "Aye, sire. Any other orders?"

The Invader paused. "Yes. Triple the guard, and instigate random weapon searches of guests in and around the courtyard. I expect they'll make an earlier attempt, now that we've found their spy." His captain bowed and backed off a respectable distance before turning to trot away.

Staring after him, the Invader thought, *I know you're out there, Dominic. I'll find you soon, and we'll have a nice long talk.*

Part 16

Ros leaned against the wagon, arms crossed, giving the appearance of nonchalance as she stared at the castle before her. Behind her, the troupe gathered about the fire, their demeanor subdued. Word had passed among them about their current predicament, and all of them were worried about the coming morning.

They were scheduled to present themselves before the Invader at midday, the third act of the day. Plans were in place, and they were packed to leave immediately after their performance. Ros learned from contacts among the other troupes that upon completion of their act, they'd be given a healthy stipend and the necessary papers to leave the city. A few troupes had elected to remain, entertaining the Dulceans who dared to venture onto the field and receiving extra monies in return.

While it seemed obvious that Dominic hadn't betrayed Katerin's presence, Ros was still nervous. *You'd be on edge anyway*, she reminded herself, *going into the lion's den*.

She had spent a long hour in the wagon with Em, Phizo, and Katerin, discussing their options, while Daiki and Martim idled outside on guard. To Ros' annoyance, the older couple agreed with Katerin that they should stay until after their presentation. Her suggestion to have Kat hide with another troupe for the time being was met with resistance.

"*If the worst should happen and I'm discovered, it will be easier for you to deny knowledge of my true identity,*" Katerin insisted. "To hide me would imply *knowledge and, therefore, your guilt and collusion.*"

There was no arguing with that, and Em had supported Katerin.

Ros grimaced at the sour taste in her mouth and spat on the ground before her.

"You're brooding again."

Not bothering to turn, Ros said, "Aye, and with good reason."

Em moved forward, placing a companionable arm about the younger woman's waist. "Aye. Good reason you have, even without Kat." She looked up at Ros. "Being forced into an audience with the Invader can be dangerous."

Ros only nodded, and they stood for long moments. "I remember you as a young girl," Em said, voice low. "Scared of your own shadow; so uncertain. You've grown up well. Your da would be proud."

Ros swallowed. "Would he?" she whispered.

Smiling, the old woman said, "Aye. He would. You've surpassed all his dreams for you." She hugged her charge. "Your entire family would be."

Snorting, Ros nevertheless put her arm around Em's shoulders. "I find that difficult to believe, but I won't argue."

"Just as well," the old woman stated firmly. "You haven't won an argument with me yet."

"First time for everything," Ros retorted, her jibe not carrying much force.

Em hugged her again. "Remember your fears," she said. "Go to Katerin. She needs you."

Finally looking away from the castle, Ros looked into her friend's eyes. "Aye," she said. "You're right. Thank you."

"You'd have thought of it soon. I didn't raise you to be half-witted." Em received a chuckle and a squeeze before Ros released her. She watched Ros enter her wagon, hearing Kat's low greeting before returning to her family at the fire.

* ~ * ~ * ~ * ~ *

As Liam awaited the arrival of his "generals" — four men who had spent more time on the farm than on the battlefield — he stared at nothing. Dominic had returned from his outing in a strange mood. The aide tried to give the impression of somber worry, but after several months of living with him, Liam could see something else beneath the mask — a measure of satisfaction or smugness; he couldn't tell which. No amount of prying could get Dominic to discuss it, however, until the others arrived. Cloaked in silent contemplation, Liam waited until everyone had assembled.

"Travis has been compromised. I'm sure of it."

Liam sighed heavily, his thoughts a blur. *Why would Dom be happy with that?* He recalled a conversation or two with some of his more vocal supporters, all pronouncing Dominic a traitor. *Could they be right? Could he be setting a trap for me even as he ostensibly works toward setting me on the throne?*

"We can't stop now," Torlief insisted, leaning forward with a thump. "If your spy has been discovered, how much can he tell?"

Dominic, his face a mask of disgust, said, "He knows me. He knows the time and date. Travis was to tell us where the Invader would be at our attack."

Cursing was followed by apologetic looks at the prince. Liam waved them down. "We have several alternatives here," he said. "Speed, sloth, or suspension." His generals erupted in another bout of curses. *I wonder which Dominic will support.*

"No!"

"We can't stop now!"

"Perhaps if we waited..."

Dominic thumped the table with open palms. "The Invader knows the only option open to us is speed. If we wait, he'll have more time to prepare. And we certainly can't stop. Our people have worked hard for this moment; to halt now would demoralize them. We'd have a devil of a time gathering our resources again."

"You have an idea?" Liam asked.

Dominic nodded. He looked at the others, ensuring he had their attention. "With some hard work, we can have the courtyard set for tomorrow at midday."

"*Tomorrow?*" one general said. "Are you daft?"

I should think not, Liam considered. Forestalling further argument, he raised his hand. "Nay. It can work. If the Invader knows only our planned time to strike, the earlier we attack, the better. It will be difficult getting the word out, but I think we've proved ourselves willing and able."

The men watched him, and he was suddenly struck by the oddity of a fourteen-year-old boy ordering these grizzled farmers to their potential deaths. *You'll do it many times in the next few days*, Liam chided himself. *Don't become jaded. Always remember they have families, even if you don't.* The generals following his lead, the prince turned his attention to Dominic.

Oh, yes. Liam's the one. As Dominic outlined the plan, his thoughts continued along a different path. *Sabine might be the elder, but she could never command the same respect as he does. No one would follow her. But they will follow a prince.* He answered a question from one of the generals, glad to see Liam jump into the conversation with his own offerings. *But can she be used as easily? I doubt it; I seem to recall rumors of her willful ways. Too much like her mother.*

"I'll lead the men in the courtyard."

"My liege, no!" Dominic insisted, returning full attention to the planning. "We can't risk your getting killed in the skirmish!" *And I can't risk your seeing your sister alive after I've assured you of her demise.*

Liam made a face. "Dom, I can't sit outside while my people shed their blood for my restoration. If I'm to be king, I must *lead*!" *And if this is a trap laid for me, I'll be damned if I'll be where you expect me to* be.

Unexpectedly, the generals agreed with Dominic. A long debate ensued as the men refused to change their minds on the issue. No amount of arguing would alter things — not even the threat of royal disfavor.

Slumping, Liam refused to pout. "Fine. Enjoy your victory, gentlemen. I promise you, it won't happen again."

A deep sigh echoed around the table.

"More importantly, sire," Torlief said, "you'll be alive to enjoy *your* victory."

Dominic regained their attention. "Then it's agreed? Midday tomorrow, everything will be in place. I'll arrange a distraction in the courtyard."

There was consensus. The sound of chairs scraping the floor filled the room as the men prepared to leave. They went out the door at intervals, going in different directions. As Dominic closed the door on the last man, he thought, *I know just the distraction. I'm sure the Invader would be more than happy to have Princess Sabine in his hands. The courtyard will be a killing field; it will be simple to remove her body before anyone's the wiser. As far as Liam will know, Sabine* did *die a year ago.*

Liam stared into the fire. *No doubt about it. I'll be in the courtyard at midday, irrespective of Dominic's wishes. I* will *lead my army to victory.*

* ~ * ~ * ~ * ~ *

The armored man pulled off his helmet. His air of command reminded her of her father, though he wasn't as handsome. An ugly scar ran across his face from the base of his nose to curve down and around his cheek. He was saying something, his voice so low that she couldn't make it out.

When the blade pierced her mother's chest, pinning the babe to it, her scream matched theirs.

Fighting out of her nightmare, Katerin struggled with the blanket. Hands on her upper arms startled her, and she shrieked, batting them away.

"Shhh," Ros whispered. "It's a bad dream, Kat! You're safe!"

Realizing the truth of her lover's words, Katerin slumped into the embrace with a shaky breath. "I'm sorry," she murmured. "I hope I didn't wake anyone else."

Ros leaned back, taking Katerin with her. "I doubt any of us are getting much sleep this night," she said.

Katerin snuggled against Ros, draping her arm across the lean belly. She pillowed her head on Ros' breast, tentative feelings of safety washing over her as her lover encircled her with long arms. "You too?" she asked.

Reluctant, Ros nodded. "Aye, me too."

Curiosity drove away the dwindling fear. Katerin's nightmares were her own, the reason for their existence self-evident. Despite many nights of discussing them with Ros, all her attempts to alleviate their severity met with limited success.

Her lover's nightmares, although less frequent, were just as uncompromising. Ros would wake, sometimes with a yell and always terrified. The few times Katerin tried to gain insight, her lover insisted she couldn't remember the dream.

"Do you remember this one?" Katerin asked on a lark.

"No" was the immediate answer.

So fast. No pause. You do *remember.* Squeezing Ros, Katerin let the suspicions go. "Tomorrow night, we'll be away, and all will be well."

"Aye," Ros said, returning the hug. "The last of the packing will be done in the morning. We'll leave when the performance is finished."

Katerin smiled. "A reverse parade," she said. "Everyone in costume and makeup as we flee with festive abandon."

Snorting at the image, Ros nodded. "Let's just hope Usiku has time to don his breeches first," she said, referring to the dark-skinned man's buffoon act.

The women chortled in the darkness, holding each other for strength and support.

* ~ * ~ * ~ * ~ *

Looking over Firemount Field, the tyrant could see the fires of various camps. It appeared that a few troupes had gathered to sing and dance the night away. *Tomorrow will be my celebration.* Drinking from a cup of wine, the Invader contemplated the view, but his eyes were on a future prize.

Given the circumstances and the information from the uncovered spy, he was certain Dominic would attempt a coup soon. The exact time was unknown, but the Invader doubted that it would be much longer. To that end, he had prepared his finest archers to be present along the ramparts of the courtyard. In addition, a good number of the Royal Guard were instructed to wear civilian clothes and mingle with the lords and ladies of court during the day's performances.

You're no match for me, you worthless traitor, he thought. *Strength of arms will prevail.*

* ~ * ~ * ~ * ~ *

"That one?"

"Yes. That's the wagon," Dominic agreed, his voice as low as his comrade's. "She's small-boned, dark of hair and eye."

"And the prince wants her taken to the Invader?" the greasy man asked, tugging at his ear with a frown.

"Isn't that what I said?" Dominic asked. "If you get caught, the less you know, the better. Just get the girl and bring her to the guard at the castle. She's to be a diversion." *Fool! Do as you're told!*

Now he was sucking his teeth. "I'll not be responsible for an innocent woman's death," he said.

"Freya's tears," Dominic cursed. "She's *not* an innocent, and she's *not* going to die! If we're to be successful, however, you must do this by midday. Will you?" *Gods save me from well-meaning villains.*

"You swear she'll be safe?"

Dominic barely refrained from rolling his eyes. Instead, he mustered all the sincerity he could. "Yes, I swear." *I swear she'll be put out of my misery.*

With reluctance, the greasy man nodded acceptance of his task. "I'll have her at the gate by the appointed time."

Taking his leave, Dominic fairly cackled. *Soon, King Liam will be on the throne, and I will stand beside him.*

Part 17

Sitting outside Phizo and Em's wagon, Katerin fiddled with her project. She was learning to knit, but it wasn't going well. Holding up a malformed sock, she tsked under her breath. "This is so much harder than it looks."

"Aye, it can be," Em agreed from her stool. She too was knitting, her endeavor much more aesthetically pleasing.

Katerin eyed the sock balefully before raising her eyes to scan the field.

Chuckling, the older woman said, "It's been less than an hour, Kat."

Katerin dropped her gaze, blushing, and sighed. "I know. But the waiting is hard. I'd much rather have it over and be gone." She made a halfhearted attempt at knitting.

Phizo, perched in the door of the wagon, smoking a pipe, said, "Aye. As would we all. But no fears, Kat. They'll be finished in no time, and we'll be long gone by nightfall."

"Yes, I know," Katerin murmured. She concentrated on her task once again, frowning in disgust. With a snort, she dropped her needles into her lap. "Oh, honestly! This is giving me fits!" Transferring the project to her basket, she rose and dusted off her skirts. "I'll return momentarily. I've a mind to work on my sewing instead."

"You want company?" Phizo asked, preparing to rise.

"No, thank you," Katerin said, mindful of the old man's aching joints. She gave him a reassuring smile. "It will be just a moment while I fetch the other."

Masculine honor appeased, Phizo relaxed and nodded, missing Em's mischievous wink. Suppressing a giggle, Katerin picked up her basket and left them.

The immediate encampment was still, wagons packed in preparation for a speedy departure, the few horses that were not needed for Willem's performance already hitched. Beyond their troupe, other camps were rehearsing for their audience with the Invader or entertaining those brave locals who wandered around the field. Only a handful had left, and Katerin was glad they would be joining them soon.

Opening the wagon door, Katerin stepped inside. There was little space to move because of the outdoor accouterments. Stools, small tables, an oiled canvas awning and poles cluttered the entry. She eased past them, reaching the cupboard she used for her ongoing handicrafts. Katerin quickly found what she was looking for, setting her knitting basket inside before closing the door. Squinting in the late morning light, Katerin shut the wagon door firmly behind her. She stared at the castle, a mix of emotion in her heart — wistful nostalgia tainted with a healthy dose of fear. *Just a bit longer, and we'll be free of this danger.*

"Milady!"

Startled, Katerin turned from her thoughts, grabbing her skirts in one hand, preparing to flee. A man, flushed and panting from running, slid to a stop before her.

Knuckling his forehead in respect, he said, "Forgive me, Milady; I didn't mean to frighten you."

Heart still thumping, Katerin reacted to his deference with proper royal snobbery. "It is well you didn't, then, isn't it?"

"Aye, Milady," the man agreed, ignoring the lie. "I was sent when it happened. There's been an accident! You're to come to the castle immediately!"

"Accident?" Katerin blanched, her sewing project falling out of her numb fingers. "What happened? Is Ros involved?" she demanded, grabbing the messenger's arm.

"I don't know, Milady," he answered, pulling back, drawing the woman with him. "I didn't see. I was only told that someone is calling for you."

Katerin felt a wave of nausea rush over her. *Oh, gods! Not again! I don't think I can handle more death.* Steeling herself, she said, "Take me to her!"

"Aye, Milady. This way."

* ~ * ~ * ~ * ~ *

"But, *sire*," the lieutenant whispered.

"I'm not changing my mind, Ian," Liam said. "Save your breath and follow orders."

Silently cursing upstart princes, the sole remaining Dulce guardsman nodded. "Aye, sire."

Liam grasped the man's upper arm. "Remember, you'll be the captain of my guard when this is over."

"Thank you, my liege. But if you don't survive, I'll never see it."

Chuckling, Liam released his man. "Then we'd best get on with it, eh?" At Ian's nod, he said, "I'll see you on the other side."

The guard nodded. "Aye, sire, you will."

Liam watched him drift away into the crowd, preparing his peasant army to storm the gates. *An army I'm supposed to be leading from afar.*

Loitering at the courtyard entrance, Liam searched for a way past the Invader's guards. No commoners were allowed inside — only those with royal invitations, and a fair number of those were being searched. He had been there most of the morning, watching. At last, he saw an opportunity.

As the next group of performers passed, Liam pulled up his hood and put his shoulder against the second of two wagons, keeping himself out of sight of the circus people. They were stopped at the gate, and a blonde woman producing their invitation before being waved through.

"Here! Are you with this troupe?" a guard asked as Liam went through.

With a snort, he pointed at the tiger pacing inside. "You think I'd be pushing this cage if I wasn't?"

Accepting his claim, not willing to upset the animal, the guard waved him on with a sour expression.

Once inside, Liam eased away from the agitated cat. *Gods, I hope that thing's not loose when the call to arms sounds.* He kept his hood up, letting it partially obscure his face. While Liam didn't know most of the lords and ladies present, chances were good that some would recognize him. For all he knew, they were part of this rebellion, too.

"The Adamsson Circus," a court herald announced.

His attention diverted to the center of the courtyard, Liam noted the Invader's location near the main doors. Ignoring the burst of adrenaline, he eyed the man responsible for his nearly mortal wound. *Have to keep him from escaping in that direction.* Liam forced himself to locate his people and the guards — a welcome distraction from his urge to run forward and kill his enemy.

~~*~*~*

Dominic, dressed in the Invader's livery, waved a lord through the door he was manning. "Be welcome, sir," he greeted with a slight bow. The courtier ignored him and sidled into the courtyard just as the next act began. Withholding a sneer, the adviser entertained himself with thoughts of how differently these people would treat him by day's end. *If they survive.*

Dominic scanned the courtyard for the rebels, noting their proper placement. Above them were fifteen of the Invader's finest archers, casually watching the crowd. When the call came, the archers would be first to die. Secreted about the yard were several weapons, including crossbows. Liam's spies in the castle had smuggled them in weeks earlier and hid them over recent days; however, some had been discovered since Travis' disappearance. Dominic could only marvel that the Invader's sheer stubbornness was at work as the ruler sat blithely watching the displays, *knowing* the danger against him.

All we need now is our diversion, he thought. *It's a shame she'll die in the melee.* The Invader would be certain he'd won, never knowing his failure with Liam until it was too late.

~~*~*~*

They had gotten some way before Katerin's suspicions surfaced. She'd been raised in this city — this castle. The courtyard was in another direction; she was sure of it. *Would the Invader have the circus enter elsewhere?* Try as she might, Katerin couldn't see why.

Her guide ducked around a corner. "This way, Milady."

"I think not." Katerin looked about nervously. The man had led her to a little-used lane. *This is the way to the servants' entrance.* If she didn't miss her guess, the guarded gate was a little farther. *Is this a trap?*

Realizing she was no longer with him, the man returned. "Milady? We must hurry!"

"Who are you?" Katerin demanded, backing away.

"A valet, Milady," he said, "sent to fetch you. The accident—"

"You'd do well to explain this 'accident'. I don't recall your saying exactly what transpired." *My gods! Am I such a gullible fool?* She continued moving away, the man following.

His face lost its earnestness, and he scowled. "I'm sorry, Milady, but my superiors insisted that I fetch you. You won't be hurt; I swear it."

That was all Katerin needed to hear. Grabbing her skirts, she turned to flee, running directly into another man, who held her firm. Her struggles were useless, the behemoth being three times her size and weight. She couldn't even make noise past the meaty hand held over her mouth.

Her erstwhile guide glanced about in search of trouble. Finding none, he turned his attention to the scuffling woman. "Be still," he insisted. "You'll not be hurt. By the end of the day, there'll be a new king on the throne."

New king? These men are from the rebellion! Katerin froze. *Dominic!*

"Aye. Just be careful, and you'll be fine." To the bigger man, he said, "Let's go."

Katerin fought once more, her captor carrying her before him like a sack of squiggling puppies.

"Here!" the smaller man shouted at the guards as they rounded the corner. "I've a present for the Invader!"

* ~ * ~ * ~ * ~ *

An ornate chair had been brought out for the occasion, and the Invader lounged upon it, a canopy raised above him to shade him and his guests. A few of the highest lords and their ladies were honored to sit on the makeshift dais, watching as yet another circus set up before them.

Biting back a yawn, the Invader scanned this newest offering. *I certainly hope Dominic gets on with it,* he thought. *The sooner this is quashed, the better.* His eyes fell on the circus leader, and his boredom washed away. It was the woman he'd seen registering in the field a day or so earlier. Tall, thin, with a mop of blonde hair that apparently couldn't be tamed, she looked as much a rogue without her weapon as she had with it. *I wonder if she knows how to use that sword I saw her with?* he idly mused. Noting her swagger, he concluded she probably did.

The woman made a formal bow to the crown before beginning her speech. Her voice was rough, deeper than the Invader expected and filled with a vigor he found surprising. Heedless of her words, he leaned on one arm and waved his hand servant closer. "Who is she?"

"I'm not sure, sire. They were announced as the Adamsson Circus."

Adamsson. The name didn't ring a bell. However, the longer he watched the woman, the more familiar she became. *Who are you?* "Find out a name," he ordered.

"Aye, Your Majesty." Bowing, the servant backed away.

The Invader leaned back in his chair, ignoring the nervous glances of those seated closest to him. When the woman finished her introduction, bowing to one side as a family of three began riding trick horses, his eyes followed her. *From where do I know you?* His mind puzzled over it for some time, all avenues of search failing him. He was beginning to believe the woman simply had one of those faces that reminded him of another.

When the trick riding was over, the woman returned to the center of the courtyard and began another speech — something about flights. He paid her words no mind, hearing only the voice, the tones echoing faintly in his memory. A silver tray holding a parchment was thrust at his face and the Invader jerked away in annoyance, his concentration broken.

Scowling, he snatched the folded paper and glanced inside. All concerns regarding the woman were gone in an instant. Oblivious to the performance before him, he looked over his shoulder at the aide. "Are you certain of this?"

"Aye, sire," the man bowed. "It's her."

So, the Princess Sabine is involved in this. Slowly scanning the courtyard, the Invader noted the many unfamiliar faces, wondering which were involved in Dominic's little scheme. *When will you attack? Do you know she's been taken? Or is this a ruse?*

"Sire? What do you want us to do with the prisoner?"

Yes, Dominic. What do you want me to do? The Invader finally said, "Bring her here. Now." As the aide left to do his bidding, he stroked his chin in thought.

* ~ * ~ * ~ * ~ *

Ros introduced the next act, one in which she would be participating. Her troupe crowded forward and began an inverted human pyramid, using their strongman as the base and pinnacle. Their time was limited, a full three-hour show uncalled for, and she'd chosen those acts that would take the least in the way of props. When this act was finished, Cristof would bring the tiger out for a quick bit, and they would leave.

The Invader's initial overt interest in her was distracted by a message, and she breathed a sigh of relief. That his interest was in her specifically unsettled Ros, and she wondered how she would get through this. It was bad enough being in the den without drawing the undue attention of the lion.

Ros watched an aide scamper away and the Invader's eyes return to the performance, though without the intensity of a few moments earlier. Martim and Tommaso were linked arm in arm, standing on Abdullah's shoulders, free arms out to balance each other. Amar, a thinner man, was clambering up the human chain with the help of the others.

Working out the angles, Ros waved Minkhat closer, and the pair made a show of fixing the fulcrum and board they would use for their trick. When it was in place, she checked on her people's progress. Habibah and Sati were now balanced upon Amar's shoulders, and the dwarf, Sameer, was clambering up the chain. Once he was set, he gave a yell and Abdullah, at the base, turned slowly, garnering applause for the mass of humanity on his shoulders.

In the meanwhile, Minkhat and Usiku took their places and

joined arms, helping Willem climb above them. As they held him tight at the ankles, Ros made her foray up the smaller pyramid. It took some work to find the proper placing and balance to get there, but soon, she was atop his shoulders, arms out in balance. Abdullah finally settled into place, and after a nod from him, Ros called out.

Young Wilm scampered forward from among the horses. With a mischievous grin, he tumbled about until he landed on one end of the board that had been placed between the two groups. Though he was on the opposite side, standing in front of Abdullah, he faced Ros' pyramid. When everyone gave the go-ahead, Ros yelled again and jumped.

Landing on the opposite end of the board, Ros sent the young lad flying. Abdullah shuffled about, keeping an eye on the airborne boy until he landed safely on Sameer's shoulders, high above the audience. Then all of them posed for their applause, smiling before beginning the process of clambering down. When they were all on the ground, they lined up and bowed to the crown as the clapping continued.

A door to the side opened, and two guards appeared, towing a dark-haired prisoner. Her wrists bound before her, she struggled between them as she was dragged toward the Invader.

The applause faded at this new entertainment, and Ros looked for the interruption. *Bleeding Sif! What's* she *doing here?* She took a step forward, Willem and Usiku having the presence of mind to hold her back.

Across the courtyard, Liam tensed as the prisoner was brought before the Invader and forced to kneel. *That can't be!*

Dominic, a fleeting smile crossing his lips, firmly closed the door by which he was positioned. With smooth precision, he slid a wooden bar into iron slots, locking it. Turning, he noted that his compatriots were doing the same. No one was aware as yet, all eyes on the throne.

The Invader, a pleased smile on his face, rose and stepped forward. "Princess Sabine, it's so good to finally meet you." He drew his sword. "Unfortunately, your audience will be short."

Part 18

As the Invader prepared to deliver the death blow, Dominic watched, waiting for the proper moment. Katerin, refusing to bow her head to the usurper, glared at the man who had massacred her family.

Liam frantically looked about, locating his aide and realizing with sick horror that Dominic planned to do nothing. Lips thinning in anger, he threw off his cloak and shouted, "For Liam and Dulce! To me!" Pulling a short sword from his waist, he pushed forward to save his sister.

The call to arms sounded prematurely and Dominic cursed, looking for the cause. "Damned royal bratling will be my undoing!" Regardless, he grabbed a hidden sword and waded into the fight.

The rebels echoed Liam's cry, firing crossbows at the overhead archers, who returned arrows with deadly intent. Several people fell in the courtyard, fighters and bystanders alike. Immediately, the lords and ladies stampeded toward the now-locked doors. The only unguarded exit was the main gate, and they wasted no time in finding it, leaving sword-wielding rebels to their posts with little complaint.

Ros stopped struggling against her friends as the courtyard erupted in violence. Arrows rained from above, and the scattered guard on the ground began fighting the rebels around them. Ros pushed her people toward safety. "Get out! Don't stop! Protect the boy!" The troupe needed no further urging, though Amar had to drag Cristof away from his tiger.

Daiki tried to bring Ros along, but she pulled away. "I have to save Kat!" Ignoring his glare, she said, "I'll not leave her to him!"

The old man growled in frustration, ducking as an arrow barely missed its mark. "Be careful!" he warned, turning away to follow the others.

Seeing her people safely in retreat, Ros turned to the dais. Three of the Royal Guard surrounded the Invader, determined to protect their liege. No thought was given to the prisoner outside their defensive circle. Katerin had fallen to one side, wrestling with her bonds while the rebellion raged around her. Ros, recognizing her opportunity, leapt forward. *If I can just get her out of here...*

The fighting on the dais was fierce as the rebels endeavored to win their cause. Katerin edged away from the proceedings, squirming as she painstakingly moved. She grunted when someone stepped on her thigh but didn't cease in her attempt to escape. Her only hope was that her friends and Ros were able to make it out of the castle.

Ros ducked a sword, dropping into a protective heap over Katerin and startling the smaller woman into a muffled shriek. "It's *me*, Kat!" Her lover nodded recognition as Ros planned a course of action. Removing Katerin from her bindings was out of the question; there was no time. Instead, Ros began pulling them both out of the immediate melee, avoiding being trampled as best she could. Katerin did her best to assist in their escape, scrabbling along as directed.

At the same time, the Invader knew his prey was escaping. He couldn't leave her demise to chance; her tenacity was already a burr in his side. The prophecy of his youth loomed over him, and he knew the princess must die by his hand. With a rough curse, he pushed past his guard, looking for the woman he must slay to stay alive. *Ah, there she is! You'll not crawl away from me, Sabine! I have a destiny to fulfill!* Once more, he raised his sword, intent on killing both women to ensure his success.

* ~ * ~ * ~ * ~ *

Liam was almost there, heart in his throat, when Dominic stepped into his path. "Get out of the way, Dom! We must save Sabine!"

"No, Your Majesty," the aide said, raising a sword to block another's attack. "It's out of our hands!" He gutted the soldier and turned to the prince. "You shouldn't be here! We need you safe!" Dominic tried to grab the young man's arm, barely pulling away from the vicious slash his prince directed at him.

Backing away, Liam pointed his blade at the older man. "Is this why you didn't want me in the courtyard?" he demanded. "You *knew* Sabine was alive and that she'd be here today. You were going to *sacrifice* her to put me on the throne!"

* ~ * ~ * ~ * ~ *

Ros, concentrating on pulling them away from the storm of violence, looked up in time to see the Invader's gleeful look of triumph as he prepared to spit them both. She froze in horror, and their eyes locked. He faltered, an expression of recognition on his face. A rebel attacking from the side distracted him and forced him to defend himself.

Gods be damned, that was too close! Ros scrambled further away, helping Katerin to her feet. Looking at the chaos between them and the gate, she cursed and scooped up a sword dropped by a fallen rebel.

Katerin realized their fight for survival had just begun and that she was utterly useless with her hands bound. She brought her wrists to her mouth and began prying at the ropes with her teeth.

* ~ * ~ * ~ * ~ *

Glancing past the aide, Liam could see that someone had intercepted the Invader. *I have some time. Not much.* "I was told you were here the day *after* my family was killed. That you had an audience with the Invader," Liam said, returning his attention to the older man. "Is this true?"

"Of *course* not, my liege," Dominic scoffed. "Now hurry! You must leave here!" *Kemplak's hells! How can I make this royal bratling see reason?*

Narrowing his eyes, Liam knew Dominic for the liar he was. With no further word, he attacked the traitor.

* ~ * ~ * ~ * ~ *

"Are you all right?" Ros yelled over the clash of weapons.

Still chagrined about being tricked, about nearly dying, Katerin only nodded.

Ros pulled on her lover's arm, holding up the short sword. "Let's get you loose and to the gate! I told the others to get out! We need to find them!" Ros looked into her lover's frightened eyes and fought the urge to kiss her. *Now is definitely* not *the time!*

Before she could follow Ros' direction, Katerin's eyes became round as she looked over her shoulder. Ros turned, raising her sword, clumsily blocking the Invader's swing.

"The celebration is just beginning," he said with an evil smile. "It's not time to leave just yet."

* ~ * ~ * ~ * ~ *

Dominic blocked Liam's sword. "Your Majesty, this is pointless! I'm *not* your enemy!" He struck aside another attack. "Please! Listen to reason!"

The pair circled one another warily. "Tell me true, Dom," Liam said.

"I *am* speaking true, my liege," the aide insisted, his voice earnest. He snarled as he fended off another attack. "Bleeding Sif! Why won't you listen? You're as pigheaded as your mother."

Liam, dark eyes cold, paused to salute Dominic with his blade. "I'll take that as a compliment."

* ~ * ~ * ~ * ~ *

It had been a while since Ros had fought with a sword, despite the fact that she normally carried one, and she was driven back repeatedly, Katerin behind her.

"And who are you?" the Invader asked. "I realize that now isn't the proper time for introductions, but I'm sure I've seen you someplace before." He continued advancing, almost negligent in his attacks. *Let us see how good you are with that sword.*

Slowly, Ros regained her equilibrium, her defense strengthening against the onslaught. "I am no one, sir. Just allow us to leave, and we'll not set foot in your realm again." She parried a vicious thrust, barely avoiding the blade that whisked by her ear.

Katerin was hard pressed not to yank Ros back by her shirt. Though she knew that her lover had experience with a sword, Ros' level of skill certainly couldn't match that of a man who lived by one. Still, Katerin resolved to stay out of the way, keeping a watchful eye on the other skirmishes around them to warn Ros if necessary as she continued trying to free her hands.

The Invader laughed. "You'll excuse my doubts. Princess Sabine and I have unfinished business to attend to. You'd do well to stand aside." To prove his point, he pressed his attack, attempting to rattle her with a blindingly fast frontal assault.

Ros could feel Katerin's presence behind her, and it encouraged her. She stood firm, still on the defense but no longer retreating. "You're mistaken, sir. She is not a princess and is no threat to you."

* ~ * ~ * ~ * ~ *

Liam forced his opponent back another step. Despite their difference in age, Dominic and the prince were evenly matched. The aide's lack of formal instruction leveled the field with Liam's lack of practical experience. Regardless, the aide was being pushed back.

"Please, my liege," he said, making one final attempt to attain his goal. "We *must* stand together. Your kingdom awaits you; there can be no doubt of your succession."

The prince's lips were tight and fire sparked in his eyes. "You would have me slay my family to ensure my crown?" he demanded. Not awaiting an answer, Liam attacked fiercely, his sister all but forgotten in a wave of fury.

* ~ * ~ * ~ * ~ *

Surprised that Ros held her ground, the Invader said, "You fight well. I didn't expect a woman to have much skill."

"I was taught by my da and my father." Finally becoming accustomed to the shorter blade, Ros began pressing forward. There was no way the Invader would just let them go; this she knew. All she could do was kill him or die trying.

Forced to defend himself, the Invader narrowed his eyes. Again, he attacked, only to take a step backward. "Perhaps I know your father?" he asked from between clenched teeth.

"You did," Ros agreed. Her initial fear for Katerin was fading, replaced by a grim joy as she traded blows with this thief who called himself a king. Advancing again, she easily blocked his defense, the tip of her blade catching his arm.

The Invader refused to respond to the sharp pain. Regardless of his apparent retreat, he had knowledge of his fate and a prophecy to bolster his resolve. His attacks turned vicious, but the woman held her ground. "That must be why I find you familiar," he continued conversationally. "You must take after your father."

"Aye, I do." For Ros, the world dissipated. The courtyard and its battles were long past affecting her. Feeling like an observer rather than a participant in a desperate fight, she noted the Invader was favoring his left. *An old injury? He's got to be wearing down. He's old enough to be my da.*

* ~ * ~ * ~ * ~ *

As the rebels gained the upper hand in the courtyard, those who had instructions to secure the castle did so. A few were left in the courtyard to keep a main defense at the gate and guard their companions' backs. Discovering two of their own trading blows was startling.

Liam noted the attention of his people, vaguely aware of their bafflement. *Let's see to whom you are loyal.* Stepping out of the melee, he called out, "Arrest this man for treason."

Dominic's eyes widened in sudden apprehension, and he waved his sword frantically around the ever-growing circle of rebels. "*Get 'im!*"

Pausing only long enough to see his order obeyed, Liam remembered his sister's danger. He cursed, pointing at two men. "With me!" he said, leading them toward the place where he'd last seen Sabine. *Gods! I hope I'm not too late!*

* ~ * ~ * ~ * ~ *

The pair circled, slashing at each other with brutal resolve, unmindful of their growing audience. Katerin remained behind Ros, not allowing the Invader anywhere near her to finish the assassination. Given the opportunity, she was sure he'd gut her in an instant, even if it meant his eventual demise at the hands of her lover.

Sweat began beading on his forehead, and the Invader wondered why the engagement was taking so long. He had to give the woman her due; she was a fine sword fighter. *I don't have time for this.* Beginning a complicated series of thrusts and feints to distract his opponent, he said, "Perhaps you could tell me your father's name?"

Ros felt a thrill as she defended, seeing the opening so clearly that she was momentarily amazed the Invader didn't notice. She made a quick parry and then slid the blade home, neatly slicing through his ribs.

The Invader stood in shock as his sword clattered to the floor. He felt numbness washing over him before a hot/cold agony lanced through his body. He heard the old witch's prophecy just as she'd spoken it to him so many years ago. *"You will die by a sword, kingling. It will be wielded by the child of your enemy, one of royal blood who will avenge those you have wronged."*

Ros watched the Invader fall to his knees, still holding her blade. She followed him down, staring into puzzled eyes, kneeling at his side, watching blood bubble from his lips.

"Wh...who *are* you?"

Ros leaned closer, whispering into his ear almost as a lover would. "My name is Rosmerta Lisbet Helena Klasyne, rightful heir to the throne of Barentcia. You slaughtered my father and the rest of my family more than twenty years ago." With a snarl on her face, she twisted the blade, yanking it to the right and slicing into the Invader's heart.

* ~ * ~ * ~ * ~ *

Hands grabbed her, and Katerin cried out, violently spinning around to face her attacker. The sight that met her was an impossibility. "L...Liam?" she asked, voice rasping.

"Sabine." His dark eyes, so like hers, were shining with tears as he reached out.

They fell together, each happily reassuring the other of being hale and hearty.

~~*~*

Ros stood, leaving the sword in its human sheath. The smell of death was strong, and she realized her hands were sticky with blood. Behind her, the incongruous sounds of laughter caught her attention, lapping like waves against the shores of utter emptiness. She was surprised to find that she wasn't as alone as she felt.

"Aye, you spit him good," a grizzled farmer said. Around him, others gathered, nodding and murmuring agreement.

"That I did," Ros said.

The old man nodded in admiration. "He deserved it: stolen property, stolen crowns, stolen lives. He'll have much to account for in the afterlife."

A smile grew on Ros' face, the simple words easing an ache she hadn't known was there. "Aye. That he will. And better him than me."

That brought a chuckle from the men. Another spoke up. "You're a hero, you know. What's your name, so we can get the tale down proper?"

What's my name? Ros said, "I am called Ros. I own the Adamsson Circus in my da's name." She heard someone calling and turned, seeing a mirror image of her lover in the teenaged boy beside her. Smiling, she stepped forward to be introduced to the next king of Dulce.

Epilogue

Moist fog, muffled sound, a minstrel's voice calling.

Blindly, she focused on the song and its sedate beat, moving with care over the uneven terrain. As she neared the music, she could discern other sounds: the tumbling of water, and dove calls, gentle in the slight breeze. Her slippered foot stumbled over a rock, and she could hear it clatter against others, splashing. The wind picked up, brushing a lock of hair across her forehead, dissipating the mist before her. Flickering light beckoned her closer as she picked her way across a stream.

As she struggled with the familiar nightmare, barely coming to consciousness, she could feel fingers caress her forehead.

"Shhh. It's just a bad dream," Katerin's voice murmured. "You're safe now."

Sighing, Ros relaxed back into sleep.

D. Jordan Redhawk lives in Portland, Oregon where she makes her living in the hospitality industry. (But don't make the mistake of thinking she's hospitable.) Her household consists of her wife of eighteen years, four attack cats that rampage through the house at all hours of the day and night, two Hermit crabs, and a white buffalo Beanie Buddy named Roam.

You can reach D. Jordan Redhawk through her website: http://www.djordanredhawk.net

Printed in the United States
95484LV00004B/224/A